iBT 新多益口說

李育菱 ◎著

獨立＋整合題型

28天拿下高分

旋風突破 **iBT** 口說 **22** 分、**新多益** 口說 **150** 分以上的關鍵就是：

「答題內容切題」、「豐富多元的生活實例」和「表達流暢、語調清晰平穩」

But How to Do It？

⊚ **洗腦式關鍵解析：**由開頭、主體、結論**3**大區塊剖析**18**組高分答案的架構
　→ 答題內容有層次、順序和脈絡可循，考官一聽就懂！

④ **熟讀500**必備應考字彙和**50**組以上的答題模板套用＋**84**組的換句話說
　→ 回答「獨立 ＋ 整合」題型時，不怕詞窮！

✎ **加分元素：**
　→ 高分答案、模板套用和換句話說有專業外師錄音，用聽的來記憶考點，
　　 聽力、口說也同步晉級！

　→ 另於**18**組「獨立」題型中後附上第二種答題範文，
　　 答案不會只有「模板套用」和「換句話說」，而是更加 活潑、多變、自然！

MP3

Author's words 作者序

Thanks to my family's support and nurturing. This book comes with their efforts, too. My husband, Justin helped with revising and final checking throughout this book. Most importantly, he was always there when I needed him. Every time I was stuck somewhere, my lovely darling's smile always warmed my heart. The strength would come back to me again. Also, my host family, the Craig-Meyer family, was the biggest inspiration to me. Their love and care during my stay in USA encouraged me to complete this book with faith and patience. The Meyer family, pastor Chen's family and pastor Rowold, all stand in a very special place in my heart and guide me through every confusion I have in my life. Last but not least, Nugent family surprised me with every tiny happy moment and shared with me big life events. Just say, my other home is in USA. Rain or shine, all those significant moments in my life turned out to be those English stories and words you are about to own by reading this book. It's my great honor to share them with you. I hope this book can bring you to the place you want to be. This book will serve you well if you are dedicated and would like to achieve an impressive TOEFL or TOEIC score before embarking on your adventures in any English speaking country as well as accurate and fluent English communications in your business career. Go get them with fun and faith!

感謝家人的支持與培育，這本書的完成也歸功於他們的成就。Justin 在寫書的過程中協助了所有重要的修改及最後校正，最重要的是，當我需要他的時候他總是在我身邊。過程中，或許失落沒有信心，小可愛的笑容總是讓我的心再度充斥著滿滿的熱情與力量。此外，在美國的 Craig-Meyer 家庭是鼓舞我最大的動力。無論我身在台灣或美國，他們的關愛與支柱就是讓我完成這本書的信念與耐心。Meyer 家庭、陳牧師一家以及羅牧師（Mr. Rowold），他們在我生命中站了一席重要及特別的位置，在我困惑或需要引導的時候陪伴著。最後也很重要的是 Nugent 家庭，他們總是與我分享生命中的許多小美好幸福及重要時刻，就像我在美國的家。晴或雨，這些歡欣或重要時刻都變成這本書的每一篇故事及文字。親愛的讀者們，藉著閱讀它們，您也將擁有這些故事。這是我的榮幸與您們一起分享我的所學及生活。最重要的是，這本書可以讓您在準備托福以及多益口說時，從亂無章法中摸索出得高分的關鍵！讓您大步前往托福以及多益口說高分族群一員，不僅僅奠定您順利進入任何英語系國家文化及學習的旅程，也讓您的商業職場英文口說溝通無往不利！以無比的勇氣及信心去贏得您閃亮的托福以及多益口說佳績吧！

本書主軸雖為新托福口說部分，但透過每單元的學習方式和步驟，讀者也能漸漸掌握新多益口說測驗的拿分技巧，特別是看表格並回答相關問題的整合題型。關於學習方式，本書除了道地英語口說詞彙或常用語句的整理蒐集，每個單元都有針對托福口說題型的實力養成方向、應試技巧以及關鍵字的彙整，讓讀者從基礎打好底子，再廣泛的涉獵個人需要的關鍵字，逐步建構個人的托福口說詞彙資料庫。在句型方面，本書也提供了一句多方說的示範。句型表達是活的，透過每個單元的反覆重整句型，相信會帶給讀者深入英語口語表達的多種風貌，讓您百說無失誤！

透過各單元平易近人的英文小品文，讓您在閱讀不同的文化或生活風情的同時，能夠旁徵博引、觸類旁通您身邊唾手可得的各大托福口說題材，舉凡逛夜市、慢跑、登山、浪漫巴黎旅遊、藝文美術館、書香咖啡館、熱情南灣沙灘海景，甚至是挑戰我們思維的教育議題、出遊行程、大學生生活或科技網路等探討，還有真實英語系國家學校布告欄或校園生活大小事，都在此書歷歷在目的呈現。新托福和新多益口說的初衷，就是希望在英語系國家的留學辛辛學子或在工作生活時，英語能力實實在在的活用在生活裡，讓您在正式踏入英語系國家生活或求學時，求學路途順利，工作或生活能短時間入境隨俗、如魚得水（feel like home）。

李育菱

Contents 目次

PART **3** 口說活用篇

PART 1
個人生活篇

Unit 01
個性特點
Personal Traits

準備方向提示

1. 此類型題目焦點為對人物特徵及個性（personal traits, personalities）的描述，平時需累積對人物特徵正面描述的形容詞彙。

2. 平時可讓自己多關心自己身邊的人事物，想想誰是身邊的貴人朋友、哪些人深深啟發自己、哪些事物陪伴成長茁壯……（how influential, inspirational or impressive things are）等，以及為什麼的主要理由。

3. 培養自己在觀賞英文電影或影集時（movies or TV shows），聽旁白對人物主角的描述（narrators' words），提供自己在於對不同人物身上，可有些啟發式的腳本，進而作為自己對遇此題目觸類旁通的描述。

Question: Who has the greatest influence on your life? Why? Please give specific examples to support your reasons.

對你影響最深的人是誰？為什麼？請提供特定的例子來支持你的理由。

參考範文

My grandmother Ruth is the person who influenced me the most in my life. She is the most caring, generous, and compassionate person I ever knew. Never did I see her showing less concern and loving care to whoever she met. One day of my childhood, an old lady whom I never saw came to our house to show her gratitude for the help she got from my grandmother ten years ago. Besides, she was also energetic and hard-working as well. She assisted my grandfather with his leadership and management of the whole village: a very great example she set for all of our family members to follow in life. Her faithful attitude toward the world inspires me to act with sincerity and enthusiasm towards whichever matters. If there's anyone who ever dives that deep into my life, no one can overpass her influence on me.

中文翻譯

　　Ruth 祖母是影響我生命最深的人，她為人體貼、慷慨、有同理心，無人能比。對任何人，我從沒看她少付出過關懷。在我兒時的一天，一位我從未謀面的女士出現在我家門口，她是要來向 10 年前從祖母那得來的協助表示感謝的。此外，她也是一個充滿活力、認真工作的人。她協助我的祖父領導並管理整個里，這件事為整個家族樹立了很棒的模範，讓我們追隨。她對世界的虔誠態度啟發了我，讓我對任何事情都抱著真誠和熱情。要說誰對我的生命影響最深，沒有人能超越她對我的影響。

單字、片語說分明

① influence *v.* 影響

② caring *adj.* 關懷的

③ generous *adj.* 慷慨的

④ compassionate *adj.* 有同理心的

⑤ loving *adj.* 慈愛的

⑥ energetic *adj.* 精力豐沛的

⑦ leadership *n.* 領導

⑧ management *n.* 管理

⑨ faithful *adj.* 忠誠的

⑩ attitude *n.* 態度

⑪ overpass *v.* 通過、度過

⑫ show one's concern... *ph.* 對……表達關心

⑬ show one's gratitude to... *ph.* 對……表達感激

⑭ set a good example for... *ph.* 為……建立良好榜樣

新托福口說參考範文解析與評點

托福口說答題拿分首要掌握以下要點

1. **What（內容資訊）**：本範文完全針對題目回答了所需的內容資訊。

2. **How（再解釋 1）**：文法上沒有錯誤，語意上可以理解，文章內有使用連接語詞（如 Besides, also）；語意間內容本身也有承接，使聽者容易跟隨講者的話題內容。使用常用簡單明瞭的英文詞彙及句型片語。

3. **Why**（再解釋 2）：本範文沒有離題，絕對針對題目回答，也沒有答非所問。文章使用了許多各型描述的形容詞（如 caring, generous, compassionate, hard-working, loving, energetic, faithful），清楚栩栩如生地描繪出所景仰人物的人格特質及事蹟。所描繪的情境先後皆有連貫關係，明顯連續指出二至三種不同的支持論點及理由。

在描述內容資訊時，本範文首先提出

1. My grandmother Ruth is the person who **influenced** me the most in my life. She is the most **caring**, **generous**, and **compassionate** person I ever knew. Never did I see her **showing less** concern and **loving** care to whoever she met. → 開頭馬上不拖泥帶水的提出所景仰的人物，同時將人物的性格特徵清晰一一描述出來。

2. 並再以自己的親身經歷及成長過程加強描述做此答案的證據與原因。→ One day of my childhood, an old lady whom I never saw came to our house to **show her gratitude** for the help she got from my grandmother ten years ago.

3. 支持論點二不但再度提出景仰人物令作者仿效的正面人格特質，也描述了具體例證及輔佐說明。→ Besides, she was also **energetic** and hard-working as well. She assisted my grandfather with his **leadership** and **management** of the whole village: **a** very great **example she set for** all of our family members to follow in life. Her **faithful attitude** toward the world inspires me to act with sincerity and enthusiasm towards whichever matters. If there's anyone who ever dives that deeply into my life, no one can **overpass** her influence on me.

4. 此範文也從對社區社群的實質貢獻方面、心理層面、以及個人成長

經驗不同方面點出回答者本身做此選擇的原因理由，並點出了以下個人做此選擇的原因：在對社區社群的**實質貢獻**方面（如**...assisted my grandfather with his leadership and management of the whole village; set a very noble and humble example...**）、個人成長經驗（**childhood; a lady came to show gratitude**），以及心理層面（**inspires me to act with sincerity and enthusiasm...**）。

5. 結尾結論句的重申及巧妙的重新潤飾表示出答題者對題目的了解，因此掌握良好。→ Her **faithful attitude** toward the world inspires me to act with sincerity and enthusiasm towards whichever matters. If there's anyone who ever dives that deeply into my life, no one can **overpass** her influence on me.

托福口說論述的架構組成單位

1. 開頭介紹（**Introduction**）：

   My grandmother Ruth is the person who **influenced** me the most in my life.

2. 文章主體（**Body**）：

   A. 支持論點一（Supporting idea 1）：

   I. 支持句一（Supporting sentence 1）：

   She is the most **caring**, **generous**, and **compassionate** person I ever knew. Never did I see her **show less** concern and **loving** care to whoever she met.

   II. 支持句二（Supporting sentence 2）：

   One day of my childhood, an old lady whom I never saw came to our house to **show her gratitude** for the help she got from my grandmother ten years ago.

B. 支持論點二（Supporting idea 2）：

　I.　支持句一（Supporting sentence 1）：

　　　Besides, she was also **energetic** and hard-working as well.

　II.　支持句二（Supporting sentence 2）：

　　　She assisted my grandfather with his **leadership** and **management** of the whole village: **a** very great **example she set for** all of our family members to follow in life.

C. 結尾結論（Conclusion）：

　　Her **faithful attitude** toward the world inspires me to act with sincerity and enthusiasm towards whichever matters. If there's anyone who ever dives that deeply into my life, no one can **overpass** her influence on me.

　　此題目要求的是考生表達人物或事件描述的能力，因每個人各有所司，因此對所景仰人物或影響自己深刻**的人物，自然會因為考生的成長背景及學歷背景而選擇不同。不過，**訣竅在於多多補充對人物個性特徵的描述（如：**optimistic**、**energetic**、**insightful**、**dynamic**、**delightful...**），**考試時適時抓出幾個來彰顯所景仰人物或影響自己最深刻的人物。**開頭及結尾則著重在描述此人的重要性、無懈可擊的影響力等潤述。而要掌握好這些要點，就是考生在一定時間內快速整述主體人物的綜合口語能力了。

以上述短文為例，相關議題可依以下短文解析做變化，遇此類托福口說題目時就可侃侃而談、迎刃而解。未劃底線的部分可不需更改，**劃底線**部分可替換為考生本身的經驗以及欲描述的項目。

開頭

1. My grandmother Ruth is the person who influenced me the most in my life. She is the most caring, generous, and compassionate person I ever knew. Never did I see her showing less concern and loving care to whoever she met.

   → 將劃底線的部分改為考生（您）的**景仰的人以及他們的個性**的描述，如：

   → Director Fernando is the person who influenced me the most in my life. He is the most friendly, generous, and compassionate person I ever knew. Never did I see him showing less passion and care to whoever and whatever he met and knows.

2. One day of my childhood, an old lady whom I never saw came to our house to show her gratitude for the help she got from my grandmother ten years ago.

   → 將劃底線的部分改為考生（您）與**景仰的人**相關的生活經驗，如：

   → When he first saw me, I was a little girl gobbling my ice cream. He told me that I was his imagination coming to life. He has a very strong faith in his movie production industry.

主體

1. Besides, she was also energetic and hard-working as well. She assisted my grandfather with his leadership and management of the whole

village: a very noble and humble example she set for all of <u>our family</u> <u>members to follow in life</u>.

→ 將劃底線的部分改為考生（您）景仰人物的其他個性特質以及貢獻的方面，如：

→ Besides, he is also <u>energetic and optimistic</u> as well. He <u>showed his</u> <u>genuine talent for film productions by presenting the true feelings</u> <u>and features of universal human nature</u>.

2. A very <u>great</u> example she set for all of <u>our family members to follow in</u> <u>life</u>.

→ 將劃底線的部分改為考生（您）景仰人物所有的獨特的貢獻以及貢獻的領域。

→ A very <u>amazingly breathtaking</u> example he set for all of <u>us future</u> <u>motion industries</u> to follow in <u>film field</u>.

結尾

　　之後再編述一項理由支持所提出的論點。可以此句再加強所景仰之人對自己的影響及幫助，間接引導至結論句。為近似所景仰之人的正面個性特質。

1. If there's anyone who ever dives that deep into my life, no one can overpass <u>her</u> influence on me.

→ 將劃現部分改成考生（您）的景仰人物，女性或男性人物，最後結論句以不同方式重述重點句。此結論句為萬用型結論句：

→ If there's anyone who ever dives deep into my life, no one can overpass <u>his</u> influence on me. This kind of <u>positive energy and</u> <u>optimistic attitude</u> surely encourages me whenever I hit some bumpy roads.

此類考題應考時準備筆記關鍵字

1. 描述個人特性的正面形容詞

   He or she is admirable, adventurous, caring, compassionate, intelligent, dynamic, earnest, elegant, hearty, moderate, prudent, reliable, sharing, steady, trusting, wise, understanding...

2. 個人相關成功事蹟

   He or she excels in leadership, good management; **he or she has run a successful business; he or she has achieved** a great success in investment, academic area...

3. 彰顯所景仰人物事蹟的詞彙

   appreciate, admire, impress, influence, encourage, inspire, inspirational, insightful, respectful...

F 換句話說補一補 Track 03

My grandmother Ruth is the person who influenced me the most in my life.
我的祖母 Ruth 對我的生命影響最深遠。

1. I admire my grandmother Ruth for her deep influence on my life.
   我敬佩我的 Ruth 祖母，因為她對我的生命影響深遠。

2. My grandmother Ruth has a great influence on me in life.
   我的 Ruth 祖母深深影響了我的生命。

If there's anyone who ever dives that deep into my life, no one can overpass her influence on me.
假如要說誰深深觸動我的生命，無人可超越她。

1. I'm doubtful anyone could dive into my life that deeply like my grandmother did.
   我恐怕找不到像我祖母那樣深深觸動我生命的人。

2. If I have to name someone who impacts me the most, nothing beats her royal example to me.
   假如要說誰深深觸動／影響我的生命，沒有人可以取代她建立起的典範。

Director Fernando has impressed me the most and inspired me a lot in many aspects of my life. When he first saw me, I was a little girl gobbling my ice cream. He told me that I was his imagination coming to life. He has very strong faith in his movie production industry. A gentleman like him with generous and friendly manners never fails in showing his genuine talent in film productions. His works present the true feelings and features of universal human nature. He used to say that the key to success is to never give up our inner childlike heart, and he believes that at certain point of time, life will shine like a supernova along the journey. This kind of positive energy and optimistic attitude surely encourages me whenever I hit some bumpy roads. Thanks to his presence, I earn more than just acting skills.

Part
1

Part
2

Part
3

> 單字小解

① **impress** *v.* 影響

② **inspire** *v.* 啟發

③ **aspect** *n.* 方面

④ **gobble** *v.* 大口吃、狼吞虎嚥

⑤ **faith** *n.* 信仰、信念

⑥ **generous** *adj.* 慷慨的

⑦ **genuine** *adj.* 真正的

⑧ **talent** *n.* 才華

⑨ **feature** *n.* 特質

⑩ **universal** *adj.* 共通的、共有的

⑪ **supernova** *n.* 超新星

⑫ **bumpy** *adj.* 顛簸的

> 中文翻譯

　　Fernando 導演是影響我最深的人，我生命的各個層面都深受他的啟發。他第一次見到我時，我還是一個大口吃著冰淇淋的小女孩。他說我就像是他想像中的人物。他對他的電影事業有著很深的信念，一個像他這樣慷慨、友善的人，必定也會將他的才華展現在電影製作上。他的作品呈現了人類共有的天性，也就是真誠的感受和特質。他曾說成功的關鍵在於永遠保有我們內在的童心，他也相信在某個時間點，生命會在這趟旅途上像顆超新星一樣，綻放最閃耀的光芒。在我走在顛簸的路上時，這樣正面且樂觀的態度大大鼓舞了我。感謝他的出現，我得到的不只演技，而是更多。

Unit 02
個人興趣 1
Personal Habits 1

🅐 準備方向提示

1. 此類型題目焦點為對自己所愛的活動或嗜好（personal interest）的描述，平時可思考自己喜歡做什麼、為什麼有此選擇或者是與此有關的學習。

2. 累積描述正面心情的詞彙（如 cool down, bring me peace, chill out），可增強説明所喜好活動的理由。

3. 可以多方聽聽名人演講（Travel and Living Channel, celebrity speeches），學習他／她們如何面對生活的壓力或如何將生活安排得更美好，如此在選擇活動方面可有些啟發式的腳本，作為自己遇此題目觸類旁通的描述。

B 模擬題目 🎧 Track 05

Question: What do you do when you have free time? Why do you like it? Please give specific examples to support your reasons.

平日喜歡做的事？為什麼喜歡？請提供特定的例子來支持你的理由。

參考範文

　　When I have free time, I draw and create some artworks. I enjoy watching different artwork online or in any art galleries or exhibitions. When I was studying in the states, my host father created artwork whenever he was available too. At the end of year, he would set an art gallery and invited all the family members or friends to come over for a visit. He seemed to enjoy sharing that part of him with everyone, which made me connect art with satisfaction and happiness. Also, I'm very interested in art therapy. I believe that art and music are fabulous human legacies throughout history. Personally, artworks show so many feelings deep down in us, and we may not even notice about that. Drawing and painting can help me cool down and bring me peace and comfort, so I would like to have my life surrounded with artistic aroma by creating artworks.

中文翻譯

　　只要有時間，我會畫畫和創作。我很喜歡上網或到任何藝廊、展覽觀賞藝術作品。過去在美國留學的時候，我寄宿家庭的爸爸只要一有空也會創作，而且在年底的時候，他還會辦藝術展，並邀請所有的家庭成員或朋友來參觀，他似乎很喜歡將這個部份的自己和所有人分享，讓我覺得藝術可以帶來滿足和幸福。我對藝術療法也很有興趣，我相信藝術和音樂是人類歷史上的美麗傳承。對我來說，藝術作品展現了我們深藏內心的許多感受，我們甚至都沒發現。塗鴉和繪畫有助我冷靜，並帶給我平靜和舒適，所以我希望能透過創作活在身邊皆是藝術氛圍的生活裡。

單字、片語說分明

① **gallery** *n.* 藝廊、畫廊

② **exhibition** *n.* 展覽、展示

③ **available** *adj.* 可得的；空閒的

④ **therapy** *n.* 治療、療癒方法

⑤ **fabulous** *adj.* 美好的；美麗的

⑥ **legacy** *n.* 傳統；文物遺產

⑦ **artistic aroma** *n.* 藝術氣息、藝術氣氛

C 新托福口說參考範文解析與評點

托福口說答題拿分首要掌握以下要點

1. **What（內容資訊）**：本範文完全針對題目回答了所需的**內容資訊**。

2. **How（再解釋 1）**：文法上沒有錯誤，語意上可以理解，文章內有使用**連接語詞**（如 Also, so）；語意間內容本身也有承接，使聽者容易跟隨講者的話題內容。使用常用簡單明瞭的英文詞彙及句型片語，則能提升口語上的流暢度。

3. **Why（再解釋 2）**：本範文沒有離題，絕對針對題目回答，也沒有答非所問。文章使用了個人經驗以及本身教育背景的詞彙（**art galleries, exhibitions, art therapy**），清楚栩栩如生地描繪出自己的興趣及經驗的結合。所描繪的情境先後皆有連貫關係，明顯連續指出二種不同的支持論點及理由。

> 在描述內容資訊時，本範文首先提出

1. When I have free time, I draw and create some artworks. → 開頭馬上開門見山提出空閒時的活動。

2. 並解釋為什麼喜歡這個空閒活動的理由，並加入自己的親身經歷與這個活動帶來的美好感受。

   → I enjoy watching different artworks online or in any art **galleries** or **exhibitions**. When I was studying in the states, my host father created art works whenever he was **available** too. At the end of year, he would set an art gallery and invited all the family members or friends to come over for a visit. He seemed to enjoy sharing that part of him with everyone, which made me connect art with satisfaction and happiness.

3. 支持論點二不但再度以個人經驗提出描述了具體例證及輔佐說明。

   → Also, I'm very interested in **art therapy**. I believe that art and music are **fabulous** human **legacies** throughout history. Personally, art works show so much inside feelings deep down in us, and we may not even notice about that.

4. 此範文也從個人成長經驗及興趣方面、專業領域層面、以及心理層面不同方面點出回答者本身做此選擇的原因理由，並點出了以下個人做此選擇的原因：在對個人成長經驗及興趣方面（**host family; art galleries and exhibitions...**）、專業領域層面（**art therapy**）以及心理層面（**cool down; art shows inside of us**）。

5. 結尾結論句的重申及巧妙的重新潤飾表示出答題者對題目的了解，因此掌握良好。

   → Drawing and painting can help me cool down and bring me peace and comfort, so I would like to have my life surrounded with **artistic aroma** by creating artworks.

托福口說論述的架構組成單位

1. 開頭介紹（**Introduction**）：

   When I have free time, I draw and create some art works.

2. 文章主體（**Body**）：

   A. 支持論點一（Supporting idea 1）：

   I. 支持句一（Supporting sentence 1）：

      I enjoy watching different art works online or in any art **galleries** or **exhibitions**.

   II. 支持句二（Supporting sentence 2）：

      When I was studying in the states, my host father created art works whenever he was **available** too. At the end of year, he would set an art gallery and invited all the family members or friends to come over for a visit. He seemed to enjoy sharing that part of him with everyone, which made me connect art with satisfaction and happiness.

   B. 支持論點二（Supporting idea 2）：

   I. 支持句一（Supporting sentence 1）：

      Also, I'm very interested in **art therapy**.

   II. 支持句二（Supporting sentence 2）：

      I believe that art and music are **fabulous** human **legacies** throughout history. Personally, art works show so much inside feelings deep down in us, and we may not even notice about that.

3. 結尾結論（**Conclusion**）：

   Drawing and painting can help me cool down and bring me peace and comfort, so I would like to have my life surrounded with **artistic aroma** by creating art works.

　　此題目要求考生在一定時間內快速整述自己喜歡的活動，以及對自己的正面影響，也就是對自己喜歡的活動的描述能力。答案常常是因人而異，會依考生的經驗及背景而選擇不同。不過，**訣竅在於累積不同活動經驗的描述，以此融入對自己生命及心靈洗滌的描述（如 bring me peace; cool me down...）**；考試時若能適時運用這些描述自己正面能量的詞彙，並說明做此選擇的原因，就能在類似題目拿到高分。

D 新托福口說答題模板套用 🔵 Track 06

　　以上述短文為例，相關議題可依以下短文解析做變化，遇此類托福口說題目時就可侃侃而談、迎刃而解。未劃底線的部分可不需更改，**劃底線**部分可替換為考生本身的經驗以及欲描述的項目。

開頭

1. When I have free time, I draw and create some artworks. I enjoy watching different art works online or in any art galleries or exhibitions.
   → 將劃底線的部分改為考生（您）**喜歡從事的運動或活動**的描述。
   → When I have free time, I join runner groups. I enjoy jogging a lot.

2. When I was studying in the states, my host father created artworks whenever he was available too. At the end of year, he would set an art gallery and invited all the family members or friends to come over for a visit. He seemed to enjoy sharing that part of him with everyone, which made me connect art with satisfaction and happiness.
   → 並簡短描述個人的相關經驗。將劃底線的部分改為考生（您）**個人的經驗**。
   → When I was still a student, I like to jog whenever I was available

too. Pretty much every month, I would join a runner's group and invited all the family members or friends to come over for a try as well. I was happy and enjoyed sharing that part of me with friends.

主體

1. Also, I'm very interested in art therapy. I believe that art and music are fabulous human legacies throughout history.
   → 將劃底線的部分改為考生（您）另外一個喜歡從事的運動或活動的方面。
   → Also, I'm very interested in sport management. I believe that sports and exercise are fabulous human activities throughout history.

2. Personally, artworks show so many feelings deep down in us, and we may not even notice about that.
   → 將劃底線的部分改為考生（您）喜歡的運動或活動，以及這些活動帶給您的感受。
   → Personally, body movements show so many feelings deep down in us, and we may not even notice about that.

結尾

之後再編述一項理由支持所提出的論點。

1. Drawing and painting can help me cool down and bring me peace and comfort, so I would like to have my life surrounded with artistic aroma by creating artworks.
   → 將劃底線的部分改為考生（您）重視的活動或運動，最後結論句以不同方式重述重點句。
   → Running and exercising can help me cool down and bring me peace and comfort, so I would like to live my life in an athletic life style by jogging.

E 此類考題考前及應考時準備筆記關鍵字

Part 1

1. 不同的休閒活動

   I enjoy hiking, mountain climbing, listening to music, reading, photographing, bicycling, watching TV, mediation ...

2. 對個人有正面影響（如心靈或生理方面）的詞彙

Part 2

   It helps me cool down, refresh my mind, re-energize, relax, break my running records; **It brings me** new ideas and peaceful moment; **It is** inspiring, ...

3. 興趣相關的專業領域詞彙

Part 3

   I'm also interested in art therapy, massage, aroma therapy, mediation ...

F 換句話說補一補  Track 07

He seemed to enjoy sharing that part of him with everyone.
他似乎很喜歡將這個部份的自己和所有人分享。

1. Sharing that part with everyone he knows seemed to bring him happiness.
   將這個部分和所有人分享似乎帶給他快樂。

2. Happiness is what he got when he shared that part with his friends.
   只要和朋友分享這個部分他就會得到快樂。

Personally, artworks show so many feelings deep down in us, and we may not even notice about that.
藝術作品展現了我們深藏內心的許多感受，我們甚至都沒發現。

1. I personally feel that artworks show inside of us so much that we don't even realize.

   我認為藝術作品大大展現了我們的內心深處，甚至連我們自己都沒發現。

2. To me, artworks show so much inside of us and we may not realize it.

   對我來說，藝術作品大大展現了我們的內心深處，甚至連我們自己都沒發現。

Drawing and painting can help me cool down and bring me peace and comfort, so I would like to have my life surrounded with artistic aroma by creating art works.

塗鴉和繪畫有助我冷靜，並帶給我平靜和舒適，所以我希望能透過創作活在身邊皆是藝術氛圍的生活裡。

1. I feel some calmness and peace when drawing and painting, so I would like to have my life surrounded with artistic aroma by creating art works.

   我在塗鴉和繪圖時感到平靜，所以我希望能透過創作活在身邊皆是藝術氛圍的生活裡。

2. Creating artworks brings me calmness and peace, for instance, drawing and painting.

   像是塗鴉和繪圖的創作會帶給我平靜。

想想看還能怎麼答 Track 08

Painting is always my number one free time activity after work. Whenever I'm available, I paint, draw or create some artworks. Other than my regular teaching job, I am also trying as possible as I could to create some space and time for my hobby. Teaching sometimes can be very tiring and frustrating when out of passion and motivation; however, painting, drawing and creating some artworks can always help have my energy back for me to face another few week's workload, and at the same time, bring me some inner refreshment and inspiration. Artistic works I made also become a good resource of teaching materials. Sometimes I share my artworks with my students if possible to cultivate their ability to appreciate art. At this time, the classroom's atmosphere became livelier and relaxing, which surprisingly and greatly improve students' learning efficiency. Art no doubt plays an important role in my life.

單字小解

① **motivation** *n.* 動機

② **refreshment** *n.* 提振精神

③ **inspiration** *n.* 靈感

④ **cultivate** *v.* 培養

⑤ **appreciate** *v.* 欣賞

⑥ **livelier** *adj.* 較活潑的

⑦ **efficiency** *n.* 效率

中文翻譯

　　繪畫是我最喜愛的休閒娛樂。每當我有空時，我嘗試繪畫及創作些藝術作品。除了專職的教學工作，只要一有空，我會撥時間空間做藝術品。教學工作有時會因失去熱情與動機而感疲倦，但繪畫及創作藝術作品常常能幫我恢復精力儲備另一週的工作能量，同時啟發我並帶來煥然一新的感受。我做的藝術作品也是我教學上的好素材，若有機會有時我會和學生分享我的創作，來培養學生欣賞藝術的能力，這時課堂的氣氛會變得有生氣且清鬆，而且更讓我驚喜的是，這還大大改善了學生的學習效率。藝術無疑在我的生命中扮演很重要的角色。

Unit 03
個人興趣 2
Personal Habits 2

A 準備方向提示

1. 此類型題目焦點為對自己平常喜好的地點或活動（**activities, sports, habits, locations**）的描述。

2. 除此之外，此類題目為向人描述喜好活動或地點的介紹文，因此需累積一些戶外室內活動（**outdoor and indoor activities**）的英文詞彙以及相關景點（**breathtaking scenery**）（如 **go hiking, bicycling, Taipei 101, the Great Wall, or the Grand Canyon**）的描述。

3. 強烈建議多多觀看英文旅遊節目（**TLC, sport programs**）唷！既可增廣見聞，又可學好英文。聽旁白對景點的描述，可提供自己對不同景物或地標有些啟發式的腳本，如此也能作為自己對遇此題目觸類旁通的發揮。

模擬題目 Track 09

Question: Please share with us a place you would like to go when you have free time and why? Please give specific examples to support your reasons.

請分享你有空喜歡一個人去的地方？為什麼？請提供特定的例子來支持你的理由。

參考範文

When I have some free time, I would like to visit the lakes. It's really easy to fall in love with lakes. Lake area provides a great variety of water activities, for example, water skiing, boating, canoeing and kayaking. Its breathtaking scenery provides peaceful atmosphere. Moreover, the beautiful wildlife offers a relaxing resort. That's why whenever I need some peaceful moment, I visit the lakes alone. Perhaps sometimes I would like to have some day-offs from daily work. The lakes offer me some space to go bicycling, hiking, camping or birdwatching. Magically, I feel my whole body would be reenergized after the lake trip. One of the marathon events I just finished is also held in the lake area. The impression of the fresh air and blissful climate around the lake area is still very vivid to me, and I guess other runners would agree with me about that. With all the excitements and relaxation, if I can't relax here, I may need therapy.

33

>― 中文翻譯

　　我一有空的時候，就會去湖邊。愛上湖水真的很容易，而且湖邊可以做許多活動，例如滑水、划船、團體或單人泛舟等。湖邊的景色令人驚嘆，塑造寧靜的環境。此外，美麗的野生動植物生態讓這裡成為能放鬆心情的地方，適合旅遊度假，這也是為什麼在我需要寧靜時，我都會獨自一人到湖邊去。可能有時候在工作之餘，我會想要幾天休假，湖邊正好是我騎單車、健行、露營或賞鳥的好去處。從湖邊活動回來後，我全身都能再次充滿活力，真的很神奇。我剛結束一個辦在湖邊的馬拉松活動，所以我想跑者也會同意湖邊有新鮮空氣和宜人的氣候吧。湖邊讓人振奮也讓人放鬆，如果連在裡都無法放鬆，我可能需要接受治療了吧。

>― 單字、片語說分明

① **waterskiing** *n.* 滑水

② **boating** *n.* 划船

③ **canoeing** *n.* 團體泛舟

④ **kayaking** *n.* 單人泛舟

⑤ **breathtaking** *adj.* 令人驚嘆的

⑥ **day-off** *n.* 休假

⑦ **re-energize** *v.* 重新充滿活力

⑧ **blissful** *adj.* 愉悦的

新托福口說參考範文解析與評點

>― 托福口說答題拿分首要掌握以下要點

　　1. What（內容資訊）：本範文完全針對題目回答了所需的**內容資訊**。

　　2. How（再解釋 1）：文法上沒有錯誤，語意上可以理解，文章內有使用**連**

接語詞（如 **Moreover, so**），語意間內容本身也有承接，使聽者容易跟隨講者的話題內容。使用常用簡單明瞭的英文詞彙及句型片語也能有助於口語上的流暢度。

3. **Why**（再解釋 **2**）：本範文沒有離題，絕對針對題目回答，沒有答非所問。文章使用了許多戶外活動的詞彙（**biking, hiking, waterskiing, canoeing and kayaking**），確實描述可在湖邊做的活動。所使用的詞彙解釋了講者喜歡湖邊的理由之一，緊密連結本題的主旨。

在描述內容資訊時，本範文首先提出

1. When I have some free time, I would like to visit the lakes. It's really easy to fall in love with lakes. → 開頭立即闡述有閒暇時最喜歡到湖濱區。

2. 根據自己的經驗提出具體活動，使聽者更能了解考生的湖濱閒適之行，加強描述做此答案的原因。→ Lake area provides a great variety of water activities, for example, **water skiing, boating, canoeing** and **kayaking**. Its **breathtaking** scenery provides peaceful atmosphere.

3. 支持論點二 → Moreover, the beautiful wildlife offers a relaxing resort. That's why whenever I need some peaceful moment, I visit the lakes alone.

4. 支持論述三結合前述的兩點再度提出湖濱區的活動及跟自己的緊密關係，整合具體例證及輔佐說明。→ Perhaps sometimes I would like to have some **day-offs** from daily work. The lakes offer me some space to go bicycling, hiking, camping or birdwatching.

5. 此範文也從**親身經驗**、**個人心理層面**，以及**具體的湖濱活動**等不同

方面點出回答者本身做此選擇的原因理由：在**親身經驗**方面（**my whole body reenergized**）、個人心理層面（**peaceful moment; relax**）以及具體湖濱活動（**water skiing, boating, canoeing and kayaking; or bicycling, hiking, camping or birdwatching...**）。

6. 結尾結論句的重申及巧妙地重新潤飾表示出答題者對題目的了解，因此掌握良好。同時有運用口語化反說式的輕鬆語句正面描述出湖濱區著實引人入勝。→ With all the excitements and relaxation, if I can't relax here, I may need therapy.

> **托福口說論述的架構組成單位**

1. 開頭介紹（**Introduction**）：

    When I have some free time, I would like to visit the lakes. It's really easy to fall in love with lakes.

2. 文章主體（**Body**）：

    A. 支持論點一（Supporting idea 1）：

       I. 支持句一（Supporting sentence 1）：

          Lake area provides a great variety of water activities, for example, **water skiing, boating, canoeing** and **kayaking**.

       II. 支持句二（Supporting sentence 2）：

          Its **breathtaking** scenery provides peaceful atmosphere.

    B. 支持論點二（Supporting idea 2）：

       I. 支持句一（Supporting sentence 1）

          Moreover, the beautiful wildlife offers a relaxing resort.

       II. 支持句二（Supporting sentence 2）：

          That's why whenever I need some peaceful moment, I visit the lakes alone.

C. 支持論點三（Supporting idea 3）：

I. 支持句一（Supporting sentence 1）：

Perhaps sometimes I would like to have some **day-offs** from daily work. The lakes offer me some space to go bicycling, hiking, camping or birdwatching.

II. 支持句二（Supporting sentence 2）：

Magically, I feel my whole body would be **reenergized** after the lake trip.

III. 支持句三（Supporting sentence 3）：

One of the marathon events I just finished was also held in the lake area. The impression of the fresh air and blissful climate is still very vivid to me, and I think other runners would agree about that.

D. 結尾結論（**Conclusion**）：

With all the excitements and relaxation, if I can't relax here, I may need therapy.

　　此題目要求的是考生表達對一個喜愛的地點或想介紹地點的描述的能力，因個人經驗不一，所選擇的地點當然不同。**訣竅在於對不同景點情境的描述，可分山景及海景、大都市中的書店或咖啡店、湖濱、鄉野或大自然美景**。準備方向為針對這些景物進行描述及觀察，補充描述山及海洋等自然美景對自己的影響。**開頭及結尾皆點出所選景點，並描述出此情此景對自己的意義及心靈陶冶**。因此，掌握好這些要點，就是考生在一定時間內快速整述場景地點的綜合口語能力了。

新托福口說答題模板套用　Track 10

　　以上述短文為例，相關議題可依以下短文解析做變化，遇此類托福口說題目時可侃侃而談對題目迎刃而解。未劃底線的部分可不需更改，<u>劃底線</u>部分可替換為考生本身的經驗以及欲描述的項目。

開頭

1. Lake area provides a great variety of <u>water activities</u>, for example, <u>water skiing, boating, canoeing and kayaking</u>. Its breathtaking scenery provides peaceful atmosphere.

   → 將劃底線的部分改為考生（您）所設想的景點的描述。

   → <u>Kenting</u> provides great variety of <u>water activities</u>, for example, <u>water skiing, boating, canoeing and kayaking</u>. Its breathtaking scenery provides peaceful atmosphere.

2. Moreover, the beautiful wildlife offers a relaxing resort. That's why whenever I need some peaceful moment, I visit <u>the lakes</u> alone.

   → 繼續將劃底線的部分替換描述場地或景點對考生（您）**親身經歷或心靈層面**的洗滌。

   → Moreover, the beautiful wildlife offers a relaxing resort. That's why whenever I need some peaceful moment, I visit <u>Kenting</u> alone.

主體

1. Perhaps sometimes I would like to have some **day-offs** from daily work. <u>The lakes</u> offer me some space to go bicycling, hiking, camping or birdwatching. Magically, I feel my whole body would be **reenergized** after the trip. One of the marathon events I just finished was also held in <u>the lake area</u>, so I guess runners agree with the fresh air and **blissful** climate around <u>the lake area</u> as well.

   → 將劃底線的部分改為考生（您）的所想描述的**景點或私人秘密景點**。

   → Perhaps sometimes I would like to have some **day-offs** from daily work. <u>Kenting</u> offers me some space to go bicycling, hiking, camping or birdwatching. Magically, I feel my whole body would be **reenergized** after the lake trip. One of the marathon events I just finished was also held in <u>Kenting</u>, so I guess runners agree with the fresh air and **blissful** climate around <u>Kenting</u> as well.

結尾

　　之後再補上此萬用景點或場地的結論句就可巧妙地彰顯考生（您）的口語技巧，並能流暢答題囉。

1. With all the excitements and relaxation, if I can't relax here, I may need therapy.

小提示：此題的論點具體描述比較多，因此結論句相對就可以單刀直倏地只放入喜歡的景點或私人秘密散步小徑的萬用句，簡潔有利的結尾論述。

E 此類考題考前及應考時準備筆記關鍵字

1. 對自然美景的描述

   This place has beautiful scenery, broad wild life; a blissful, breathtaking sunset; wonderful sunshine, waves...

2. 此景此點對個人的意義及心靈陶冶

   This is a place where I can enjoy peaceful moment; chilling out, relaxing; relaxation; **getting rid of** stress; therapy; cooling down; calming one's mind; being reenergized...

3. 各種不同的戶內戶外活動因應場景需求

   I love water skiing, boating, canoeing and kayaking, bicycling, hiking, camping or birdwatching...

F 換句話說補一補 🔵 Track 11

It really easy to fall in love with lakes.
愛上湖濱區很容易。

1. I'm sure you will love lakes.
   你一定會愛上湖濱區。

2. Lakes will certainly amaze you.
   湖濱區將使你驚豔!

That's why also whenever I need some peaceful moment, I visit the lakes alone.
這也是為什麼在我需要寧靜時,我都會獨自一人到湖邊去。

1. This also explains why I visit the lakes alone whenever I need some peaceful moment.
   這也解釋了在我需要寧靜的片刻時,我會想要獨自一人的原因。

2. Whenever I need some time alone, I visit the lakes, and that's why.
   當我需要一人獨處時,我就會到湖邊,這就是原因。

If I can't relax here, I may need therapy.
如果連在裡都無法放鬆,我可能需要接受治療了吧。

1. Here is my relaxing paradise.
   這裡是我放鬆的樂園。

2. Chilling out is just what this place offers.
   這個地方能讓人聊天放鬆。

 **G 想想看還能怎麼答** Track 12

　　Wisconsin has the greatest natural resource and is the largest inland chain of lakes in the world. It is filled with great lakes with great views and great fishing. The lakes provide sufficient space for water skiing and boating as well as canoeing and kayaking. Whenever I seek an active vacation or just want to relax, I go to the lakes. It's easy to fall in love with Wisconsin's lakes. Their breathtaking scenery provides peaceful atmosphere. And the beautiful wildlife offers a relaxing resort. Not only residents but also visitors can fish or boat, and if you would like to go bicycling, hiking, camping, birdwatching or taking pictures, it all serves you well. I also just finished a 3K run-for-kids marathon around the lakes last Christmas. Trust me, the lake area has some magical attraction letting us go back to visit again and again and never feel tired of it.

單字小解

① **resource** *n.* 資源
② **chain** *n.* （連成串的）鍊
③ **sufficient** *adj.* 充足的
④ **resident** *n.* 居民
⑤ **attraction** *n.* 景點
⑥ **sth serves one's well** *ph.* 對……適用

中文翻譯

　　威斯康辛的天然資源相當豐盛，擁有全球最大的內陸島湖鍊。這裡有最棒的湖、最棒的景色，是最適合釣魚的地方。湖濱區腹地廣大，可用來做滑水、划船、單人或雙人泛舟等的活動。每當我想要替假期安排許多活動，或只是想要放鬆時，我都會來到湖邊。你馬上就會愛上威斯康辛的湖濱區，這裡的景色讓人驚嘆，給人閑靜平和的氣氛。美麗的野生動植物生態讓這裡成為適合度假的地方。當地居民和遊客都能來此釣魚或划船，如果你想要騎單車、健行、露營、賞鳥或拍照，那也沒問題。上個聖誕節我才在湖濱區剛完成一趟三公里為孩童而跑的馬拉松，相信我，湖濱區散發神奇的吸引力，總能讓人們一去再去而不會感到厭煩。

Unit 04
該具備的能力
Required Abilities

🅰 準備方向提示

1. 此類型題目焦點為對不同角色所需具備特質或能力的描述，平時可多觀察各行各業，並以不同行業或職位的立場多方思考（**Try to think about what kind of capacities, skills or requirements one career or position needs.**）。

2. 累積不同職稱的詞彙（如 **CEO, firefighters, nurses, teachers, plumbers, architects...**），以及各行各業工作所需的特質、能力或工作內容（如 **decision-making; take the day / night shift; drafting; repairing / maintaining pipes; nursing care; design new projects...**）。

3. 現在有許多針對各行各業的實境秀（如 *Million Dollar Decorators, The Apprentice, Bakery Boss...*），多看這些在選擇角色特點或能力需求上，會比較了解，同時也可有些啟發式的腳本，作為自己對遇此題目觸類旁通的描述。

B 模擬題目 Track 13

Question: What kinds of skills should a college student be required? And why? Please give specific examples to support your reasons. 大學生該具備什麼樣的技能，為什麼？請提供特定的例子來支持你的理由。

參考範文

A college student should be required to have basic life skills, socializing skills and individual professional skills from my point of view. Whichever major we might choose in college will eventually require us to communicate with people when we join the society. Also, we will have to deal with different affairs in daily life whether we want or not, so basic life skills are required. Additionally, we can't forget to improve our professional skills since they are the very foundation of our career. College education may just simply be the baby step of our career not to mention that we are all freshmen in the society after we graduate. From the above reasons, college students should try to make themselves engross in academic learning, handling their own life, and socializing with college mates or some coworkers if they have part-time job after school. Busy, fascinating though.

中文翻譯

　　大學生應有基本生活能力、人際相處溝通能力以及個人專業技能。無論是哪一種學術專業，終會有面對社群需溝通的時候，而且我們每天都要面對不同的事情，這是無法避免的，所以基本的生活能力不可少。此外，必須要精進專業知能及學習，因為大學所學只是職業生涯根本。大學教育充其量只是專業生涯的起步，更別

説我們這些剛畢業的社會新鮮人了。從以上所述理由,大學生應試著致力於念書、管理自己的生活還有在課後打工時與人互動溝通。很忙碌,但很棒!

單字、片語說分明

① socialize (socializing) *v.* 人際溝通;社交

② individual *adj.* 個人的

③ additionally *adv.* 此外

④ improve *v.* 進步;增進

⑤ foundation *n.* 基礎;根本

⑥ career *n.* 生涯

⑦ mention *v.* 提到、提及

⑧ graduate *v.* 畢業

⑨ academic *adj.* 學術的

⑩ handle (handling) *v.* 處理;掌握

⑪ college mate *n.* 大學同學

⑫ fascinating *adj.* 令人著迷的;美好的;燦爛的

⑬ from one's point of view *ph.* 從某人的觀點而言

⑭ deal with *ph.* 處理

補充:表達人事物的美好、燦爛及令人傾心:fascinating=fabulous=wonderful=amazing=enchanting=thrilling=delightful

新托福口說參考範文解析與評點

托福口說答題拿分首要掌握以下要點

1. **What(內容資訊)**:本範文完全針對題目回答了所需的**內容資訊**。

2. **How(再解釋 1)**:文法上沒有錯誤,語意上可以理解,文章內有使用連

接語詞（如 **Also, Additionally, From the above reason**）；語意間內容本身也有承接，使聽者容易跟隨講者的話題內容。使用常用簡單明瞭的英文詞彙及句型片語也能有助於口語上的流暢度。

補充：本文章為列點式或順序性口説的典型。

3. **Why**（再解釋 2）：本範文沒有離題，絕對針對題目回答，沒有答非所問。文章以連接語條列了問題所問的答案，針對所條列各點增加具體理由支撐句，強化所列舉的項目。**語句段落間先後皆有連貫關係，論述二種不同的支持論點及理由。**

> ⟩ **在描述內容資訊時，本範文首先提出**

1. A college student should be required to have basic life skills, **socializing** skills and **individual** professional skills **from my point of view**. → 開頭立即順序性的點出大學生應有的基本技能及所需的能力培養。

2. 並概觀經驗及個人見解闡述加強描述做此答案的原因。 → Whichever major we might choose in college will eventually require us to communicate with people when we join the society. Also, we will have to **deal with** different affairs in daily life whether we want or not, so basic life skills are required.

3. 支持論點二再度以個人宏觀經驗針對所提出的幾點，提出描述了具體例證及輔佐説明。→ **Additionally**, we can't forget to **improve** our professional skills since they are the very **foundation** of our **career**. College education may just simply be the baby step of our career not to **mention** that we are all freshmen in the society after we **graduate**.

4. 此範文也在專業學術、職涯領域上（individual professional skill; career...）以及人際溝通方面（communicate with people...）點出回答者本身做此回答的原因。

5. 結尾結論句的重申及巧妙地重新潤飾表示出答題者對題目的了解，因此掌握良好。→ **From the above reasons**, college students should try to make themselves engross in **academic** learning, **handling** their own life, and socializing with **college mates** or some **coworkers** if they have part-time job after school. Busy, **fascinating** though.

新托福口說論述的架構組成單位

1. 開頭介紹（Introduction）：

　　A college student should be required to have basic life skills, **socializing** skills and **individual** professional skills **from my point of view**.

2. 文章主體（Body）：

A. 支持論點一（Supporting idea 1）：

　　I.　支持句一（Supporting sentence 1）：

　　　　Whichever major we might choose in college will eventually require us to communicate with people when we join the society.

　　II.　支持句二（Supporting sentence 2）：

　　　　Also, we will have to **deal with** different affairs in daily life whether we want or not, so basic life skills are required.

B. 支持論點二（Supporting idea 2）：

I.　支持句一（Supporting sentence 1）：

Additionally, we can't forget to **improve** our professional skills since they are the very **foundation** of our **career**.

II.　支持句二（Supporting sentence 2）：

College education may just simply be the baby step of our career not to **mention** that we are all freshmen in the society after we **graduate.**

3. 結尾結論（**Conclusion**）：

From the above reasons, college students should try to make themselves engross in **academic** learning, **handling** their own life, and socializing with **college mates** or some **coworkers** if they have part-time job after school. Busy, **fascinating** though.

　　此題目詢問考生大學生需要有哪些能力需求，考生依此需快速擇取相關條件、具有邏輯性的列點、舉相關具體理由來整述所要求的內容。**建議考生在平時準備論述性問題時，訓練自己快速列點及寫下各點的關鍵字，增強面對托福口說測驗時，詞彙搜尋的能力。**

例如：

1. 專業能力方面（professional skills）：**Additionally**, we can't forget to **improve** our professional skills since they are the very **foundation** of our **career**.

2. 基本能力方面（basic skills）：Also, we will have to **deal with** different affairs in daily life whether we want or not, so basic life skills are required.

3. 溝通技巧方面（communicating skills）：Whichever major we might choose in college will eventually require us to communicate with people when we join the society

　　所需列舉的關鍵字只有三組：professional skills、basic skills、communicating skills，其餘句型在組成和論述時，皆需將既定的想法及英文口說能力密切結合。**考生於平時訓練即時英文口說能力時，要試著將關鍵字融入英文即時口說中，不用太多思索，如此多加練習後，在考時就能盡情發揮。**

D 新托福口說答題模板套用  Track 14

　　以上述短文為例，相關議題可依以下短文解析做變化，遇此類托福口說題目時可侃侃而談對題目迎刃而解。未劃底線的部分可不需更改，**劃底線**部分可替換為考生本身的經驗以及欲描述的項目。

開頭

1. A college student should be required to have basic life skills, socializing skills and individual professional skills from my point of view.
   → 將劃底線的部分改為考生（您）**所描述的角色所需求的條件或特質的描述。**
   → A detective should be required to have observatory skills, analytical capability and capability to think logically from my point of view.
2. Whichever major we might choose in college will eventually require us to communicate with people when we join the society. Also, we will have to deal with all the affairs in daily life whether we want or not, so basic life skills are required.
   → 並**追加與所欲描述的角色的相關特質、優點或狀況。**同樣將劃線的部分改成考生（您）**對該角色的理解。**

→ Whichever underline{difficult case a detective might encounter} will eventually require him or her to observe the spot in the first place. Also, he or she will have to deal with all the affairs with the evidence collected whether he or she wants or not, so analytic and reasoning capacities are required too.

主體

1. Additionally, we can't forget to improve our professional skills since they are the very foundation of our career.

   → 繼續將劃底線的部分改為考生（您）所欲描述的角色的必要特質或能力方面。

   → Additionally, they can't forget to utilize their logic capacities in that they are the very foundation of their career.

2. College education may just simply be the baby step of our career not to mention that we are all freshmen in the society after we graduate.

   → 將劃底線的部分改為考生（您）所欲描述的角色的相關特質以及其所會面對的可能最困難的部份。

   → Being observatory and innovative may just simply be the baby step of their career not to mention that they are all beginners in this area when they deal with their first case.

結尾

   之後再編述一項理由支持所提出的論點。

1. From the above reasons, college students should try to make themselves engross in academic learning, handling their own life, and socializing with college mates or some coworkers if they have part-time job after school. Busy, fascinating though.

   → 將劃現部分改成考生（您）所欲描述的角色以及他／她們的必要特質

或能力方面，最後結論句以不同方式重述重點句。

→ From the above reasons, <u>detectives</u> should try to make themselves engross in <u>keeping their minds fresh and sharp, having their own insights, and making sure that everything goes in the order</u> if they want to maintain their reputation and working efficiency. Busy, fascinating though.

E 此類考題考前及應考時準備筆記關鍵字

1. 不同的職稱或工作類型（job, work, title）

   I work as a CEO, basketball player, movie star, doctor, writer, firefighter...

2. 不同的職稱或工作類型的概要工作內容

   I need to make a major decision; a good point guard needs strong defense; an actor needs good acting skills; a doctor needs to diagnose the disease directly; a good columnist needs to be insightful; a writer has to be good at words...

3. 不同的工作類型所需的相關專業領域能力

   You are required to have the ability of management; leadership; to be energetic; sharp in observation; fashionable; determined; insightful; cautious; brave, inspiring; sensitive...

F 換句話說補一補 Track 15

A college student should be required to have basic life skills, socializing skills and individual professional skills from my point of view.
大學生應有基本生活能力、人際相處溝通能力以及個人專業技能。

Part
1

Part
2

Part
3

1. In my opinion, a college student should be required to have basic life skills, socializing skills and individual professional skills.

   我認為大學生應有基本生活能力、人際相處溝通能力以及個人專業技能。

2. It seems to me that a college student should be required to have basic life skills, socializing skills and individual professional skills.

   大學生應有基本生活能力、人際相處溝通能力以及個人專業技能，我似乎是這麼想的。

Additionally, we can't forget to improve our professional skills since they are the very foundation of our career.

此外，必須要精進專業知能及學習，因為大學所學只是職業生涯根本。

1. Moreover, we should improve our professional skills because it is the very foundation of our career.

   此外，我們必須要精進專業知能及學習，因為大學所學只是職業生涯根本。

2. Furthermore, improving our professional skills is strongly suggested in that they are a very foundation of our career.

   此外，必須要精進專業知能及學習，因為那只是職業生涯根本。

   補充：除此之外：**Moreover, Furthermore, Likewise, Also, Besides, As well, In addition, Still...**

From the reasons above, college students should try to make themselves engross in academic learning, handling their own life, and socializing with college mates or some coworkers if they have part-time job after school.

從以上所述理由，大學生應試著致力於念書、管理自己的生活還有在課後打工時與人互動溝通。

1. Therefore, taking a part-time job after school encourages college students to socialize with coworkers. Also, academic learning and handling their own life provide them with the chance to communicate with college mates.

   也因此，課後的兼職有助於學生和同事間互動；學術上的學習和處理自己的生活則讓他們有機會和大學同學溝通。

2. For the reasons outlined above, it's better that college students are busy at academic learning, handling their own life, and socializing with college mates or some coworkers if they have part-time job after school.

   由以上所述原因，大學生最好忙於念書、於念書、管理自己的生活還有在課後打工時與人互動溝通。

想想看還能怎麼答 Track 16

Going to college is a huge step in life. It's a smart choice to make it count instead of fooling around during college time. So if there's some list that I would suggest for college students, I would say that perhaps academic studying, socializing, and international views are the skills required and to be developed in college based on my experience. I feel that academic studying is a way to build professional skills so we will have some fundamental knowledge by the time we leave college. Also, communicating with people well can facilitate our professional skills to be noticed and contributed to the institution, community and society efficiently we are engaged with. Additionally, probably it is a current trend that knowing different cultures and respecting different kind of views are inevitable skills for a promising career. Those skills take some work to build but it is worthwhile for sure.

單字小解

① **academic** *adj.* 學術的

② **socialize (socializing)** *v.* 人際溝通；社交

③ **international** *adj.* 國際的

④ **professional** *adj.* 專業的

⑤ **institution** *n.* 機構

⑥ **inevitable** *adj.* 不可或缺的

⑦ **promising** *adj.* 有前景的

⑧ **career** *n.* 生涯

⑨ **international view** *ph.* 國際觀

⑩ **contribute to...** *ph.* 貢獻於……

Part
1

Part
2

Part
3

中文翻譯

　　上大學是人生中重要一步。既然如此，當然就要讓此經驗值得票價。若真的要給大學生一張必做的事項清單，我認為念好學術課目、學習人際溝通以及培養國際觀是一定要的。念好學術科目是累積專業技巧的方式，並為畢業後打好基礎。同時，與人溝通能夠增進我們專業的能見度，並將這些專業有效貢獻給社群、社會及我們工作的機構。此外，了解並尊重各種不同的文化和看法已是當前的趨勢，同時也是有前景的工作上必備的技巧。這些技巧培養需花時間，但絕對值得。

Unit 05
未來目標
Future Goals

A 準備方向提示

1. 此類型題目為對未來的憧憬及描述性質，平時多思考個人的興趣或對未來願景（Personal interests, future visions）。

2. 平時需累積對個人學習領域的英文單字量，遇此題目就可放在自己在未來對社會的貢獻、對自己的期許、或夢想實現（Contributions, expectations, dreams）等。

3. 保持對**國際新聞或知識接觸的習慣**（**International news and knowledge**），遇此題目可發展觸類旁通的敘述，當做是影響自己對未來做此選擇的基礎或理由。

模擬題目 Track 17

Question: Imagine what you will be doing 10 years from now. What's the difference that will be made about yourself?

十年後會做什麼？自己有什麼改變？

Part 1

Part 2

Part 3

參考範文

　　From what I picture my future in ten years, I will be taking a promising job in marine industry and contributing what I learned to the society. My major is Marine Biology and honestly speaking I love what I'm studying. I enjoy spending time reading Marine Biology and getting a profound understanding of the ocean biological system. The more I learn from those studies, the more I would like to take action in developing a coexisting friendly environment to marine creatures. My mom was a passionate biologist and practiced her dream in Australia. Her adventures inspired me so much since I was a little kid. Our family also moved to Australia for her marine project. That's why I'm not strange to dolphins and whales. I'm glad to be a Marine Biology major. Thus, I imagined myself doing research on creating greater marine environment and upgrading ocean to a better place.

中文翻譯

　　我想像十年後，我將會有一個前途似錦的海業工作並且在此領域內對社會貢獻我所學。我喜歡我的主修海洋生物學。我喜歡研究海洋生物學並對此領域有更深度的了解。所學越多，我越想為海洋生物發展出最美好的生態環境。我的母親是一位海洋生物學者，並在澳洲實現她的夢想。她的海洋工作生涯冒險在我年幼時大大啟發了我的視野。為此我們全家還一起搬到澳洲。海豚及鯨魚就如同我的朋友般，我真的喜歡海洋生物學。因此，未來十年的我將會研究如何晉升海洋生態系統赴付諸行動。

單字、片語說分明

① **promising** *adj.* 有前景的、前途似錦的

② **marine industry** *n.* 海洋工業

③ **major** *n.* 主修

④ **Marine Biology** *n.* 海洋生物學

⑤ **contribute to** *ph.* 對……有貢獻

⑥ **take action in** *ph.* 在……方面行動

⑦ **do research on** *ph.* 在……方面做研究

新托福口說參考範文解析與評點

托福口說答題拿分首要掌握以下要點

1. **What（內容資訊）**：本範文完全針對題目回答了所需的**內容資訊**。

2. **How（再解釋 1）**：文法上沒有錯誤，語意上可以理解，同時語意本身就有因果關係，使聽者容易跟隨講者的話題內容。使用常用簡單明瞭的英文詞彙及句型片語，則能夠增加口語的流暢性。

3. **Why（再解釋 2）**：本範文沒有離題，絕對針對題目回答，沒有答非所問。它使用了連接語詞 thus 點出最後的結論句。句與句之間有強烈因果關係或故事情境先後連貫關係，明顯連續指出二至三種不同的支持論點及理由。

在描述內容資訊時，本範文首先提出

1. My **major** is Marine Biology and honestly speaking I love what I'm studying. I enjoy spending time reading **Marine Biology** and getting profound understanding of the ocean biological system. The more I learn from those studies, the more I would like to **take action in** developing a coexisting friendly environment to marine creatures. → 也就是先點出是自己非常有興趣的主修及關心的議題。

2. 並再以自己的親身經歷及成長過程加強描述做此答案的原因 → My mom was a passionate biologist and practiced her dream in Australia. Her adventures inspired me so much since I was a little kid. Our family also moved to Australia for her marine project. That's why I'm not strange to dolphins and whales.

3. 此範文也從實質貢獻方面、心理層面、以及個人成長經驗不同方面點出回答者本身做此選擇的原因理由，並點出了以下個人做此選擇的原因：在**實質貢獻方面**（**contribute to society; developing a coexisting friendly environment to marine creatures**）、個人成長經驗（**mom's adventures inspire me...; Australian life experience**），以及心理層面（**I love Marine Biology; ...not strange to ocean creatures...**）。

4. 結尾結論句的重申及重新潤飾表示出答題者對題目的了解因此掌握良好。

新托福口說論述的架構組成單位

1. 開頭介紹（**Introduction**）：

   From what I picture my future in ten years, I will be taking a **promising** job in **marine industry** and **contributing** what I learned to the society.

2. 文章主體（**Body**）：

   A. 支持論點一（Supporting idea 1）：

   I. 支持句一（Supporting sentence 1）：

   My **major** is Marine Biology and honestly speaking I love what I'm studying. I enjoy spending time reading **Marine Biology** and getting profound understanding of the ocean biological system.

   II. 支持句二（Supporting sentence 2）：

   The more I learn from those studies, the more I would like to **take action in** developing a coexisting friendly environment to marine creatures.

   B. 支持論點二（Supporting idea 2）：

   I. 支持句一（Supporting sentence 1）：

   My mom was a passionate biologist and practiced her dream in Australia. Her adventures inspired me so much since I was a little kid. Our family also moved to Australia for her Marine project.

   II. 支持句二（Supporting sentence 2）：

   Our family also moved to Australia for her marine project. That's why I'm not strange to dolphins and whales.

3. 結尾結論（**Conclusion**）：

　　I'm glad to be a Marine Biology major. Thus, I imagined myself **doing research on** creating greater marine environment and upgrading ocean to a better place.

　　此篇是有關於對於未來的一切的想像及假想題目，想當然爾就不會有一個所謂的標準答案。**重點一樣是放在對事物描述的能力，強調易於理解、有邏輯性、對一個假設性議題在一定時間裡綜合整述的能力。**

Part
1

Part
2

Part
3

D 新托福口說答題模板套用 🅐 Track 18

　　以上述短文為例，相關議題可依以下短文解析做變化，遇此類托福口說題目時可侃侃而談對題目迎刃而解。未劃底線的部分可不需更改，**劃底線**部分可替換為考生本身的經驗以及欲描述的項目。

開頭

1. From what I picture my future in ten years, I will be taking a promising job in marine industry and contributing what I've learned to the society.
　→ 將劃底線的部分改為考生（您）的**志向**以及**對夢想情境**的描述。
　→ From what I picture my future in ten years, I will be homeschooling my own children and teaching in a public school.

主體

1. My major is Marine Biology and honestly speaking I love what I'm studying. I enjoy spending time reading Marine Biology and getting a profound understanding of the ocean biological system.
　→ 將劃底線的部分改為考生（您）的**主修或專長描述**以及有熱忱的方面。
　→ My major is Secondary Education and honestly speaking I love what I'm studying. I enjoy spending time with learners and getting a profound understanding of facilitating learning.
2. The more I learn from those studies, the more I would like to take action in developing a coexisting friendly environment to marine creatures.
　→ 將劃底線的部分改為考生（您）可提供的**貢獻**以及**專長呈現**。

→ The more I learn from those studies, the more I would like to take action in helping learners overcome their learning difficulty.

結尾

之後再編述一項理由支持所提出的論點。

1. Thus, I imagined myself doing research on creating greater marine environment and upgrading ocean to a better place.

　　→ 將劃底線的部分改成考生（您）的志向以及對夢想情境的描述，和開頭類似，但不同的地方在於最後結論句以不同方式重述重點句。

　　→ Thus, I imagined myself homeschooling and helping other kids' learning in order to maintain my passion in life and career.

E 此類考題考前及應考時準備筆記關鍵字

1. 志向以及對夢想情境的描述

I want to be an engineer; a pediatrician; a teacher; an accountant; a chef, a CEO...

2. 主修或專長描述以及有熱忱的方面

I have passion about engineering; education; accounting, cuisine, international business...

3. 貢獻以及專長呈現

I aim to contribute to the society; facilitate learning, provide a variety of teaching materials; surprise people; increase job opportunities...

F 換句話說補一補 🌐 Track 19

From what I picture my future in ten years, I will be taking a promising job in marine industry and contributing what I learned to the society.
十年後的我會在前景看好的海洋業工作,並將我的所學貢獻社會。

1. I will be taking a promising job in marine industry and contributing what I learned to the society from my version of my future ten years from now.
   十年後,我會在海洋業服務,這是一個很有前途的工作,同時我也會將我所學貢獻給社會。

2. I have a vision of taking a promising job in marine industry and contributing what I learned to the society ten years later in my fature.
   我能想像十年後的未來,我會在前途似錦的海洋業就職,並將所學貢獻給社會。

My major is Marine Biology and honestly speaking I love what I'm studying.
我主學海洋生物學,而且老實說,我愛我的所學。

1. Honestly, I love my major Marine Biology.
   老實說,我很愛我的主修,海洋生物學。

2. Marine Biology is definitely my favorite major.
   海洋生物學絕對是我最愛的主修。

That's why I'm not a stranger to dolphins and whales.
因此,我對海豚和鯨魚並不陌生。

1. That's why I know dolphins and whales very well.
   那就是為什麼我非常了解海豚和鯨魚。

2. That's why dolphins and whales are no foreign words to me.
   因此,海洋和鯨魚對我來說不是天方夜譚。

G 想想看還能怎麼答 Track 20

Painting is always my number one free time activity after work. Whenever I'm available, I paint, draw or create some artworks. Other than my regular teaching job, I am also trying as possible as I could to create some space and time for my hobby. Teaching sometimes can be very tiring and frustrating when out of passion and motivation; however, painting, drawing and create some artworks can always help have my energy back for me to face another few week's workload, and at the same time, bring me some inner refreshment and inspiration. With this kind of life style, I imagine myself creating artworks in my own studio room. If I would like to, I also share my artworks with my students from special class demands. That is to say, I will have my own studio and get some art business going on 10 years from now.

單字小解

① **motivation** *n.* 動機
② **refreshment** *n.* 提振精神
③ **inspiration** *n.* 靈感
④ **studio** *n.* 工作室

中文翻譯

　　繪畫是我最喜愛的休閒娛樂。每當我有空時，我嘗試繪畫及創作些藝術作品。除了專職的教學工作，只要一有空，我會撥時間空間給自己的興趣。教學工作有時會因失去熱情與動機而感疲倦，但繪畫及創作藝術作品常常能幫我恢復精力儲備下幾週的工作能量，同時啟發我並帶來煥然一新的感受。這樣的生活方式讓我想像我在工作室創作的樣子，如果我想，我還能和特教的學生分享我的作品，也就是說，10 年後我會有我自己的工作室，可能還會經營和藝術相關的生意。

Part 1

Part 2

Part 3

Unit 06
生活經驗 1
Experiences 1

A 準備方向提示

1. 此類型題目結合了最喜歡或最常去的地點、最喜歡從事的一些活動,以及這些地點或活動等對自己的意義的綜合型的答題(activities, places, best time in life)。

2. 將本書其他相關地點、活動、人物等描述的文章、重點提示以及準備方向皆熟讀,在這類型的題目上進行整合發揮。

3. 平時可收看 CNN 旅遊報導、相關英文旅遊節目、閱讀英文旅遊雜誌介紹、瀏覽英文旅遊網站(travel channel, travel magazines, travel website, travel introduction)、各國或各洲的旅遊觀光局的英文導覽網站,相信會對此題目有不同凡響的心得描述!

B 模擬題目 Track 21

Question: When and where in your life have you been the happiest? Use reasons and details to support your response.

目前人生最快樂的一段時光。請解釋並詳述來支持你的回答。

參考範文

Staying in Australia was the most wonderful experience I had in my life. At a beach town with changing weather, I could always get to the ocean just fifteen minutes by bicycling. And as I remembered, it only took me fifteen minutes to go back and forth between the beach and where I lived. The story went far more than that because by the time I got to the beach, what amazed me the most was the coral reefs! Also, when seasons changed, jelly fish was EVERYWHERE sometimes. If anyone asked me if I wanted to go to the South Pole for penguins, I would say "No". I didn't need to brave the freezing weather to see the cute penguins. They could be found in Australia, New Zealand and Tasmania as well. Here, I could see penguins coming out of the water and it was rare since only a small number of penguins living here. When recalling those days in Australia, I would say that was the best time of my life.

中文翻譯

待在澳洲的那段時光是我人生中最美好的經驗。那裡鄰近海邊，氣候多變，騎單車只要 15 分鐘就能到達。我還記得往返沙灘和我住的地方也只要 15 分鐘。不僅如此，一到沙灘後，最讓我驚豔的是珊瑚礁！此外，隨著氣候的變化，水母有時隨處可見。若有人問我要不要到南極看企鵝，我會說「不」；我不用忍受寒冷的天

氣就能看到可愛的企鵝。企鵝在在澳洲、紐西蘭和塔斯馬尼亞都能找得到。在這裡我能夠看到企鵝浮出水面這樣難得的景象，因為這裡的企鵝數量非常的少。每當回想起待在澳洲的那日子，我會說那是我人生中最棒的時光。

單字、片語說分明

① back and forth *adv.* 往返

② amaze *v.*（讓人感到）驚艷

③ coral reef *n.* 珊瑚礁

④ jelly fish *n.* 水母

⑤ brave *v.* 忍受、面對（難題、挑戰或困境）

⑥ freezing *adj.* 寒冷的

新托福口說參考範文解析與評點

托福口說答題拿分首要掌握以下要點

1. **What（內容資訊）**：本範文完全針對題目回答了所需的內容資訊。

2. **How（再解釋 1）**：文法上沒有錯誤，語意上可以理解。本篇因為是地點、事物的綜合描述發揮，因此語氣呈現活潑，語意間內容本身也有承接（如使用連接作用的句子：**The story is far more than that...**），使聽者容易跟隨講者的話題內容。使用常用簡單明瞭的英文詞彙及句型片語（如 **amaze; go back and forth...**），可增加口語上的流暢度。

3. **Why（再解釋 2）**：本範文沒有離題，絕對針對題目回答，沒有答非所問。文章描述了許多誘人的活動及小趣聞（如 **penguins, coral reef, jelly fish**），栩栩如生描述出澳洲生活的曼妙精采，令聽者意猶未盡！二至三種不同的支持論點及理由也同時描繪出來。

> 在描述內容資訊時，本範文首先提出

1. Staying in Australia was the most wonderful experience I had in my life. → 開頭馬上不拖泥帶水的點出最精采的一段生活是在澳洲。

2. 並再以自己的親身經歷的小鎮風情加強描述做此答案的原因 → At a beach town with changing weather at the same time, I could always get to the ocean just fifteen minutes by bicycling. And as I remembered, it only took me fifteen minutes to go **back and forth** between the beach and where I lived.

3. 支持論點二接著提出迷人的珊瑚礁及俏皮的水母，為景點澳洲提出具體例證及輔佐說明 → The story went far more than that because by the time I got to the beach, what **amazed** me the most was the **coral reefs**! Also, with the change of season, **jelly fish** was EVERYWHERE sometimes.

4. 支持論點三再根據作者所見所聞，**繼續舉出獨一無二的企鵝**，為景點澳洲再度提出具體例證及輔佐說明 → If anyone asked me if I want to go to the South Pole for penguins, I would say "No". I didn't need to **brave** the **freezing** weather to see the cute penguins. They could be found in Australia, New Zealand and Tasmania as well.

5. 支持論點三的補述強調 → Here, I could see penguins coming out of the water and it was rare since only a small number of penguins living here.

6. 此範文也從對**實際生活方面、心理層面、以及個人經驗的小鎮風情、趣聞**等不同方面點出回答者本身做此選擇的原因理由，並點出了以下個人做此選擇的原因：如在對**實際**生活方面（**going back and forth between the beach and where I lived**）、心理層面（**...what amazed most...**）以及個人體驗過的事及趣聞（**coral reef...jelly fish...penguins...**）。

7. 結尾結論句清楚明確重申（此類題目的萬用結論句），反映出答題者對題目的掌握良好 → When recalling those days in Australia, I would say that was the best time of my life.

新托福口說論述的架構組成單位

1. 開頭介紹（**Introduction**）：

　　Staying in Australia was the most wonderful experience I had in my life.

2. 文章主體（**Body**）：

A. 支持論點一（Supporting idea 1）：

I. 支持句一（Supporting sentence 1）：

　　At a beach town with changing weather at the same time, I could always get to the ocean just fifteen minutes by bicycling.

II. 支持句二（Supporting sentence 2）：

　　And as I remembered, it only took me fifteen minutes to go **back and forth** between the beach and where I lived.

B. 支持論點二（Supporting idea 2）：

I. 支持句一（Supporting sentence 1）：

　　The story went far more than that because by the time I got to the beach, what **amazed** me the most was the **coral reefs**!

II. 支持句二（Supporting sentence 2）：

Also, with the change of season, **jelly fish** was EVERYWHERE sometimes.

C. 支持論點三（Supporting idea 3）：

I. 支持句一（Supporting sentence 1）：

If anyone asked me if I want to go to the South Pole for penguins, I would say "No". I didn't need to **brave** the **freezing** weather to see the cute penguins.

II. 支持句二（Supporting sentence 2）：

They could be found in Australia, New Zealand and Tasmania as well. Here, I could see penguins coming out of the water and it was rare since only a small number of penguins living here.

D. 結尾結論（Conclusion）：

When recalling those days in Australia, I would say that was the best time of my life.

　　此題目要求的是考生描述地點、事件、或人物（有的話）的表達能力，是地點、事件、人物描述的綜合發揮。本書的人物篇中都有各項的範例及準備方向，在考前研讀本書循序漸進的準備，考試時適時抓出幾個來彰顯最深刻的景點、喜歡的活動、趣聞事件或影響自己最深刻的人物。**開頭及結尾可著重在重新潤飾重申（有萬用句）**，掌握好這些要點，就是考生在一定時間內快速整述的綜合口語能力了。

D 新托福口說試題範文模板套用 Track 22

以上述短文為例，相關議題可依以下短文解析做變化，遇此類托福口説題目時可侃侃而談對題目迎刃而解。未劃底線的部分可不需更改，**劃底線**部分可替換為考生本身的經驗以及欲描述的項目。

開頭

1. Staying in <u>Australia</u> was the most wonderful experience I had in my life. At <u>a beach town</u> with changing weather at the same time, I could always <u>get to the ocean just fifteen minutes by bicycling. And as I remembered, it only took me fifteen minutes to go back and forth between the beach and where I lived.</u>

→ 將劃底線的部分改為考生（您）**所欲描述的景點特性、地形、或活動重心。**

→ Staying in <u>Jamaica</u> was the most wonderful experience I had in my life. At <u>a beach town</u> with changing weather at the same time, I could always <u>get to the ocean just fifteen minutes by bicycling. And as I remembered, it only took me fifteen minutes to go back and forth between the beach and where I lived.</u>

備註：Australia 及 Jamaica 皆在海洋型休閒娛樂景點著稱，剛好 有許多點可相通。**建議考生可以依照海洋型或山岳型城市或區域景點為兩大重點來準備。Part 1 Unit 03** 的想想看還可以怎麼答的部份另有湖泊型的景點區域提示範本可參考！

2. The story went far more than that because by the time I got to the beach, what amazed me the most was the <u>coral reefs</u>! Also, <u>when seasons changed, jelly fish</u> was EVERYWHERE sometimes.

→ 並描述更真實的相關活動經驗，劃底線的部分可以套用相關的景點。

→ The story went far more than that because by the time I got to the beach, what amazed me the most was <u>the sanshine on the island</u>! Also, <u>due to its geographical feature</u>, <u>white or golden sand beach</u> was <u>spreading ahead of me</u>, which was fantastic.

主體

1. If anyone asked me if I wanted to go to <u>the South Pole for penguins</u>, I would say "No". I <u>didn't need to brave the freezing weather to see the cute penguins. They could be</u> found in <u>Australia, New Zealand and Tasmania as well.</u>

   → 將劃底線的部分改為考生（您）的**重點景點及活動細項、趣聞、或特色**方面。

   → If anyone asked me if I wanted to go to <u>Starbucks for fresh coffee or to any night club for Reggae music</u>, I would say "No". I <u>didn't fear to brave the blazing sunlight and felt excited to participate in parties held in beach bars. Those interesting experiences could only</u> be found in <u>Jamaica</u>.

2. Here I could <u>see penguins coming out of the water</u> and it was <u>rare since only a small number of penguins living here</u>.

   → 劃底線的部分改為考生（您）所選景點或活動上獨特的地方。

   → Here, I could taste <u>the freshest coffee and enjoy the unique Reggae music</u> and it was <u>great since Jamaica is the birthplace for the both things</u>.

結尾

1. When recalling those days in <u>Australia</u>, I would say that was the best time of my life.

   → 可以此萬用型結論句在結尾再度重申，劃底線部分換地方即可。

   → When recalling those days in <u>Jamaica</u>, I would say that was the best time of my life.

E 此類考題考前及應考時準備筆記要點

1. 描述地點的詞彙

   admirable, adventurous, caring, compassionate, intelligent, dynamic, earnest, elegant, hearty, moderate, prudent, reliable, sharing, steady, trusting, wise, understanding...

2. 個人相關成功事蹟

   excellent leadership, good management, successful career, investment, academic success, guru, show talent on~, in the history of~ ...

3. 彰顯所景仰人物事蹟的詞彙

   appreciate, admire, impress, influence, encourage, inspire, inspirational, insightful, respectful ...

F 換句話說補一補　Track 23

Staying in Australia was the most wonderful experience I had in my life.
待在澳洲的那段時光是我人生中最美好的經驗。

1. The most wonderful experience I had is when I was in Australia.
   我最美好的經驗是我待在澳洲的那段時光。

2. I highlight my staying in Australia as the most wonderful experience.
   我要特別提出我待在澳洲的那段時光是最美好的經驗。

It only took me fifteen minutes to go back and forth between the beach and where I lived.

往返沙灘和我住的地方也只要 15 分鐘。

1. I could be in the beach in just fifteen minutes since it was not far away from my place.

   海邊離我住的地方不遠，15 分鐘就能到了。

2. The beach was only fifteen minutes away from where I lived.

   海邊離我住的地方只要 15 分鐘。

The story went far more than that because by the time I got to the beach, what amazed me the most was the coral reefs!

不僅如此，一到沙灘後，最讓我驚豔的是珊瑚礁！

1. The story hadn't ended yet because by the time I got to the beach, the coral reefs were amazing!

   不僅如此，一到海邊後，那珊瑚礁真是讓人驚艷！

2. The story went on since by the time I got to the beach, the coral reefs were wonderful!

   不僅如此，一到海邊後，那珊瑚礁真是太美了！

Part 1

Part 2

Part 3

I have been studying in USA for a while; however, the happiest time is not when I am studying there. Weird, isn't it? Students' life is always supposed to be the period of time that provides us the most pleasure in life. Strangely but understandingly, my working hours are actually the happiest time because all those life experiences inspire me the most and whisper some encouraging words to support me. In other words, those days are the days I peacefully live day by day and know my goals for future. For instance, I help a few groups of young kids learn English and new things. Long time ago, if you asked me why I was doing what I was doing right now, I would not know how to answer. For now, I think I know the answer, which is that I want to see people's smiles. You know why. When we make people happy, we make ourselves happy as well. Easy as that, but we are not that smart to realize it immediately. And those experiences in the States have impressed me the most and inspired me a lot in many aspects of my life.

單字小解

① **for a while** 一陣子

② **strangely** *adv.* 奇怪地

③ **understandingly** *adv.* 可以理解地

④ **whisper** *v.* 呢喃

⑤ **encouraging** *adj.* 振奮人心的

⑥ **impress** *v.* 留下印象

中文翻譯

　　我曾經在美國留學一陣子，但最快樂的時光和念書無關，很奇怪，對吧？學生生活通常是一段讓我們最快樂的時光呀。對我來說，工作的時光其實才是最快樂的，很奇怪吧，但其實是能夠理解的，那些工作帶來的生活體驗深深啟發了我，並用鼓勵的話語來支持我。也就是說，我平靜地度過那段時光的每一天，並了解我未來的目標還幫忙一群孩子學習英文和新的事物。不久之前若你問我為什麼要做我現在正在做的事，我可能不知道要如何回答。但現在，我想我知道答案了，那就是我想要看到人們的笑容。你知道為什麼，當我們讓人們快樂時，我們也會快樂，就這麼簡單，但我們卻無法馬上了解。我一直記著那些在美國的經驗，而這些經驗也影響了我生命的各個層面。

Unit 07
生活經驗 2
Experiences 2

A 準備方向提示

1. 此類型題目要求考生分享各國風情、地標或習俗活動（festivals, activities, landmarks, tourist attractions）。

2. 累積可描述自己國家的文化（cultures）、著名景點（landmarks）、或年度活動（annual festivals）的英語詞彙。

3. 可固定閱讀英語學習雜誌（English learning magazines），或訂閱每週每日新消息或了解新活動；各式英語學習雜誌皆是為台灣考生量身訂做的優質日常口説資源。

 模擬題目 Track 25

Question: Where do you recommend the most to your friends from the other countries? Use reasons and details to support your response.

最值得介紹給外地人的地方？請解釋並詳述來支持你的回答。

參考範文

Kenting is a wonderful Taiwan tourist destination that I would put in the must-see list in Taiwan. It's a beautiful city in the Southern Taiwan with tropical climate. The flora of Kenting consists of coastal and terrestrial plants. Thus, the variety of fruits and vegetables amazingly attributes to Southern Taiwan's tropical weather. Enjoying the sea breeze by taking a peaceful scooter ride reenergizes your body on a cozy holiday. Also, whether you're a water sport enthusiast or not, you can try snorkeling, speed boating or banana boating, all kinds of water sports here. B&B can provide you with a great ocean view from the patio or balcony. A beach is just like a back garden located behind where you are staying. Some featured theme restaurants surprise their customers with innovative tropical fruit cocktails or drinks. To sum up, sightseeing here is definitely taking your breath away. Kenting is the paradise of leisure and fun.

中文翻譯

墾丁是台灣很棒的旅遊景點，是我會放在台灣必去清單裡的。這裡是南台灣的美麗熱帶城市，植物包含沿海和陸地的植物，因此這裡多樣的水果和蔬菜都要拜南台灣熱帶氣候所賜。在天氣涼爽的假日騎車迎著海風讓全身充滿力量。還有不管你是不是海上運動的愛好者，你都能嘗試潛水、水上快艇或香蕉船等各種海上活動。邊烤肉還能在庭院或陽台飽覽美麗的海景，海灘就像是你家的後花園。這裡的主題餐廳的創意熱帶水果雞尾酒或飲品讓顧客驚艷。總而言之，在此觀光絕對能讓人驚嘆不已，墾丁是休閒時光和樂趣的天堂。

單字、片語說分明

① **tourist destination** *n.* 旅遊景點

② **tropical** *adj.* 熱帶的

③ **flora** *n.* 植物

④ **consist of** *v.* 組成

⑤ **costal** *adj.* 沿岸的

⑥ **terrestrial** *adj.* 陸地的

⑦ **attribute to** *v.* 歸因於

⑧ **enthusiast** *n.* 熱愛者

⑨ **snorkeling** *n.* 浮潛

⑩ **provide sb with sth** *ph.* 提供

⑪ **patio** *n.* 庭院

⑫ **balcony** *n.* 陽台

⑬ **theme** *n.* 主題

⑭ **innovative** *adj.* 創新的

⑮ **cocktail** *n.* 雞尾酒

⑯ **to sum up** 總結

⑰ **sightseeing** *n.* 觀光

⑱ **leisure** *n.* 休閒時光

新托福口說參考範文解析與評點

托福口說答題拿分首要掌握以下要點

1. **What**（內容資訊）：本範文完全針對題目回答了所需的內容資訊。

2. **How**（再解釋 1）：文法上沒有錯誤，語意上可以理解，文章內有使用連接語詞（如 **Thus; Also; To sum up...**）語意間內容本身也有承接，使聽者容易跟隨講者的話題內容。使用常用簡單明瞭的英文詞彙及句型片語（如 Kenting is a wonderful Taiwan **tourist destination**; It's a beautiful city in the Southern Taiwan.），可增加口語上的流暢度。

3. **Why**（再解釋 2）：本範文沒有離題，絕對針對題目回答，沒有答非所問。景點介紹的文章著重於描述性質，有焦點句、主題句、活動或節慶內容描述、景點特色描述，堆疊而成具體理由以及支持論點。

在描述內容資訊時，本範文首先提出

1. Kenting is a wonderful Taiwan **tourist destination** that I would put in the must-see list in Taiwan. → 開頭立即點出目標地點。

2. 描述概觀的氣候及目標地特色 → It's a beautiful city in the Southern Taiwan with **tropical** climate. The **flora** of Kenting **consists of coastal** and **terrestrial** plants. Thus, the variety of fruits and vegetables amazingly **attributes to** Southern Taiwan's tropical weather.

3. 再度以個人宏觀經驗針對所提出的幾點，提出描述了具體例證及輔佐說明 → Enjoying the sea breeze by taking a peaceful scooter ride reenergizes your body on a cozy holiday.

4. 繼續提供另外相關景點活動 → Also, whether you're a water sport **enthusiast** or not, you can try **snorkeling**, speed boating or banana boating, all kinds of water sports here.

5. 強調景點吸引人入勝之處 → B&B can **provide** you **with** a great ocean view from the **patio** or **balcony**. Beach is just like a back garden **located** behind where you are staying. Some featured **theme** restaurants surprise their customers with **innovative** tropical fruit **cocktails** or drinks.

6. 此範文在氣候文化方面、引人入勝的活動、以及心理層面不同方面點出回答者本身做此選擇的原因理由，並點出了以下個人做此選擇的原因：在氣候文化方面（**tropical climate**）、引人入勝的活動（**snorkeling, speedboating, B&B, cocktails...**）以及心理層面（**reenergize; taking your breath away...**）。

7. 結尾結論句的重申及巧妙的重新潤飾表示出答題者對題目的了解因此掌握良好 → **To sum up, sightseeing** here is definitely taking your breath away. Kenting is the paradise of **leisure** and fun.

新托福口說論述的架構組成單位

1. 開頭介紹（**Introduction**）：

   Kenting is a wonderful Taiwan **tourist destination** that I would put in the must-see list in Taiwan.

2. 文章主體（**Body**）：

   A. 支持論點一（Supporting idea 1）：

   I. 支持句一（Supporting sentence 1）：

       It's a beautiful city in the Southern Taiwan with **tropical** climate.

II. 支持句二（Supporting sentence 2）：

The **flora** of Kenting **consists of coastal** and **terrestrial** plants.

III. 支持句三（Supporting sentence 3）：

Thus, the variety of fruits and vegetables amazingly **attributes to** Southern Taiwan's tropical weather.

B. 支持論點二（Supporting idea 2）：

I. 支持句（Supporting sentence）：

Enjoying the sea breeze by taking a peaceful scooter ride reenergizes your body on a cozy holiday.

C. 支持論點三：

Also, whether you're a water sport **enthusiast** or not, you can try **snorkeling**, speed boating or banana boating, all kinds of water sports here.

D. 支持論點四：

I. 支持句一（Supporting sentence 1）：

B&B can **provide** you **with** a great ocean view from the **patio** or **balcony**.

II. 支持句二（Supporting sentence 2）：

Beach is just like a back garden **located** behind where you are staying.

III. 支持句三（Supporting sentence 3）：

Some featured **theme** restaurants surprise their customers with **innovative** tropical fruit **cocktails** or drinks.

E. 結尾結論（**Conclusion**）：

To sum up, **sightseeing** here is definitely taking your breath away. Kenting is the paradise of **leisure** and fun.

此題目其實很好發揮。建議考生您可準備至少三個最喜歡的台灣景點，將景點的特色、氣候、每年的活動、地點吸引人的賣點等預備三篇類似文章，練習時放鬆心情閉上眼睛，想像您享受期間的時刻，將這些美好時光鋪成為短篇的英語口說文章，準備好需要的關鍵字（依景點不同會有些許差異，都是正面的景觀描述語），即使托福考試期間是如臨大敵的生死關頭，這短暫的幾十秒口說發揮，反而會讓您稍稍有溫暖的小憩角落陽光喔。

D 新托福口說答題模板套用 Track 26

以上述短文為例，相關議題可依以下短文解析做變化，遇此類托福口說題目時可侃侃而談對題目迎刃而解。未劃底線的部分可不需更改，**劃底線**部分可替換為考生本身的經驗以及欲描述的項目。

開頭

1. <u>Kenting</u> is a wonderful Taiwan tourist destination that I would put in the must-see list in Taiwan. It's a beautiful <u>city</u> in the <u>Southern</u> Taiwan with <u>tropical climate</u>.

→ 將劃底線的部分改為考生（您）所欲描述的目標景點及氣候。

→ <u>Yangming Mountain</u> is a wonderful Taiwan tourist destination that I would put in the must-see list in Taiwan. It's a beautiful <u>place</u> in the <u>Northern</u> Taiwan with <u>mild subtropical climate</u>.

備註：開頭萬用句：**Kenting** is a wonderful Taiwan **tourist destination** that I would put in the must-see list in Taiwan.

主體

1. The flora of <u>Kenting</u> consists of <u>coastal and terrestrial</u> plants. Thus, the variety of <u>fruits and vegetables</u> amazingly attributes to Southern Taiwan's <u>tropical weather</u>.

→ 隨後繼續追述所欲描述景點相關景點、景點特色、或狀況，並將劃底
線的部分換成其他景點的特色和氣候。

→ The flora of Yangming Mountain consists of mountain and continental plants. Thus, the variety of flora amazingly attributes to the Northern Taiwan's tropical weather.

2. Enjoying the sea breeze by taking a peaceful scooter ride reenergizes your body on a cozy holiday.

→ 將劃底線的部分改為考生（您）所欲描述的景點引人入勝之處方面。

→ Enjoying the romantic night view by having milk aroma oolong tea reenergizes your body on a cozy holiday.

3. Also, whether you're a water sport enthusiast or not, you can try snorkeling, speed boating or banana boating, all kinds of water sports.

→ 此段改為考生（您）所欲描述目標景點的著名年度活動。

→ Also, annual Yangming Mountain Flower Festival and hot spring offers you a relaxing walk and spa surrounded by fresh mother nature scenes.

4. B&B can provide you with a great ocean view from the patio or balcony. A beach is just like a back garden located behind where you are staying. Some featured theme restaurants surprise their customers with innovative tropical fruit cocktails or drinks.

→ 根據以上段落追加補述更多目標景點為優選的理由。將劃上底線部分改成考生（您）目標景點的其他特點。

→ B&B can provide you with a fascinating night view from the patio or balcony. Mother nature melody and flora area are just like in the back garden located behind where you are staying. Some featured theme restaurants surprise their customers with innovative cocktails or drinks.

備註：陽明山的話可改為：aroma of oolong tea。此段也很適合描述九

份夜景以及民宿。

萬用句：

→ Some featured theme restaurants surprised their customers with innovative cocktails or drinks.

結尾

1. To sum up, sightseeing here is definitely taking your breath away. <u>Kenting</u> is the paradise of leisure and fun.

   → 最後結論句以不同方式重述重點句，並將劃現部分改成考生（您）所欲描述的目標景點。

   → To sum up, sightseeing here is definitely taking your breath away. <u>Yangming Mountain</u> is the paradise of leisure and fun.

結尾萬用句：

→ To sum up, sightseeing is definitely taking your breath away. Yangming Mountain is the paradise of leisure and fun.

目 此類考題應考時準備筆記

1. 不同目標景點（landmarks, tourist attractions）

   I love Beitou spring; Wulai spring; Chinging Farm; The Botanical Garden; Yeh-Liu（a theme park in the Northern Taiwan）; Mt. Ali, Window on China（a theme playground in Taiwan）; Hsi-Tzu-Wan Beach, Kaohsiung; Love River; Tung-Shan River; Old Fort of Anping, Tainan; Taroko Gorge; Maokong...

2. 不同水陸上活動、節慶、年度活動或各地方代表性特色 tung blossom; beehive fireworks in Tanshui; neo-clasical Chinese architecture; flowers and jades; a traditional market; the world's tallest skyscrapers; I could go hiking; cycling; scuba diving; tea tasting

there...

3. 美景令人陶醉、有益身心或心曠神怡相關詞彙

The views and activities there help shape your body; **this place provides** you a good site to see the night view; **to experience** distinctive culture popular, gourmet; **to reenergize** my body; **to refresh** my mind; **to appreciate enchanting music...**

 換句話說補一補 🔘 Track 27

Kenting is a wonderful Taiwan tourist destination that I would put it in the must-see list in Taiwan.
墾丁是台灣很棒的旅遊景點,是我會放在台灣必去清單裡的。

1. When you have a chance to visit Taiwan, Kenting is a must-see in this charming country.
   若你有機會拜訪台灣這迷人的國家,墾丁就是你一定要去的地方。

2. Kenting is an intoxicating tourist attraction, so be sure to give it a try when Taiwan is on your way to visit.
   墾丁是一個非常迷人的景點,如果你正好會來台灣一趟,一定要來墾丁一趟。

Enjoying the sea breeze by taking a peaceful scooter ride reenergizes your body on a cozy holiday.
在天氣涼爽的假日騎車迎著海風讓全身充滿力量。

1. The sea breeze reenergizes your body if you take a peaceful scooter ride.
   您可邊騎車享受單車之旅,邊讓海風為自己補充能量。

2. The peaceful cycling along the beach reenergizes your body.
   在海邊來趟單車之旅能幫自己充滿能量。

Some featured theme restaurants surprise their customers with innovative tropical fruit cocktails or drinks.

這裡的主題餐廳的創意熱帶水果雞尾酒或飲品讓顧客驚艷。

1. Innovative tropical fruit cocktails or drinks surprise their customers at some featured theme restaurants.

   創意熱帶水果雞尾酒或飲品讓來訪主題餐廳的訪客驚艷。

2. Many tourists also highlight some featured theme restaurants because of their tropical fruit cocktails or drinks.

   主題餐廳的熱帶水果雞尾酒是許多觀光客大力推薦的。

想想看還能怎麼答 Track 28

I've been to Chicago, New York and Boston some metropolitan cities. Chicago is world known for its aesthetic architecture. New York embraces a variety of multicultural styles. Boston presents country's grand academic and classical ambience. From where I grow up, Taiwan, I would like to say that Taipei consists of all above features and still is developing into a capital city with the mix of modern and tradition. Here are some examples. Taipei 101 will surely surprise visitors with its spectacular night view. Jio-Fen and Wu-Lai's old streets probably show you some secret ancient treasures and traditional Taiwanese street foods. If you see a group of students visiting those places and saying hi to you, yap, Taipei is also the most packed city with universities and colleges. Be sure to say hi back to them, you may end up with a local tourist guide showing you around.

單字小解

① **be known for** 以（……）知名
② **aesthetic** *adj.* 有美感的
③ **embrace** *v.* 擁抱
④ **present** *v.* 呈現
⑤ **ambience** *n.* 氣氛

中文翻譯

　　我曾去過芝加哥、紐約和波士頓等的大城市；芝加哥的建築極富美感，世界有名；紐約擁有文化多元風格；波士頓展現宏偉的學術和古典氣氛。而我成長的台灣台北則擁有以上的特質，且不斷發展成為現代與傳統兼容的首都。這裡有一些例子，台北 101 大樓的夜景很壯觀，肯定讓訪客眼睛為之一亮。九份和烏來老街帶你看古老的神秘寶藏，品嚐台灣傳統街邊美食。若你偶然看到一群學生跟你打招呼，是的，台北市人口密集，到處都有大學和技術學院，那你也別忘了回聲嗨，然後你可能就會有當地的導遊帶你走走逛逛。

Unit 08
生活經驗 3
Experiences 3

A 準備方向提示

1. 此類型題目焦點描述世界著名景點或地標的描述（tourist attractions; landmarks; architecture）。

2. 累積可描述景點特色、節慶活動或愜意享受生活的詞彙（如 **tropical, historical, festivals, chill out, relaxation, peaceful...**）等，可增強說明所喜好活動的理由。

3. 結合前幾章描述性質題目參考答案，並於平時廣泛閱讀英文旅遊介紹的雜誌或影視娛樂節目，都可以為自己累積啟發式的腳本，在遇此題目時能有觸類旁通的描述。

B 模擬題目 🌐 Track 29

Question: Where is your favorite place to visit? Use reasons and details to support your response.
你最喜歡去的地方？請解釋並詳述來支持你的回答。

> ### 參考範文

The most interesting tourist attraction I've been to is the Phuket Ocean Resort in Thailand. Born in Taiwan surrounded by ocean, I'm not stranger to a big wide beach and sea. Surprisingly, the Phuket experience is still totally amazing even though I'm familiar with ocean and beach. I truly enjoyed seeing the sunset at Patong beach and walking along the beautiful fine sand beach. After then, served by pineapple tropical fruit tea, I was like in the heaven. Maybe it's because that we can never have enough ocean treat from Mother Nature, so the Patong beach and ocean adventure still impressed me the most during my Thailand trip. Patong is absolutely an interesting tourist attraction I've been to.

> ### 中文翻譯

　　我去過最有趣的旅遊景點是泰國的普吉海洋度假村。我出生在四面環海的台灣，對於沙灘和海並不陌生，但讓我驚訝的是，普吉島的體驗對熟悉海洋和沙灘的我來說依然驚奇。我很喜歡欣賞芭東海灘的夕陽，並沿著細沙海灘漫步。在享受一杯鳳梨熱帶水果茶後，我簡直就是在天堂了。或許是因為海洋帶給我們的享受我們永遠都感受不完，所以芭東沙灘和海洋冒險依然讓我在泰國之行中留下深刻印象。芭東島絕對是我去過最有趣的景點了。

單字、片語說分明

① **Phuket Ocean Resort** *n.* 普吉海洋度假村

② **tropical** *adj.* 熱帶的

③ **adventure** *n.* 冒險

④ **impress** *v.* 留下深刻印象

⑤ **absolutely** *adv.* 絕對地

新托福口說參考範文解析與評點

托福口說答題拿分首要掌握以下要點

1. **What（內容資訊）**：本範文完全針對題目回答了所需的內容資訊。

2. **How（再解釋 1）**：文法上沒有錯誤，語意上可以理解，採取的是語意間內容的上下連貫承接，使聽者容易跟隨講者的話題內容。使用常用簡單明瞭的英文詞彙及句型片語，可增加口語上的流暢度。

3. **Why（再解釋 2）**：本範文沒有離題，絕對針對題目回答，沒有答非所問。**文章使用了個人經驗**（如 **walked into the ocean, pineapple fruit tea...**），清楚生動地勾勒出旅行普吉島的風味之行。所描繪的情境先後皆有連貫關係，明顯連續指出不同的支持論點及理由。

在描述內容資訊時，本範文首先提出

1. The most interesting tourist attraction I've been to is the **Phuket Ocean Resort** in Thailand. → 開頭馬上不拖泥帶水的提出目標地標或景點。

2. 並再以自己的親身經歷及成長過程加強描述做此答案的原因 →

Born in Taiwan surrounded by ocean, I'm not stranger to a big wide beach and sea. Surprisingly, the Phuket experience is still totally amazing even though I'm familiar with ocean and beach. I truly enjoyed seeing the sunset at Patong beach and walking along the beautiful fine sand beach. After then, served by pineapple **tropical** fruit tea, I was like in the heaven.

3. 此範文也從個人成長經驗、興趣方面以及心理層面不同方面點出回答者本身做此選擇的原因理由，並點出了以下個人做此選擇的原因：在對個人成長經驗及興趣方面（**grow up in Taiwan; no stranger to a big wide beach and sea; walking along the beach; pineapple juice...**），以及心理層面（**amazed; like be in the heaven...**）。

4. 結尾結論句的重申及巧妙的重新潤飾表示出答題者對題目的了解，因此掌握良好 → Maybe it's because that we can never have enough ocean treat from mother nature, so the Patong beach and ocean **adventure** still **impressed** me the most during my Thailand trip. Patong is **absolutely** an interesting tourist attraction I've been to.

新托福口說論述的架構組成單位

1. 開頭介紹（**Introduction**）：

　　The most interesting tourist attraction I've been to is the **Phuket Ocean Resort** in Thailand.

2. 文章主體（**Body**）：

　A. 支持論點一（Supporting idea 1）：

　　I. 支持句一（Supporting sentence 1）：

　　　　I truly enjoyed seeing the sunset at Patong beach and

walking along the beautiful fine sand beach. After then, served by pineapple **tropical** fruit tea, I was like in the heaven.

B. 支持論點二（Supporting idea 2）：

I. 支持句（Supporting sentence 1）：

Maybe it's because that we can never have enough ocean treat from Mother Nature, so the Patong beach and ocean **adventure** still **impressed** me the most during my Thailand trip.

補充：此句已為上述的理由原因做些微的補述，同時連續語意引出結尾句。

C. 結尾結論（Conclusion）：

Patong is absolutely an interesting tourist attraction I've been to.

　　此題目要求的是考生表達對自己喜歡的世界各地景點或地標的描述能力，答案常常是因人而異，會因為考生的遊歷、經驗或社會經濟背景而選擇不同。不過，與前幾篇許多訣竅雷同，像是在於累積不同活動經驗、節慶、年度例行勝點等的描述，並以此融入對自己生命及心靈啟迪的描述（如 **It's like the heaven; fresh my mind; release my anxiety; set me free; exhausted me...**）等，考試時適時可運用這些描述提供自己正面能量的詞彙，並說明做此選擇的原因。因此，掌握好這些要點，就是考生在一定時間內快速整述自己喜歡的活動，以及對自己的正面影響的綜合口語能力了。

D 新托福口說答題模板套用 🔘 Track 30

　　以上述短文為例，相關議題可依以下短文解析做變化，遇此類托福口說題目時可侃侃而談對題目迎刃而解。未劃底線的部分可不需更改，<u>劃底線</u>部分可替換為考生本身的經驗以及欲描述的項目。

開頭

1. The most interesting tourist attraction I've been to is the Phuket Ocean Resort in Thailand.

→ 將劃底線的部分改為考生（您）喜歡的世界著名景點或地標的描述。

→ The most interesting tourist attraction I've been to is the Cape Town in South Africa.

補充：此開頭句為萬用型開頭句，劃底線的部分改成您的目標地或著名景點或地標即可。

2. Born in Taiwan surrounded by ocean, I'm not stranger to a big wide beach and sea. Surprisingly, the Phuket experience is still totally amazing even though I'm familiar with ocean and beach.

→ 並描述簡短個人經驗的相關描述，劃底線的部分改考生（您）欲描述的目標景點或世界著名地標。

→ Born in Taiwan surrounded by ocean, I'm not stranger to a big wide beach and sea. Surprisingly, the Cape Town experience is still totally amazing even though I grew up with ocean and beach.

主體

1. I truly enjoyed seeing the sunset beyond Patong beach and walking along the beautiful fine sand beach.

→ 同樣將劃底線的部分改為考生（您）的目標景點或世界著名地標。

→ I truly enjoyed seeing the sunset beyond Cape Town beach and walking along the beautiful fine sand beach. Can you believe it?

結尾

之後再編述一項理由，續上文支持所提出的論點，並悄悄的預告結尾句的來臨（此句因承接上文，也開示結尾句，因此在放到此處再度講解用途）。

1. Maybe we can never have enough ocean treat from mother nature, so the Patong beach and ocean adventure still impressed me the most during my Thailand trip.

   → 將劃現部分改成考生（您）喜歡並重視的活動或運動，最後結論句以不同方式重述重點句。

   → Maybe we can never have enough ocean treat from Mother Nature, so the Cape Town beach and ocean adventure still impressed me the most during my trip to South Africa.

2. Patong is absolutely an interesting tourist attraction I've been to

   → 將劃底線的部分改為考生（您）的目標景點或世界著名地標。

   → Cape Town is absolutely an interesting tourist attraction I've been to.

   補充：此結論句為萬用型結論句，劃底線的部分改成您的目標地或著名景點或地標即可。

E 此類考題考前及應考時準備筆記要點

1. 不同的休閒活動（sports, exercise, leisure activities）

   I like cycling, hiking, mountain climbing, clubbing, photography, bicycling, sightseeing, swimming...

2. 幫助個人放鬆或休憩的詞彙，可能是心靈或生理方面

   The massage helps me cool down, fresh my mind, reenergize, come up with new idea, relax; It's an inspiring experience...

3. 不同的風俗、建築物或觀光場景或賣點

   The time to MOMA; theatre; opera; bungee jumping; reggae music; beach party; fireworks; festivals; Memorial Hall; Wax Museum; National Park; watch dolphins, watch whales... is unforgettable.

F 換句話說補一補　🔵 Track 31

The most interesting tourist attraction I've been to is the Phuket Ocean Resort in Thailand.
我去過最有趣的旅遊景點是泰國的普吉海洋度假村。

1. The Phuket Ocean Resort in Thailand is the most interesting tourist attraction I've been to.
   泰國的普吉海洋度假村是我去過最有趣的旅遊景點。
2. I would definitely highlight the Phuket Ocean Resort in Thailand as the most interesting tourist attraction that I've been to.
   我一定會將泰國的普吉海洋度假村當作我去過最有趣的旅遊景點。

Born in Taiwan surrounded by ocean, I'm not stranger to a big wide beach and sea.
我出生在四面環海的台灣，對於沙灘和海並不陌生。

1. I was born in Taiwan surrounded by ocean, so a big wide beach and sea is not strange to me.
   我出生在四面環海的台灣，對於沙灘和海並不陌生。
2. On the island like Taiwan surrounded by ocean where I am from, I'm surely very familiar with a big wide beach and sea.
   我來自四面環海的島嶼台灣，我真的非常熟悉寬闊的沙灘和大海。

After then, served by pineapple tropical fruit tea, I was like in the heaven.
再享受一杯鳳梨熱帶水果茶後，我簡直就是在天堂了。

1. After then, the pineapple tropical fruit tea completely took me to the heaven.
   然後喝下的鳳梨熱帶水果茶完全帶我飛向天堂。

2. After then, the pineapple tropical fruit tea just brought everything to the right place.

然後一杯梨熱帶水果茶喝下後，感覺都對了。

G 想想看還能怎麼答 🌀 Track 32

　　Visiting Paris is like that my dream comes true in lifetime. We land in the evening and head to our B&B right away. The antiques and statues inside and outside the B&B already amazed us with European design style. Our tiredness soon fades away and is replaced with the excitement to explore more. The next day, we can't wait one minute more. We want to discover Paris from the River Seine. Those beautiful views along River Seine explain why poets here are all so romantic. In the following days, Champs Elysses and Nortre Dame bring us right back to the place where the history comes into being. Last but not least, the main attraction, Eiffel Tower, is beyond just a fascinating and incredible world famous architecture. The whole trip is the most enjoyable tour.

單字小解

① **B&B** *n.* 為 Bed and breakfast 的縮寫，是一種提供住宿並附早餐的酒店
② **antique** *n.* 骨董
③ **statue** *n.* 雕像
④ **be replaced with** *ph.* 被……取代的
⑤ **River Seine** *n.* 塞納河
⑥ **Champs Elysses** *n.* 香榭麗舍大街
⑦ **Nortre Dame** *n.* 聖母院
⑧ **come into being** *ph.* 存在

⑨ **fascinating** *adj.* 迷人的

⑩ **incredible** *adj.* 不可思議的

中文翻譯

　　能到巴黎就像是我人生的美夢成真一樣。我們在晚上抵達後就直接前往住宿加早餐酒店（B&B），酒店內外的骨董和雕像設計走歐式風格，已經讓我們驚豔不已。我們的疲累很快就煙消雲散，取而代之的是想要深入探索的興奮心情。隔天我們一分鐘都等不及，很想從塞納河看看巴黎。塞納河沿岸的景色美麗，難怪這裡的詩人都那麼浪漫。接下來的幾天，香榭麗舍大街和聖母院將我們帶回歷史的痕跡中。雖然最後才提，但也是很重要的，那就是主要景點艾菲爾鐵塔已經不只是一座迷人又不可思議的世界級建築了。這整趟旅行真的非常愉快。

PART**2**

獨立論述篇

Unit 09
學習方式
Learning Style

A 準備方向提示

1. 此類型題目焦點為對自己嗜好（personal habits; hobbies）、意見或想法的描述，平時可思考自己喜歡做什麼（preferences）、為什麼或者是與此有關的話題。

2. 累積描述正面或負面心情的詞彙（如 comfortableness; troublesome; convenient...）等，可增強說明所喜好或選擇的理由。

3. 可以多方閱讀或收看英文節目（English magazines, English channels），在選擇個人偏好或選擇方面可有些啟發式腳本，進而為自己對此題目培養觸類旁通的描述。

🅑 模擬題目　🕐 Track 33

Question: What kind of learning style do you prefer, studying alone and studying in a group?

你偏好何種學習方式，一個人念或一起念？

參考範文

I prefer to study alone instead of in a group. Studying alone helps me build my fundamental knowledge of what I am reading by self-reflection. If I'm studying with a group of people, I may get more ideas for sure; however, I can't listen to my own voice for this new subject and sort out problems on my own. Also, I get hungry quite easily while studying, so I need to have some sandwiches or light snacks. In case my eating or snack time might bother other learners, I feel that it's a better idea for me to just study alone. One more reason why I choose to study alone is that I read the text out loud once awhile. In order to ensure other people to have quality reading time, I don't think that reading out loud is a good idea. Eventually, studying alone offers me more comfortableness than studying with a group of people.

中文翻譯

　　我偏好一個人而不是一起念書。一個人念書有助我透過自我省思，將閱讀的內容再加以轉化我的基礎知識。和人一起念書的確會得到更多想法，但是我沒辦法聽聽我對新科目的想法，也沒辦法自己解決問題。而且我在念書的時候容易肚子餓，所以當中我需要來點三明治或小點心。由於我的點心時間可能會打擾到其他人，我覺得還是一個人念書會比較好。我過一陣子就會把文章大聲念出來是另外一個原因。為了維持其他人的閱讀品質，我覺得把文章大聲念出實在不太好。最後，比起和一群人念書的感覺，一個人念書讓我感覺更自在。

中文翻譯

① prefer *v.* 偏好

② fundamental *adj.* 基礎的

③ self-reflection *n.* 自我反省

④ sort out *v.* 解決

⑤ on one's own *adv.* 依靠自己

⑥ in case *conj.* 萬一

⑦ bother *v.* 打擾

⑧ awhile *adv.* 一陣子

⑨ eventually *adv.* 最後

⑩ comfortableness *n.* 舒適

新托福口說參考範文解析與評點

托福口說答題拿分首要掌握以下要點

1. **What**（內容資訊）：本範文完全針對題目回答了所需的內容資訊。

2. **How**（再解釋 1）：文法上沒有錯誤，語意上可以理解，文章內有使用連接語詞（如 Also; one more reason; eventually, ...）等，語意間內容本身也有承接，使聽者容易跟隨講者的話題內容。另外使用常用簡單明瞭的英文詞彙及句型片語，則能提升口語上的順暢度。

3. **Why**（再解釋 2）：本範文沒有離題，絕對針對題目回答，沒有答非所問。文章誠實的描述了個人的想法以及習慣偏好（如 hungry; snacks;

read it out loud; comfortableness... ）等，明顯連續指出二種不同的支
持論點及理由。

> **在描述內容資訊時，本範文首先提出**

1. I **prefer** to study alone instead of in a group. → 開頭馬上不拖泥
帶水的提出表明立場，下好離手。

2. 並再以自己的意見、習慣及偏好，加強描述做此答案的原因 →
Studying alone helps me build my **fundamental** knowledge of
what I am reading by **self-reflection**. If I'm studying with a group
of people, I may get more ideas for sure; however, I can't listen to
my own voice for this new subject and **sort out** problems **on my
own**.

3. 支持論點二不但再度以個人意見、想法及偏好描述了具體例證及輔
佐說明 → Also, I get hungry quite easily while studying, so I need
to have some sandwiches or light snacks. **In case** my eating or
snack time might **bother** other learners, I feel that it's a better
idea for me to just study alone.

4. 支持論點三不放棄的再度陳述個人意見、想法及偏好，描述了具體
例證及輔佐說明 → One more reason why I choose to study alone
is that I read the text out loud once **awhile**. In order to ensure
other people to have quality reading time, I don't think that
reading out loud is a good idea.

5. 此範文也從個人見解（**fundamental knowledge; self-
reflection**）、習慣（**hungry and snack...**）及偏好（**read it out
loud...**）的不同方面點出回答者本身做此選擇的原因理由，並點出
了以下個人做此選擇的原因。

6. 結尾結論句的重申及巧妙的重新潤飾表示出答題者對題目的了解，因此掌握良好 → **Eventually,** studying alone offers me more **comfortableness** than studying with a group of people.

新托福口說論述的架構組成單位

1. 開頭介紹（**Introduction**）：

   I **prefer** to study alone instead of in a group.

2. 文章主體（**Body**）：

   A. 支持論點一（Supporting idea 1）：

   I.　支持句一（Supporting sentence 1）：

   　　Studying alone helps me build my **fundamental** knowledge of what I am reading by **self-reflection**.

   II.　支持句二（Supporting sentence 2）：

   　　If I'm studying with a group of people, I may get more ideas for sure; however, I can't listen to my own voice for this new subject and **sort out** problems **on my own**.

   B. 支持論點二（Supporting idea 2）：

   I.　支持句一（Supporting sentence 1）：

   　　Also, I get hungry quite easily while studying, so I need to have some sandwiches or light snacks.

   II.　支持句二（Supporting sentence 2）：

   　　In case my eating or snack time might **bother** other learners, I feel that it's a better idea for me to just study alone.

   C. 支持論點三（Supporting idea 3）：

   I.　支持句一（Supporting sentence 1）：

   　　One more reason why I choose to study alone is that I

read the text out loud once **awhile**.

  II. 支持句二（Supporting sentence 2）：

    In order to ensure other people to have quality reading time, I don't think that reading out loud is a good idea.

  D. 結尾結論（**Conclusion**）：

    Eventually, studying alone offers me more **comfortableness** than studying with a group of people.

  此題目詢問的為考生的貼身問題，十分容易回答。完全沒有對錯，**考驗考生英語口說的反應**，還有在一定時間內做好快速整述自己想法、意見以及個人偏好的英語口語能力。平時可以多多觀察自己，研究自己的喜好以及會做的決定，不但可增進對自己的了解，也可訓練自己對身邊環境變化的反應能力！

 新托福口說答題模板套用 🎧 Track 34

  以上述短文為例，相關議題可依以下短文解析做變化，遇此類托福口説題目時可侃侃而談對題目迎刃而解。未劃底線的部分可不需更改，**劃底線**部分可替換為考生本身的經驗以及欲描述的項目。

開頭

1. I prefer to study alone instead of in a group.

 → 將劃底線的部分改為考生（您）個人的偏好、意見及想法的描述。

 → I prefer to watch a movie alone at home instead of going to see a movie with a group of people.

主體

1. Studying alone helps me build my fundamental knowledge of what I am reading by self-reflection. If I'm studying with a group of people, I

may get more ideas for sure; however, I can't listen to my own voice for this new subject and sort out problems on my own.

→ 並描述簡短個人想法或見解的相關描述，劃底線的部分改為考生（您）**想要簡述個人想法或見解。**

→ Watching a movie at home alone helps me build my own understanding of what I am watching by self-reflection. If I'm watching a movie with a group of people, I may get more ideas for sure; however, I can't listen to my own voice for this new movie and enjoy it in private.

2. Also, I get hungry quite easily while studying, so I need to take some sandwiches or light snacks. In case my eating or snack time might bother other learners, I feel that it's a better idea for me to just study alone.

→ 將劃底線的部分改為考生（您）**個人喜歡的偏好與實例分享。**

→ Also, I get hungry quite easily while watching a movie, so I need to take some sandwiches or light snack. In case my eating or snack time might bother other people, I feel that it's a better idea for me to just watch a movie alone.

3. One more reason why I choose to study alone is that I read the text out loud once awhile. In order to ensure other people to have quality reading time, I don't think that reading out loud is a good idea.

→ 將劃底線的部分改為考生（您）**個人的喜好、意見或選擇。**

→ One more reason why I choose to watch a movie alone is that I sometimes follow the movie lines and read them out loud. In order to ensure other people to have quality movie time, I don't think that reading out loud is a good idea.

結尾

1. Eventually, studying alone offers me more comfortableness than

studying with a group of people.

→ 將劃現部分改成考生（您）的選擇或意見，最後結論句以不同方式重述重點句。

→ Eventually, <u>watching a movie at home alone</u> offers me more comfortableness than watching with a group of people.

■E 此類考題考前及應考時準備筆記關鍵字

1. 不同的生活習慣（habit, preference）

   I like watching a movie alone; dinning out; cooking by myself; doing the laundry at laundry center...

2. 對個人有正面或負面影響、心靈或生理方面等的詞彙

   It provides me with comfortableness; **it's** expensive; convenient; less troublesome; **it takes** a long time; **I'm in** a rush; **I do something slowly...**

3. 相關抽象描述情緒或想法的詞彙

   I required a basic understanding of something; the foundation of something; **this helps** self-reflection; **here to show** one's gratitude to...; **I feel full of** happiness; **it has** better connection; **I feel** awkward...

■F 換句話說補一補 Track 35

One more reason why I choose to study alone is that I read them out loud once awhile.

我過一陣子就會把文章大聲念出來是另外一個原因。

1. Another reason why I choose to study alone is because I read them out loud once in a while.

   我選擇一個人念書的另外一個原因是我偶爾會把文章大聲念出來。

2. Additionally, I choose to study alone because I read them out loud once awhile.

此外，我偶爾會把文章大聲念出來，所以我才會選擇一個人念書。

In case my eating or snack time might bother other learners, I feel that it's a better idea for me to just study alone.

由於我的點心時間可能會打擾到其他人，我覺得還是一個人念書會比較好。

1. To avoid the fact that my eating or snack time bothers other learners, I take studying alone as a better idea for me to do.

我為了不讓我的點心時光打擾到其他人，我覺得一個人念書會比較好。

2. In order not to bother other learners for my eating or snack time, studying alone wins the situation.

我為了不讓我的點心時光打擾到其他人，我覺得一個人念書會比較好。

Eventually, studying alone offers me more comfortableness than studying a group of people.

最後，比起和一群人念書的感覺，一個人念書讓我感覺更自在。

1. In the end, studying alone does make me feel more comfortable than studying with a group of people.

最後，一個人念書比一群人念書更讓我覺得自在。

2. As a matter of fact, studying alone offers me more comfortableness than studying with a group of people.

事實上，比起和一群人念書的感覺，一個人念書讓我感覺更自在。

G 想想看還能怎麼答 Track 36

Studying with a group of people can always bring me better inspiration and understanding. When I just graduated from university, I invited six people to an American Literature study group. That was a great experience. We figured out the whole timeline of American Literature and shared our insights with group members to create more innovative ideas. In the end of this study group, all of us got accepted by different master degree programs. Though we are in different schools or countries, we miss each other, and keep in touch with each other. What's more, we encourage each other and help sort out many problems together while we hit some bumpy roads. From my past experience and point of view, I like to study with a group of people instead of studying alone.

單字小解

① **figure out** *v.* 解決
② **a master degree program** *n.* 碩士學位課程
③ **a bumpy road** *n.* 顛簸的道路（指挫折、困境）

中文翻譯

和一群人一起念書總能帶給我許多靈感，理解力也會變得比較好，大學一畢業後，我邀請了六個人組成美國文學讀書會。那段經驗很美好，我們整理出美國文學的時間表，互相分享我們的想法，並激發出更多創新的點子。讀書會的尾聲，我們每個人都獲准進入不同的碩士學位課程。雖然我們現在分散在不同的學校和國家，我們仍然想念著對方，至今仍有聯絡。更重要的，是我們會互相鼓勵，碰到挫折時也會幫忙一起解決問題。從過去的經驗來看，我喜歡和一群人念書，而不是一個人念。

Unit 10
論述思考
Statement Discussion

 **準備方向提示**

1. 此類型題目焦點為考生個人價值觀點的描述,平時閱讀有深度的英文文章(如 Times; newspaper)思考自己對事物的看法及選擇、為什麼或者是與此有關的知識攝取。

2. 累積描述對社群關係正面建設的詞彙(如 **communicate effectively; connect to the world; discern the intricacies, make use of community resources...**),可增強說明支持某項能力指標的理由。

3. 可多方利用社群資源、閱讀英文社論或小組討論,進而攝取不同題材的正反面説法,這樣在價值觀建立方面,可有些啟發式的腳本,作為自己對遇此題目觸類旁通的描述。

 **模擬題目** Track 37

Question: Is the literacy important in the past? Why or why not?

您覺得讀寫能力在過去重要嗎？為什麼呢？

參考範文

Not only in the past but also nowadays, I still take literacy as an important skill. School education usually focuses on the content teachers teach. How to convey content is where literacy comes in. Perhaps teachers convey the information and knowledge to their learners, while literacy allows multiple opportunities for learners to discover other information on their own. In addition, discussions and brainstorms in class also bring out creativity and new ideas for learners to think about. Writing helps us keep ideas and make connections to our own thinking and others' ideas. Literacy is the ability to read, write, speak and listen in a way that enables us to communicate effectively. As a result, literacy is certainly an essential capacity that helps us effectively connect and interpret the world we live in.

中文翻譯

不管是過去或是現在，我都認為聽說讀寫能力是非常重要的技巧。學校教育通常專注於老師教的內容，如何表達內容就需要聽說讀寫的能力。老師先將資訊和知識傳給學習者，聽說讀寫表達能力則讓學習者有許多機會自己探索其他資訊。除此之外，課堂上的討論和腦力激盪則能夠為學習者帶來創意和新的想法。寫作則有助我們記下想法，把我們的思考和其他概念連結在一起。這種聽說讀寫的能力能夠讓我們有效溝通，因此絕對是非常關鍵的能力，有助我們有效連結並解讀這個世界。

單字、片語說分明

① content *n.* 內容

② multiple *adj.* 多元的

③ brainstrom *n.* 腦力激盪

④ connection *n.* 連結

⑤ effectively *adv.* 有效率地

⑥ essential *adj.* 重要的

新托福口說參考範文解析與評點

托福口說答題拿分首要掌握以下要點

1. **What**（內容資訊）：本範文完全針對題目回答了所需的內容資訊。

2. **How**（再解釋 1）：文法上沒有錯誤，語意上可以理解，文章內有使用連接語詞（如 **other than that; as a result...**），語意間內容本身也有承接，使聽者容易跟隨講者的話題內容。使用常用簡單明瞭的英文詞彙及句型片語，則能夠提升口語上的流暢度。

3. **Why**（再解釋 2）：本範文沒有離題，絕對針對題目回答，沒有答非所問。文章使用了個人經驗以及本身教育背景的詞彙（如 **school education; discover; discussion; creativity; communicate...**）等，清楚自己想法及經驗的結合。所描繪的情境先後皆有連貫關係，明顯連續指出二三種不同的支持論點及理由。

在描述內容資訊時，本範文首先提出

1. Not only in the past but also nowadays, I still take literacy as an important skill. → 開頭馬上不拖泥帶水的清楚提出立場。

2. 並再以自己本身想法、作風經驗以及價值觀感加強描述做此答案的
原因 → School education usually focuses on the **content** teachers
teach. How to convey content is where literacy comes in. Perhaps
teachers convey the information and knowledge to their learners,
while literacy allows **multiple** opportunities for learners to
discover other information on their own.

3. 支持論點二、三不但再度以個人想法經驗及價值觀感，提出描述了
具體例證及輔佐說明 → In addition, discussions and **brainstorms**
in class also bring out creativity and new ideas for learners to
think about. Writing helps us keep ideas and **make connections
to** our own thinking and others' ideas.

4. 此範文也從個人成長經驗、教育背景、以及社會觀感不同方面點出
回答者本身做此選擇的原因理由，並點出了以下個人做此選擇的原
因：在對個人觀感（**multiple resources of material;keep
ideas...**）、教育方法（**discussion; brain storming...**）以及社會
觀感（**multiple chances**）。

5. 結尾結論句的重申及巧妙的重新潤飾表示出答題者對題目的了解，
因此掌握良好 → Literacy is the ability to read, write, speak and
listen in a way that enables us to communicate **effectively**. As a
result, literacy is certainly an **essential** capacity that helps us
effectively connect and interpret the world we live in.

托福口說論述的架構組成單位

1. 開頭介紹（**Introduction**）：

Not only in the past but also nowadays, I still take literacy as
an important skill.

2. 文章主體（**Body**）：

A. 支持論點一（Supporting idea 1）：

I. 支持句一（Supporting sentence 1）：

School education usually focuses on the **content** teachers teach. How to convey content is where literacy comes in.

II. 支持句二（Supporting sentence 2）：

Perhaps teachers convey the information and knowledge to their learners, while literacy allows **multiple** opportunities for learners to discover other information on their own.

B. 支持論點二（Supporting idea 2）：

I. 支持句一（Supporting sentence 1）：

In addition, discussions and **brainstorms** in class also bring out creativity and new ideas for learners to think about.

II. 支持句二（Supporting sentence 2）：

Writing helps us keep ideas and **make connections to** our own thinking and others' ideas.

C. 結尾結論（Conclusion）：

Literacy is the ability to read, write, speak and listen in a way that enables us to communicate **effectively**. As a result, literacy is certainly an **essential** capacity that helps us effectively connect and interpret the world we live in.

　　此題目要求的是考生表達對自己喜歡的活動的描述能力，答案常常是因人而異，會因為考生的經驗及背景而選擇不同。不過，**訣竅在於累積不同活動經驗的描述，以此融入對自己生命及心靈洗滌的描述**，考試時適時運用這些描述提供自己正面能量的詞彙，去說明做此選擇的原因。因此，掌握好這些要點，就是考生在一定時間內快速整述自己喜歡的活動，以及對自己的正面影響的綜合口語能力了。

D 新托福口說答題模板套用 Track 38

　　以上述短文為例，相關議題可依以下短文解析做變化，遇此類托福口說題目時可侃侃而談對題目迎刃而解。未劃底線的部分可不需更改，**劃底線**部分可替換為考生本身的經驗以及欲描述的項目。

開頭

1. Not only in the past but also nowadays, I still take <u>literacy</u> as an important <u>skill</u>.
  → 將劃底線的部分改為考生（您）個人價值觀感或看法（根據題意）。
  → Not only in the past but also nowadays, I still take <u>education</u> as an important <u>tool</u>.

主體

1. School education usually focuses on the content teachers teach. How to convey content is where <u>literacy</u> comes in. Perhaps <u>teachers</u> convey the information and knowledge to their learners, while <u>literacy</u> allows multiple opportunities for learners to discover other information on their own.
  → 並提供個人的想法價值觀或作風的相關描述，將劃底線的部分改為考生（您）個人價值觀感或自己的看法（根據題意）。
  → <u>Family focuses on providing children with material and mental supports</u>. How to convey content is where <u>education</u> comes in. Perhaps <u>families</u> convey the information and knowledge to their children, while <u>education</u> allows multiple opportunities for children

to discover information on their own.

2. In addition, discussions and brainstorms in class also bring out creativity and new ideas for learners to think about. <u>Writing</u> helps us keep ideas and make connections to our own thinking and others' ideas.

→ 繼續將劃底線的部分改為考生（您）個人價值觀感或自己的看法（根據題意）。

→ In addition, discussions and brainstorms in classrooms also bring out creativity and new ideas for learners to think about. <u>Education</u> helps us keep ideas and make connections to our own thinking and others' ideas.

結尾

之後再重新整述主要議題，說明支持所提出的論點。再總結式或重新潤飾支持所提出的論點。

1. <u>Literacy is the ability</u> to read, write, speak and listen in a way that enables us to communicate effectively. As a result, <u>literacy</u> is certainly an essential <u>capacity</u> that helps us effectively connect and interpret the world we live in.

→ 將劃底線的部分改為考生（您）的個人價值觀感或看法（根據題意），最後結論句以不同方式重述重點句。

→ <u>Education is a way to enable learners</u> to read, write, speak and listen in a way that enables us to communicate effectively. As a result, <u>education</u> is certainly an essential <u>tool</u> that helps us effectively connect and interpret the world we live in.

E 此類考題考前及應考時準備筆記要點

1. 各式大分類詞彙意義

   It's when numeracy, language, technology, education, poverty, crime, health, economic growth, employment, globalization, innovation, obesity, culture ... **comes in.**

2. 對個人有正面影響的詞彙

   It transforms my life; **it's** lifelong learning; it provides intellectual process; **it's necessary to** attain full language literacy; **it's a must to have** the critical analysis; **it's required to** write with accuracy and coherence, to have insights...

3. 相關領域能力的詞彙

   We all need communicative skills; creativity; critical thinking; information processing; the ability of comprehension; social and human development; access complex contexts...

F 換句話說補一補　Track 39

Not only in the past but also nowadays, I still take literacy as an important skill.

不管是過去或是現在，我都認為聽說讀寫能力是非常重要的技巧。

1. Literacy is an important skill whether in the past or nowadays.

   我都認為聽說讀寫能力是非常重要的技巧，不管是過去或是現在。

2. No matter when, literacy is an important skill.

   無論何時，聽說讀寫能力都是很重要的技巧。

Writing helps us keep ideas and make connections to our own thinking and others' ideas.

寫作則有助我們記下想法，把我們的思考和其他概念連結在一起。

1. Writing is a skill that helps us jot down the ideas and connect to our own thinking and others' ideas.

   寫作是一種幫助我們寫下想法的技巧，並透過寫作把我們的想法和其他概念結合。

2. Writing enables us to keep ideas and connect our own thinking and others' ideas.

   寫作讓我們能夠保存想法，並連結我們自己的思考和其他概念.

As a result, literacy is certainly an essential capacity that helps us effectively connect and interpret the world we live in.

這種聽說讀寫的能力能夠讓我們有效溝通，因此絕對是非常關鍵的能力，有助我們有效連結並解讀這個世界。

1. In the end, literacy is for sure an essential capacity effectively connecting and interpreting the world people live in.

   最終，聽說讀寫能力的確是非常關鍵的能力，它有助我們有效連結並解讀這個世界。

2. Essentially, literacy is surely an inevitable capacity effectively connecting and interpreting the world people live in.

   聽說讀寫能力的確是必要的能力，有助我們有效連結並解讀這個世界，這真的非常重要。

G 想想看還能怎麼答 Track 40

　　Literacy has always been and will always be important. At present, we communicate through quick blurbs and shortened phrases and truncated words. We use a lot of acronyms and abbreviations, especially with text messages on cell phones and general online messengers. Rarely do people use full sentences when typing to close friends and family. A strong enough level of literacy is important in order to understand abbreviations and acronyms because one has to understand what the shortened message represents. Whether it was carvings on cave walls, stone tablets or messages etched into tree bark, people of earlier generations had to have an understanding of such communication. Letters and characters were and still are symbols that represent a greater idea. It's in our nature as human beings to want to know and be kept updated with technology and information.

單字小解

① **blurb** *n.* 簡短的敘述

② **truncated** *adj.* 片段的

③ **acronym** *n.*（首字母的）縮寫字

④ **carving** *n.*雕刻

⑤ **etch** *v.* 蝕刻

⑥ **keep updated with** *ph.* 取得／接收最新的資訊

中文翻譯

　　聽說讀寫能力在現在和未來都很重要。現代人以簡短的字語溝通，並用到大量的縮字詞和縮寫，尤其是用手機傳簡訊或用一般的線上通訊軟體時。打字給親近的朋友或家人，人們很少會用完整的句子，為了能夠了解縮寫和縮字詞，聽說讀寫的能力要好到一定的程度，如此才能理解訊息傳達的意思。不管是洞穴牆上、石碑上的雕刻，或是刻在樹幹上訊息，早期的人類也必須要有理解這些溝通的能力。就算是過去或是現在，字母仍是涵蓋偉大概念的象徵，而想要知道最新的科技和資訊則是我們身為人類的本能。

Unit 11
資訊取得
Information Access

 準備方向提示

1. 此類型題目焦點為對自己的偏好（preferences）、生活習慣（life habits）或嗜好（habits）的描述，平時可思考自己喜歡做什麼、為什麼或者是與此有關的生活方式的選擇。

2. 累積描述正面身心的詞彙（如 good for body health; broaden horizon, cheer me up...），可增強說明做此選擇的理由。

3. 可以多方閱讀或收看英文節目（English magazine, English channel），在選擇個人偏好或選擇方面，可有些啟發式的腳本，作為自己對遇此題目觸類旁通的描述。

 **模擬題目**  **Track 41**

Part
1

Part
2

Part
3

Question: Reading news from newspapers or online, what do you prefer? Why or why not?

你喜歡看報紙還是網路新聞？為什麼？

參考範文

　　I prefer to read news from the Internet sources instead of newspapers because surprisingly the Internet spreads news faster and more precisely than we can ever have imagined. The world has become one since we can see this stream from the close interaction in the global village nowadays, so international news certainly becomes our daily concern, too. If we wait till the newspapers are printed out, it may be the next day's news. Additionally, we can just enter some key words and reach almost every story we want to read on the Internet. Besides, perhaps some more editorials available on the Internet can broaden our horizons and give fair perspectives towards the news. Reading news online doesn't physically limit us to buying a newspaper, but is workable as long as there's Internet. With all the convenience and variety, I would like to read news online.

中文翻譯

　　我喜歡閱讀新聞網路資源而非報紙，因為網路散佈新聞既快速又準確。世界已是一體，從地球村各國間的互動就可看出，我們每天必須關注國際新聞。假如我們還要等報紙印製出來，就已經是隔天的新聞了。不僅如此，我們只要輸入關鍵字，就可以找到想了解的新聞。此外，也許網路上還有許多社論，這不僅增廣讀者見聞也讓新聞多了公正度。網路上閱讀新聞並不需要親自購買報紙，只要有網路就行。有這麼多的便利性及多元性，我想要透過網路閱讀新聞。

單字、片語說分明

① **source** *n.* 資源

② **global village** *ph.* 地球村

③ **additionally** *adv.* 額外地

④ **broaden one's horizon** *ph.* 拓展視野

⑤ **limit** *v.* 限制

⑥ **workable** *adj.* 可行的

新托福口說參考範文解析與評點

托福口說答題拿分首要掌握以下要點

1. **What（內容資訊）**：本範文完全針對題目回答了所需的內容資訊。

2. **How（再解釋 1）**：文法上沒有錯誤，語意上可以理解，文章內有使用連接語詞（如. so...; additionally, ...; besides, ..），語意間內容本身也有承接，使聽者容易跟隨講者的話題內容。使用常用簡單明瞭的英文詞彙及句型片語，則能夠提升口語上的流暢度。

3. **Why（再解釋 2）**：本範文沒有離題，絕對針對題目回答，沒有答非所問。文章使用了國際觀點（global villages），清楚栩栩如生地描繪出自己興趣及經驗（enter key words...; doesn't physically limit us to...）的結合。所描繪的情境先後皆有連貫關係，明顯連續指出二種不同的支持論點及理由。

在描述內容資訊時，本範文首先提出

1. I prefer to read news from the Internet **sources** instead of newspapers because surprisingly the Internet spreads news faster

and more precisely than we can ever have imagined. → 開頭馬上不拖泥帶水的點出立場。

2. 並再以自己的想法、經驗或習慣方式加強描述做此答案的原因 → The world has become one since we can see this stream from the close interaction in the **global village** nowadays, so international news certainly becomes our daily concern, too. If we wait till the newspapers are printed out, it may be the next day's news.

3. 支持論點二、三不但再度以個人經驗提出描述了具體例證及輔佐說明 → **Additionally**, we can just enter some key words and reach almost every story we want to read on the Internet. Besides, perhaps some more editorials available on the Internet **broaden our horizons** and give fair perspectives towards the news. Reading news online doesn't physically limit us to buying a newspaper, but is **workable** as long as there's Internet.

4. 此範文也從個人經驗及偏好、社會變遷層面、以及生活實際面不同方面點出回答者本身做此選擇的原因理由，並點出了以下個人做此選擇的原因：在對個人經驗及偏好（**faster...more precisely; broaden our horizons...**）、社會變遷層面（**global village; international news...interaction...**）以及生活實際面（**doesn't physically limit us...**）。

5. 結尾結論句的重申及巧妙的重新潤飾表示出答題者對題目的了解，因此掌握良好 → With all the convenience and variety, I would like to read news online.

托福口說論述的架構組成單位

1. 開頭介紹（**Introduction**）：

　　I prefer to read news from the Internet **sources** instead of newspapers because surprisingly the Internet spreads news faster and more precisely than we can ever have imagined.

2. 文章主體（**Body**）：

A. 支持論點一（Supporting idea 1）：

　I.　支持句一（Supporting sentence 1）：

　　　The world has become one since we can see this stream from the close interaction in the **global village** nowadays, so international news certainly becomes our daily concern, too.

　II.　支持句二（Supporting sentence 2）：

　　　If we wait till the newspapers are printed out, it may be the next day's news.

B. 支持論點二（Supporting idea 2）：

　I.　支持句一（Supporting sentence 1）：

　　　Additionally, we can just enter some key words and reach almost every story we want to read on the Internet.

　II.　支持句二（Supporting sentence 2）：

　　　Besides, perhaps some more editorials available on the internet broaden our **horizons** and give fair perspectives towards the news.

C. 支持論點三（Supporting idea 3）：

　　Reading news online doesn't physically **limit** us to buying a newspaper, but is workable as long as there's Internet.

D. 結尾結論（**Conclusion**）：

　　　　With all the convenience and variety, I would like to read
news online.

　　此題目要求的是考生表達**自己的想法、經驗或習慣方式**，答案常常是因人而
異，會因為考生的經驗及背景而選擇不同。平時建立英文思考的習慣，生活中的每
件小事，只要時間空間許可，多多思考如果是英文，我該怎麼說？同時搭配本書一
直反覆使用的正面心情或身心感受的描述，加強說明自己做此選擇的最佳原因。而
掌握好這些要點，就是考生在一定時間內快速整述自己喜歡的活動，以及對自己的
正面影響的綜合口語能力了。

D 新托福口說答題模板套用　Track 42

　　以上述短文為例，相關議題可依以下短文解析做變化，遇此類托福口說題目時
可侃侃而談對題目迎刃而解。未劃底線的部分可不需更改，**劃底線**部分可替換為考
生本身的經驗以及欲描述的項目。

開頭

1. I prefer to read news from the Internet sources instead of newspapers,
   because surprisingly the Internet spreads news faster and more precisely
   than we can ever have imagined.
   → 將劃底線的部分改為考生（您）所偏好的處事風格或生活選擇（根據
   　題意）的描述。
   → I prefer to cook at home instead of dining out because surprisingly
   　cooking creates more fun and nutrition than we can ever have
   　imagined.

125

主體

1. The world has become one since we can see this stream from the close interaction in the global village nowadays, so international news certainly becomes our daily concern, too. If we wait till the newspapers are printed out, it may be the next day's news.

→ 並描述**所偏好的處事風格或生活選擇（根據題意）**。將劃底線的部分改為（您）**所偏好的處事風格或生活選擇（根據題意）**的描述。

→ Processed food is everywhere, so the nutrition and food safety certainly become our daily concern, too. If we rely on fast food or restaurant's food, we may not be provided ourselves with enough nutrition.

2. Additionally, we can just enter some key words and reach almost every story we want to read on the Internet. Besides, perhaps some more editorials available on the Internet broaden our horizons and give fair perspectives to the news.

→ 將劃底線的部分改為考生（您）**所偏好的處事風格或生活選擇（根據題意）**的描述。

→ Additionally, we can just put those food ingredients we require in our cooking. Besides, perhaps some more varieties available on food spice up our home-made dishes.

3. Reading news online doesn't physically limit us to buying a newspaper, but is workable as long as there's Internet.

→ 將劃底線的部分改為考生（您）**所偏好的處事風格或生活選擇（根據題意）**的描述。

→ Cooking at home doesn't physically limit us to going out, but is workable as long as we make sure there're vegetables, fruits, fish or meat at home.

結尾

1. With all the convenience and variety, I would like to read news online.
   → 將劃底線的部分改為考生（您）所偏好的處事風格或生活選擇（根據題意）的描述。最後結論句以不同方式重述重點句。
   → With all the convenience and variety, I would like to cook at home.

📌 此類考題考前及應考時準備筆記要點

1. 不同的生活小細節

   I love cooking; taking a walk; going to a movie theater; doing grocery shopping; being alone; with a group of people; at home, dining out; jogging; exercising at fitness center...

2. 對事物選擇負面的描述

   Something is too much to handle; **someone is** too busy; **something is** inconvenient; **takes** too much time; **it makes me feel** uncomfortable; lazy; **it stops me from** improving...

3. 對事物選擇正面的描述

   convenient; peaceful; relaxing; bring someone good idea; fresh my mind; reenergize; fast; comfortable; easy...

F 換句話說補一補　Track 43

The world has become one since we can see this stream from the close interaction in the global village nowadays, so international news certainly becomes our daily concern, too.
世界已是一體，從地球村各國間的互動就可看出。我們也不可忽視國際新聞。

1. We can envision that the world has become one from the idea of the global village, and international news surely is our daily concern as well.
   從地球村的概念就能看出世界已是一體，我們每天都要關注國際新聞。

2. The close interaction in the global village tells us that the world has become one and international news surely is our daily concern as well.
   從地球村內的密集互動就能看出世界已是一體，我們每天必須關注國際新聞。

Additionally, we can just enter some key words and reach almost every story we want to read on the Internet.
不僅如此，我們只要輸入關鍵字，就可以在網路上找到想看的新聞。

1. Entering key words is what we need to reach almost every story we would like to have on the Internet.
   只要輸入關鍵字，我們就能在網路上找到想要了解的新聞。

2. As long as we enter key words and almost every story is right there for us on the Internet.
   只要輸入關鍵字，網路上所有的新聞就會出現在眼前。

Reading news online doesn't physically limit us to buying a newspaper, but is workable as long as there's the Internet.
網路上閱讀新聞並不需要親自購買報紙，只要有網路就行。

1. As long as there's Internet, reading news online doesn't physically limit us to buying a newspaper.
   閱讀線上新聞只要有網路就行，不需要親自購買報紙。

2. The Internet allows us to read news online and doesn't physically limit us to buying a newspaper.
   網路讓人們可以閱讀新聞不需要購買報紙，只要有網路就行。

Part
1

Part
2

Part
3

Sometimes, I prefer to own a physical copy of my favorite media, such as movies, music records and video games. Many people enjoy the idea of downloading and downsizing. Most of us seem to enjoy fewer clutters, emptier cabinets and TV stands. Reading the news online means that I'll likely find something else to do instead of taking time to read. With all of the advertisements and applications in the computer, it's a challenge to maintain focus. At the same time, newspapers aren't exactly like your mom's favourite novels that she collected for 30 some years. True, some people do collect magazines and newspapers; however, this just doesn't interest me. On one hand, news tends to be a bunch of fear driven ramblings and the promotions of lifestyles that we don't necessarily need to follow. In short, perhaps reading the news online is the best because most of information can be ignored anyway.

單字小解

① **favorite** *adj.* 喜愛的
② **download** *v.* 下載
③ **downsize** *v.* 壓縮電子檔案
④ **advertisement** *n.* 廣告
⑤ **a bunch of** *ph.* 許多
⑥ **rambling** *n.* 胡言亂語
⑦ **promotion** *n.* 促銷、推銷

中文翻譯

　　有時我偏好收藏自己喜好的電影、唱片或電視遊戲等媒體的實物。許多人喜歡下載並解壓縮檔案。人們似乎大多不喜歡雜物，而偏好空間較多的櫥櫃和電視櫃。閱讀線上新聞意指我寧願做其他的事，也不願花時間閱讀。加上電腦裡一堆的廣告和應用程式，要維持專注實在是一項挑戰。另外，新聞報紙其實也不是媽媽收藏了 30 多年的小說。的確，有人會收藏雜誌和報紙，但那並不是我的興趣。再說，新聞通常充斥許多聳動的胡言亂語，所倡導的生活方式我們其實並不需要刻意去追求或模仿。總之閱讀線上新聞就是最好的選擇，反正大部分的資訊是可以忽略的。

Unit 12
居住環境
Living Environment

A 準備方向提示

1. 此類型題目焦點為對自己所偏好的活動或嗜好（personal interests）的描述，平時可思考自己喜歡做什麼、為什麼喜歡或者是與此有關的學習。

2. 累積描述正面心情的詞彙（如 bring me to heaven; refresh my mind; the luckiest person in the world...），可增強説明所偏好的活動或嗜好的理由。

3. 可以加入志工或海外遊學活動（長短期皆可）（working holidays），學習西方國家如何渡週末或長假期（holidays; vacations），或如何將生活安排的更美好愜意，了解西方文化後，在選擇活動描述方面，可有些啟發式的腳本，作為自己對遇此題目觸類旁通的描述。

 **Track 45**

Question: Where do you prefer to live? In the downtown or in the country? Why or why not?

請問您會選擇住在城市或鄉下？為什麼？

> **參考範文**

From how I grew up, I like to live in the country. Also, I believe that a countryside or a suburban area serves well for children to grow up and for retirement. Many times after a long day's work, all I want to do is sit by the riverbank or lakeside to just feel the breeze and enjoy tranquility. Mother Nature itself has its way of bringing me back to calmness and freshness. With the bliss of solitude, I feel I am ready again for tomorrow's work and battle. Neighbors know each other and watch each other's back while someone is away from home. They share their home-made cuisines and self-grown vegetables and fruits. Those greens are absolutely the best in the world because they are healthy and have no pesticides. It's always secure and peaceful no matter where I go if I live in the country.

> **中文翻譯**

　　我的成長經驗讓我選擇鄉村。我也相信鄉村適合成長中的幼兒以及退休生活。常常在一天的忙碌工作之後，我只想端坐在河畔或湖邊享受微風和寧靜。大自然有它獨特的方式帶我回到平靜及清新。在獨處的清幽中，我感覺我又準備好面對明天的工作及挑戰。鄰居互相認識；當我們不在家時，鄰居們彼此看顧家園。他們分享自己做的家庭料理以及自己栽培的青菜及水果。這些青菜無疑是全世界最棒的食材，因為他們既健康又沒有農藥。住在鄉村，不管哪裡都很安全及祥和。

① suburban *adj.* 郊外的、郊區的

② retirement *n.* 退休

③ tranquility *n.* 平靜；寧靜；安靜

④ bliss *n.* 天賜的福祐

⑤ solitude *n.* 孤獨

⑥ cuisine *n.* 料理

⑦ pesticide *n.* 殺蟲劑

新托福口說參考範文解析與評點

托福口說答題拿分首要掌握以下要點

1. **What**（內容資訊）：本範文完全針對題目回答了所需的內容資訊。

2. **How**（再解釋 1）：文法上沒有錯誤，語意上可以理解，語意間內容本身也有承接，使聽者容易跟隨講者的話題內容。使用常用簡單明瞭的英文詞彙及句型片語，則能提升口語上的流暢度。

3. **Why**（再解釋 2）：本範文沒有離題，絕對針對題目回答，沒有答非所問。文章使用了個人的成長經驗藉想法（**feel the breeze…enjoy tranquility; bring me calmness and freshness; home-made cuisine…**），清楚栩栩如生地描繪出自己經驗與趣藉想法的結合。所描繪的情境先後皆有連貫關係，明顯連續指出二種不同的支持論點及理由。

在描述內容資訊時，本範文首先提出

1. From how I grew up, I like to live in the country. Also, I believe that a countryside or a **suburban** area serves well for children to

grow up and for **retirement.** → 開頭馬上不拖泥帶水提出立場。

2. 並再以自己的親身遊歷及想法作風加強描述做此答案的原因 →
Many times after a long day's work, all I want to do is sit by the
riverbank or lakeside to just feel the breeze and enjoy **tranquility.**
Mother Nature itself has its way of bringing me back to calmness
and freshness. With the **bliss** of **solitude,** I feel I am ready again
for tomorrow's work and battle.

3. 支持論點二不但再度以個人經驗提出描述了具體例證及輔佐說明
→ Neighbors know each other and watch each other's back while
someone is away from home. They share their home-made
cuisines and self-grown vegetables and fruits. Those greens are
absolutely the best in the world because they are healthy and have
no **pesticides.**

4. 此範文也從個人的經驗方面以及心理層面不同方面點出回答者本身
做此選擇的原因理由，並點出了以下個人做此選擇的原因：在對個
人經驗方面（**From how I grew up, I like to live in the
country...**）以及心理層面（**Many times after a long day's
work, all I want to do is sit by the riverbank or lakeside to
just feel the breeze and enjoy tranquility...**）。

5. 結尾結論句的重申及巧妙的重新潤飾表示出答題者對題目的了解，
因此掌握良好 → It's always secure and peaceful no matter where
I go if I live in the country.

托福口說論述的架構組成單位

1. 開頭介紹（**Introduction**）：

From how I grew up, I like to live in the country. Also, I

believe that a countryside or a **suburban** area serves well for children to grow up and for **retirement.**

2. 文章主體（Body）：

A. 支持論點一（Supporting idea 1）：

I. 支持句一（Supporting sentence 1）：

Many times after a long day's work, all I want to do is sit by the riverbank or lake side to just feel the breeze and enjoy **tranquility**.

II. 支持句二（Supporting sentence 2）：

Mother Nature itself has its way of bringing me back to calmness and freshness. With the **bliss** of **solitude**, I feel I am ready again for tomorrow's work and battle.

B. 支持論點二（Supporting idea 2）：

I. 支持句一（Supporting sentence 1）：

Neighbors know each other and watch each other's back while someone is away from home.

II. 支持句二（Supporting sentence 2）：

They share their home-made **cuisines** and self-grown vegetables and fruits.

III. 支持句三（Supporting sentence 3）：

Those greens are absolutely the best in the world because they are healthy and have no **pesticides**.

C. 結尾結論（Conclusion）：

It's always secure and peaceful no matter where I go if I live in the country.

此題目雖屬於論述的類型，但在描述偏好的居住環境時，考生也能藉此表達自己喜歡的地方與活動，而答案會因為考生的經驗及背景而有不同的選擇。**不過，訣**

窾在於累積不同活動經驗的描述，以此融入對自己生命及心靈洗滌的描述（如 **Many times after a long day's work, all I want to do is sit by the riverbank or lake side to just feel the breeze and enjoy tranquility...** ），同時於考試時適時運用這些描述提供自己正面能量的詞彙，去說明做此選擇的原因。而能夠掌握好這些要點，就是考生在一定時間內快速整述自己喜歡的活動，以及對自己的正面影響的綜合口語能力了。

D 新托福口說答題模板套用  Track 46

　　以上述短文為例，相關議題可依以下短文解析做變化，遇此類托福口說題目時可侃侃而談對題目迎刃而解。未劃底線的部分可不需更改，**劃底線**部分可替換為考生本身的經驗以及欲描述的項目。

開頭

1. From <u>how I grew up</u>, I like to <u>live in the country</u>. Also, I believe that a country side or a suburban area serves well for children to grow up and for retirement.

　　→ 將劃底線的部分改為考生（您）個人偏好的運動、娛樂或活動（根據題意）的描述。

　　→ From <u>my studying experience</u>, I like to <u>study in the country</u>. Also, I believe that a countryside or a suburban area serves well for children to grow up and for retirement.

主體

1. Many times after a long day's <u>work</u>, all I want to do is sit by the riverbank or lakeside to just feel the breeze and enjoy tranquility. Mother Nature itself has its way of bringing me back to calmness and freshness. With the bliss of solitude, I feel I am ready again for

tomorrow's work and battle.

→ 並描述簡短個人經驗的相關描述。將劃底線的部分改為考生（您）個人偏好的運動、娛樂或活動（根據題意）的描述。

→ Many times after a long day's <u>study</u>, all I want to do is sit by the riverbank or lakeside to just feel the breeze and enjoy tranquility. Mother nature itself has its way of bringing me back to calmness and freshness. With the bliss of solitude, I feel I am ready again for tomorrow's work and battle.

補充：

Many times after a long day's work, all I want to do is sit by the riverbank or lakeside to just feel the breeze and enjoy tranquility. Mother Nature itself has its way of bringing me back to calmness and freshness. With the bliss of solitude, I feel I am ready again for tomorrow's work and battle. Neighbors know each other and watch each other's back while someone is away from home. They share their home-made cuisines and self-grown vegetables and fruits. Those greens are absolutely the best in the world because they are healthy and have no pesticides. All make me feel like home.

註解：這段也可作為所有自然美景或遊憩地點給您煥然一新的感受描述，並以這些都讓我有家的感覺（**All make me feel like home.**）作為結尾。

結尾

1. It's always secure and peaceful no matter where I go if I live in the country.
   → 將劃現部分改成考生（您）個人偏好的運動、娛樂或活動（根據題意），最後結論句以不同方式重述重點句。

→ It's always secure and peaceful no matter where I go if I <u>study</u> in the country.

E 此類考題考前及應考時準備筆記要點

1. 都市或鄉村特點描述

   city: convenient; shuttle buses; bookstore; coffee shop; excitement; easily available; public transportation; opportunities; education; big company; traffic; cinemas... **countryside:** fresh air; quietness; calmness; close to Mother Nature; relaxation; peaceful...

2. 對個人有正面影響（心靈或生理方面）的詞彙

   bring me to heaven; cool down; fresh my mind; reenergize; relaxing, inspiring; peaceful time...

3. 不同休閒活動的正反面描述詞彙

   a starry night; close to Mother Nature; avoid electronic devise; breath the fresh air; bring family closer; quality time; pollution; noises; distractions...

F 換句話說補一補 🌓 Track 47

Many times after a long day's work, all I want to do is sit by the riverbank or lakeside to just feel the breeze and enjoy tranquility.
常常在一天的忙碌工作之後，我只想端坐在河畔或湖邊享受微風和寧靜。

1. All I would like to do is sit by the riverbank or lakeside to simply feel the breeze and enjoy tranquility many times after a long day's work.
   每回忙完一天的工作後，我只想坐在河畔或湖邊享受微風和寧靜。

2. Simply feeling the breeze and enjoying tranquility is all I want by sitting along the riverbank or lakeside after a long day's work.

   我只想在忙完一天的工作後，坐在河畔或湖邊享受微風和寧靜。

With the bliss of solitude, I feel I am ready again for tomorrow's work and battle.

在獨處的清幽中，我感覺我又準備好面對明天的工作及挑戰。

1. The bliss of solitude gets me ready again for tomorrow's work and battle.

   獨處的清幽讓我感覺又準備好迎接明天的工作及挑戰。

2. The bliss of solitude reenergizes me again for tomorrow's work and battle.

   獨處的清幽讓我再次充滿能量，迎接明天的工作和戰鬥。

It's always secure and peaceful no matter where I go if I live in the country.

住在鄉村，不管哪裡都很安全及祥和。

1. Living in the country guarantees me security and peace no matter where I go.

   住在鄉下不管去哪，一定會為我帶來安全和祥和。

2. The country life ensures me security and peace wherever I go.

   住在鄉下不管去哪，肯定會為我帶來安全和祥和。

G 想想看還能怎麼答 Track 48

Ideally, I'd go with the countryside and take trips to the city at the weekends and for holidays. The country is such a beautiful place and often has the best air quality. There are times when big factories are built in the country, but that's not too common. The city is often too crowded to avoid traffic and find a parking space. The countryside offers a connection to the older days and simpler times and living expenses are cheaper, too. A lot of restaurants can be found in the city; however, they are expensive and often unhealthy. Countryside restaurants are served by local heroes with a reputation to uphold. It's even a great place to go when you want to focus on your project or when you plan to run an independent online business. At the end of the day, we all want peace and quiet and a nice place to rest our heads.

單字小解

① **countryside** *n.* 鄉村
② **traffic** *n.* 塞車
③ **reputation** *n.* 名譽、聲望
④ **uphold** *v.* 支持；品質保證的經營
⑤ **project** *n.* 計畫

中文翻譯

　　會選擇住在鄉村而在假日時到都市度假是我的理想。鄉村非常美麗，空氣也很清新。有時候工廠會建在鄉村，但這不常見。都市通常都太擁擠了，很難不遇上塞車或找不到停車位這種事。鄉村讓我們回到古早時代花費少，生活又簡單的方式。在都市可以找到許多餐廳，然而這些餐廳通常都很貴，食物也不是很健康。鄉村的餐廳通常是鄉村知名人士所開，他們很在乎維持名聲，保證能提供有品質的服務。鄉村也提供良好環境給予需要籌備計畫，抑或是經營網路生意的你我。在一天結束時，我們需要一個平和、安靜的地方來休息。

Unit 13
價值觀念
Different Values

準備方向提示

1. 此類型題目焦點為描述我們內心或許曾經掙扎過的價值觀，如成功、婚姻和職業生涯（success, marriage, career）。

2. 累積描述正面或負面心情的詞彙（如 **peaceful; gracious; regretful; brave; pity...**），可增強文章的動容性喔。

3. 欣賞劇情類、溫馨喜劇類、或史篇類等電影，練習或記下電影中感人的名句（quotes），常常在此類題目可有些啟發，作為自己對遇此題目觸類旁通的描述。

模擬題目 Track 49

Question: Do you agree or disagree with the following statement? Success only belongs to people who earn a lot of money. Use specific reasons and examples to support your answer.

你同意「成功只屬於有財富的人」的說法嗎？請詳述並舉例來支持您的論點。

參考範文

I definitely disagree with the idea that success only belongs to people who earn a lot of money; however, clearly, we all acknowledge that money is an inevitably important resource we use to obtain things. Nevertheless, the precious things in life come from those free stuffs. An outstanding photographer sometimes doesn't take a picture so to just live in the moment and enjoy it because in life, the memories we share along with people are what matter. The movie *the Secret Life of Walter Mitty* also addresses that beautiful things don't ask for attention. As long as we've been somewhere, seen things and taken enough pictures, thus, at the end of the day, we have nothing to regret and are ready to move forward. Nothing can beat this kind of peaceful mind up. Success belongs to people who truly know what happiness is and cherish it.

中文翻譯

我當然不同意成功屬於賺很多錢的人。儘管我們還是清楚知道錢是取得物品的必要資源。不過，最珍貴的事物來自那些不花錢的事物中。一個傑出的攝影師有時候只用他的心停止在最美麗的時刻，而不用相機去記錄下來，因為和人一起度過的

美好時光和回憶往往就是最珍貴的。《白日夢冒險王》這部電影提及美麗的事物不需要別人的眼光，而我們只要曾去過那些地方、看過那些事物，並拍下許多照片就夠了，那麼，在一天結束之前，我們沒有什麼可以後悔，繼續昂首跨步向前。沒有什麼事可以擊倒如此美麗的平靜心境。成功是屬於真正了解幸福以及珍惜它的人。

單字、片語說分明

① inevitably *adv.* 無可避免地；不可或缺地
② nevertheless *adv.* 儘管如此
③ photographer *n.* 攝影師
④ attention *n.* 注意；專注力
⑤ as long as *conj.* 只要
⑥ cherish *v.* 珍惜

C 新托福口說參考範文解析與評點

托福口說答題拿分首要掌握以下要點

1. **What（內容資訊）**：本範文完全針對題目回答了所需的**內容資訊**。

2. **How（再解釋 1）**：文法上沒有錯誤，語意上可以理解，文章內有使用連接語詞（如 Nevertheless; as long as; thus...），語意間內容本身也有承接，使聽者容易跟隨講者的話題內容。使用常用簡單明瞭的英文詞彙及句型片語，則能夠提升口語上的流暢度。

3. **Why（再解釋 2）**：本範文沒有離題，絕對針對題目回答，沒有答非所問。文章使用了個人所累積的至理名言、智慧話語（如 live in the moment..., beautiful things...; happiness; cherish...），巧妙的點出自己價值觀及具體名言格句的結合。所說明的論點先後皆有連貫關係，明顯連續指出二種不同的支持論點及理由。

> **在描述內容資訊時，本範文首先提出**

Part **1**

Part **2**

Part **3**

1. I definitely disagree with the idea that success only belongs to people who earn a lot of money; however, clearly, we all acknowledge that money is an **inevitably** important resource we use to obtain things. → 開頭馬上不拖泥帶水的點出立場。

2. 並再以自己的價值觀及想法加強描述做此答案的原因 → **Nevertheless**, the precious things in life come from those free stuffs. An outstanding **photographer** sometimes doesn't take a picture so to just live in the moment and enjoy it because in life, the memories we share along with people are what matter.

3. 支持論點二再度以電影名言錦句提出描述了具體例證及輔佐說明 → The movie *The Secret Life of Walter Mitty* also addresses that beautiful things don't ask for **attention. As long as** we've been somewhere, seen things and taken enough pictures, thus, at the end of the day, we have nothing to regret and are ready to move forward.

4. 此範文也從個人價值觀方面、社會觀感面以及心理層面不同方面點出回答者本身做此選擇的原因理由，並點出了以下個人做此選擇的原因：在個人價值觀方面（**live in the moment; no regret...**）、社會觀感面（**beautiful things don't ask for attention...**）以及心理層面（**know what happiness is...; cherish...**）。

5. 結尾結論句的重申及巧妙的重新潤飾表示出答題者對題目的了解，因此掌握良好 → Nothing can beat this kind of peaceful mind up. Success belongs to people who truly know what happiness is and cherish it.

托福口說論述的架構組成單位

1. 開頭介紹（**Introduction**）：

   I definitely disagree with the idea that success only belongs to people who earn a lot of money; however, clearly, we all acknowledge that money is an **inevitably** important resource we use to obtain things.

2. 文章主體（**Body**）：

   A. 支持論點一（Supporting idea 1）：

   I. 支持句一（Supporting sentence 1）：

   Nevertheless, the precious things in life come from those free stuffs.

   II. 支持句二（Supporting sentence 2）：

   An outstanding **photographer** sometimes doesn't take a picture so to just live in the moment and enjoy it because in life, the memories we share along with people are what matter.

   B. 支持論點二（Supporting idea 2）：

   I. 支持句一（Supporting sentence 1）：

   The movie *The Secret Life of Walter Mitty* also addresses that beautiful things don't ask for **attention.**

   II. 支持句二（Supporting sentence 2）：

   As long as we've been somewhere, seen things and taken enough pictures.

   III. 支持句三（Supporting sentence 3）：

   ,thus, at the end of the day, we have nothing to regret and are ready to move forward.

3. 結尾結論（Conclusion）：

Nothing can beat this kind of peaceful mind up. Success belongs to people who truly know what happiness is and **cherish** it.

此題目要求的是考生表達對自己價值觀的表述能力。**其實越是需要考生描述到與自己所信仰或內心深處的話題，常常會是一拍兩瞪眼的情況。**假如是已經有思考過的價值觀問題，非常容易對答如流，甚至侃侃而談不能自己，反之則度秒如年。建議考生（您）可參考不同的托福口說價值觀類的考古題，並且養成累積名言錦句的習慣，來源四面八方不受限！考試時適時運用加入正面態度或人生觀的詞彙，去說明做此選擇的原因。

D 新托福口說答題模板套用　🔘 Track 50

以上述短文為例，相關議題可依以下短文解析做變化，遇此類托福口說題目時可侃侃而談對題目迎刃而解。未劃底線的部分可不需更改，**劃底線**部分可替換為考生本身的經驗以及欲描述的項目。

開頭

1. I definitely disagree with the idea that <u>success</u> only belongs to people who earn a lot of money; however, clearly, we all acknowledge that <u>money is an inevitably important resource we use to obtain things</u>.

   → 將劃底線的部分改為考生（您）**自己本身的想法、作風經驗以及價值觀感**的描述。

   → I definitely disagree with the idea that <u>happiness</u> only belongs to people who earn a lot of money; however, clearly, we all acknowledge that <u>happiness has much to do with money</u>.

1. 並描述簡短個人想法、作風經驗以及價值觀感。另外加上經典引言讓口說例證更有說服力。

Nevertheless, the precious things in life come from those free stuffs. An outstanding photographer sometimes doesn't take a picture so to just live in the moment and enjoy it because in life, the memories we share along with people are what matter.

The movie *The Secret Life of Walter Mitty* also addresses that beautiful things don't ask for attention. As long as we've been somewhere, seen things and taken enough picture; thus, at the end of the day, we have nothing to regret and are ready to move forward.

結尾

　　之後再總結式或重新潤飾支持所提出的論點。

1. Nothing can beat this kind of peaceful mind up. Success belongs to people who truly know what happiness is and cherish it.

將劃底線的部分改為考生（您）自己本身的想法、作風經驗以及價值觀感的描述，最後結論句以不同方式重述重點句。

→ Nothing can beat this kind of peaceful mind up. Happiness belongs to people who truly know what happiness is and cherish it.

E 此類考題考前及應考時準備筆記要點

1. 正面人生態度的名言錦句

Don't change so people will like you; be yourself and the right people will love the real you; great things take time...

2. 累積值得、珍惜、重要等正面的詞彙

precious; matter; value the most; cherish; gain; significance; significant; benefit; worth, merit...

3. 相關正面心情或態度的詞彙

gratitude; gracious; thankful; show appreciation for; courageous; brave; fearless; heroic, ...

F 換句話說補一補 Track 51

Nevertheless, the precious things in life come from those free stuffs.
不過，最珍貴的事物來自那些不花錢的事物中。

1. Notwithstanding, those free stuffs are what value the most in life.
   不過，那些不花錢的事物中往往就是最珍貴的事物。

2. Regardless of the above, the precious things in life come from those free stuffs.
   不過，最珍貴的事物來自那些不花錢的事物中。

An outstanding photographer sometimes doesn't take a picture so to just live in the moment and enjoy it because in life, the memories we share along the way with people are what matter.
一個傑出的攝影師有時候只用他的心停止在最美麗的時刻，而不用相機去記錄下來。因為和人一起度過的美好時光和回憶往往就是最珍貴的。

1. Take a photographer for example, he / she stops taking photos and just to live in that moment because they know the memories we share along the way with people are what matter.
   就拿攝影師來說，他們不拍照而是只用心停留在那個片刻，因為他們了解和人一起度過的美好時光和回憶就是最珍貴的。

2. We can see that a photographer sometimes stops taking photos to just live in that moment because what matters in life are those memories we share along the way with people.

攝影師有時不拍照而是用心停留在那個片刻，因為和人一起分享的回憶才是人生中最重要的。

Nothing can beat this kind of peaceful mind up.
沒有什麼事可以擊倒如此美麗的平靜心境。

1. Peaceful mind wins all.
   平靜的心戰勝一切。

2. The only thing matters is the peaceful mind.
   唯一重要的是平靜。

G 想想看還能怎麼答 Track 52

　　I always like the quote "The best things in life are the people we love, the places we've seen, and the memories we've made along the way." Sometimes life is just as simple as it is. We want too much and we forgot what is the most precious things in life. Do we remember perhaps our grandmoms told bedtime stories or read books before we fell asleep when we were kids? Do we remember our efforts finally earned us baseball kits in our elementary school times? Or maybe one of those days we first kissed our new born baby when he or she finally joined our life? Success is also as simple as it is. Success is a state of mind. Are we happy? We don't need lots of money to feel successful. We just need to realize what we already possess and embrace it.

單字小解

① **precious** *adj.* 珍貴的

② **baseball kits** *n.* 棒球手套球組

③ **possess** *v.* 擁有

④ **embrace** *v.* 擁抱

中文翻譯

　　我總是喜歡這句名言『生命中最棒的事來自於我們愛的人、我們到過的地方，以及一起度過的時光』。有時候，生活就是如此的簡單。我們想要的太多，以致我們忘了生命中最重要的是什麼。是否還記得小時候奶奶的床邊故事？是否記得國小時第一次靠著努力贏得的第一套棒球手套球組？抑或是我們第一次親吻進入我們生命的小寶貝？成功也就是如此的簡單。成功是一種心境。我們是否開心？我們不需要大筆的錢才覺得開心。我們只要了解到我們擁有什麼，並且擁抱它就可以了。

Unit 14
教育問題 1 Education Issues 1 (Children Education 1)

A 準備方向提示

1. 此類型題目焦點為自己本身想法、作風經驗以及價值觀感描述，平時可思考自己喜歡做什麼、為什麼有此選擇或者是與此有關的學習。

2. 累積描述正面價值觀感的詞彙（如 **confidence; brave; responsibility; righteous; royalty, ...**），可增強說明本身想法、作風經驗以及價值觀感的理由。

3. 可以多方學習勵志類英文電影，學習他／她們如何面對生活的壓力或如何將生活安排得更美好（如 *Good Will Hunting*），在選擇說明本身想法、作風經驗以及價值觀感時，可有些啟發式的腳本，作為自己對遇此題目觸類旁通的描述。

B 模擬題目 🎧 Track 53

Question: Some people believe that it is better for children to grow up in big cities. Others believe that it is better for children to grow up in small towns or rural areas. What is your opinion and why? Use specific reasons and examples to support your response.

有些人認為孩子最好要在城市裡成長，另外也有人認為孩子最好在鄉間或郊區成長。你對此的看法是？請詳述並舉例來說明你的理由。

參考範文

I would like to have my children grow up in small towns or rural areas. The safety is the first benefit I can see if children growing up in small towns or rural areas. People know each other's name and lots of natural scenes are nearby. Presumably, it's safer than a big city. Try to imagine that a private big garden is right behind your house. It's like a great secret place for parents and children to have camping fun in summer. The other merit is that teachers will have more time to help students in a small classroom. For instance, more waiting time and more experimental discussions can happen and develop children's creativity or spontaneity for learning. Growing up in a small town or a rural area, children can become mentally and physically healthy by learning well, playing well and living in a children supporting environment.

中文翻譯

我選擇讓孩子在小鎮或鄉村成長。安全是首要的一項主要優點。鎮裡的人彼此認識，大自然美景就在身邊。鄉村應該是要比城市安全。試著想像家裡院後就有一

個私人大花園，這裡就像是父母與孩子夏日秘密的露營空間。另一個優點就是在小教室裡，老師將擁有更多的時間協助孩子。例如，老師可以有更多等待的時間，且實驗性的討論也會增加，這些都能協助發展孩子的學習創造力與自發性。在小鎮或郊區長大的孩子學得好、玩得好而且又在支持他們的環境中成長，因此他們在智能及體力上是健康的。

單字、片語說分明

① **benefit** *n.* 優點；利益
② **presumably** *adv.* 假設性地
③ **private** *adj.* 私人的
④ **merit** *n.* 優點、好處
⑤ **creativity** *n.* 創意
⑥ **spontaneity** *n.* 自發性、主動性
⑦ **mentally** *adv.* 心智地
⑧ **physically** *adv.* 體能地

新托福口說參考範文解析與評點

托福口說答題拿分首要掌握以下要點

1. **What（內容資訊）**：本範文完全針對題目回答了所需的**內容資訊**。

2. **How（再解釋 1）**：文法上沒有錯誤，語意上可以理解，文章內有使用連接語詞（如 The other merit; For instanc; Presumably, ...）語意間內容本身也有承接，使聽者容易跟隨講者的話題內容。使用常用簡單明瞭的英文詞彙及句型片語，則能夠提升口語上的流暢度。

3. **Why（再解釋 2）**：本範文沒有離題，絕對針對題目回答，沒有答非所問。文章使用了個人經驗以及本身想法作風等的詞彙（**safety concern**;

creativity; spontaneity...），清楚栩栩如生描繪出自己興趣及經驗的結合。所描繪的情境先後皆有連貫關係，明顯連續指出二種不同的支持論點及理由。

> 在描述內容資訊時，本範文首先提出

1. I would like to have my children grow up in small towns or rural areas. → 開頭立即點出立場。

2. 並再以自己本身想法、作風經驗以及價值觀感加強描述做此答案的原因 → The safety is the first **benefit** I can see if children growing up in small towns or rural areas. People know each other's name and lots of natural scenes are nearby. **Presumably**, there's greater safety than in a big city.

3. 支持論點二、三再度以個人想法經驗及價值觀感，提出描述了具體例證及輔佐說明 → Try to imagine that a **private** big garden is right behind your house. It's like a great secret place for parents and children to have camping fun in summer. The other **merit** is that teachers will have more time to help students in a small classroom. For instance, more waiting time and more experimental discussions can happen and develop children's **creativity** or **spontaneity** for learning.

4. 此範文也從**個人想法經驗作風方面、社群領域層面、以及心理層面**不同方面點出回答者本身做此選擇的原因理由，並點出了以下**個人做此選擇的原因**：在對個人想法經驗作風方面（**know each other's name; private garden**）、社群領域層面（**know each other's name; classroom; children supporting environment**）以及心理層面（**creativity..spontaneity...**）。

5. 結尾結論句的重申及巧妙的重新潤飾表示出答題者對題目的了解，因此掌握良好 → Growing up in a small town or a rural area, children can become **mentally** and **physically** healthy by learning well, playing well and living in a children supporting environment.

托福口說論述的架構組成單位

1. 開頭介紹（**Introduction**）：

    I would like to have my children grow up in small towns or rural areas.

2. 文章主體（**Body**）：

    A. 支持論點一（Supporting idea 1）：

      I.　支持句一（Supporting sentence 1）：

         The safety is the first **benefit** I can see if children growing up in small towns or rural areas.

      II.　支持句二（Supporting sentence 2）：

         People know each other's name and lots of natural scenes are nearby.

      III. 支持句三（Supporting sentence 3）：

         Presumably, it's safer than a big city.

    B. 支持論點二（Supporting idea 2）：

      I.　支持句一（Supporting sentence 1）：

         Try to imagine that a **private** big garden is right behind your house. It's like a great secret place for parents and children to have camping fun in summer.

C. 支持論點（Supporting idea 3）：

  I. 支持句一（Supporting sentence 1）：

     The other **merit** is that teachers will have more time to help students in a small classroom.

  II. 支持句二（Supporting sentence 2）：

     For instance, more waiting time and more experimental discussions can happen and develop children's **creativity** or **spontaneity** for learning.

D. 結尾結論（**Conclusion**）：

     Growing up in a small town or a rural area, children can become **mentally** and **physically** healthy by learning well, playing well and living in a children supporting environment.

此題目要求的是考生表達**自己本身想法、作風經驗以及價值觀感**的描述能力，答案常常是因人而異，會因為考生的經驗及背景而選擇不同。**不過，訣竅在於累積不同活動經驗的描述**，以此融入對自己生命及心靈成長的描述（如 **development; creativity; spontaneity; mentally and physically healthy and sound...**）。考試時適時運用這些描述並提供自己正面能量的詞彙，去說明做此選擇的原因。而掌握好這些要點，就是考生在一定時間內快速整述自己本身想法、作風經驗、價值觀感，以及對自己的正面影響的綜合口語能力了。

新托福口說答題模板套用　🔊 Track 54

以上述短文為例，相關議題可依以下短文解析做變化，遇此類托福口說題目時可侃侃而談對題目迎刃而解。未劃底線的部分可不需更改，**劃底線**部分可替換為考生本身的經驗以及欲描述的項目。

開頭

1. I would like to have my <u>children grow up</u> in small towns or rural areas.
   → 將劃底線的部分改為考生（您）**自己本身想法、作風經驗以及價值觀**感的描述。
   → I would like to have my <u>studying</u> in small towns or rural areas.

主體

1. The <u>safety</u> is the first benefit I can see by <u>growing up</u> in small towns or rural areas. People know each other's name and lots of natural scenes are nearby. Presumably, it's <u>safer</u> than a big city.
   → 並描述簡短個人想法的相關描述，將劃底線的部分改為考生（您）**自己本身想法、作風經驗以及價值觀**感。
   → The <u>peace in mind</u> is the first benefit I can see by <u>studying</u> in small towns or rural areas. People know each other's name and lots of natural scenes are nearby. Presumably, it's <u>quieter</u> than a big city.

2. Try to imagine that a private big garden is right behind your <u>house</u>. It's like a great secret place for <u>parents and children to have camping fun in summer</u>.
   → 將劃底線的部分改為考生（您）**自己本身想法、作風經驗以及價值觀**感方面。
   → Try to imagine that a private big garden is right behind your <u>living place</u>. It's a great secret place for <u>classmates, friends and professors to have BBQ or leisure gatherings</u>.

結尾

之後再總結式或重新潤飾支持所提出的論點。

1. <u>Growing up</u> in a small town or a rural area, children can become mentally and physically healthy by learning well, playing well and living in a <u>children</u> supporting environment.

→ 將劃現部分改成考生（您）自己本身想法、作風經驗以及價值觀感，最後結論句以不同方式重述重點句。

→ <u>Studying</u> in a small town or rural area, children can become mentally and physically healthy by learning well, playing well and living in an <u>academic-learning</u> supporting environment.

🔧 E 此類考題考前及應考時準備筆記要點

1. 各種成長或生活需求

safety concern; sanitary; fresh water; follow the rules/laws; financial situation; guidance; security...

2. 對個人有正面影響（心靈或生理方面）的詞彙或引言

mentally and physically healthy; Work Hard, Have Fun; creative; spontaneous...

3. 描述大自然的詞彙

remote and peaceful mountain areas; tranquil lakes; bright sunshine; romantic sunset; secret garden...

F 換句話說補一補 Track 55

The safety is the first benefit I can see by growing up in small towns or rural areas.
讓孩子在小鎮或鄉村成長，安全是首要的一項主要優點。

1. The best benefit I would say is the safety when children grow up in small towns or rural areas.
   讓孩子孩子在小鎮或鄉村成長，主要優點就是安全上的考量。

2. Growing up in small towns or rural areas offers the safety from what I can see.
   在鄉村長大，我認為是安全的。

For instance, more waiting time and experimental discussions can happen and develop children's creativity or spontaneity for learning.
例如，老師可以有更多等待的時間，且實驗性的討論也會增加，這些都能協助發展孩子的學習創造力與自發性。

1. Take more waiting time and more experimental discussions for example, both of them can develop children's creativity or spontaneity for learning.
   就拿更多等待的時間和增加的實驗性討論來說，這兩項都能協助發展孩子的學習創造力與自發性。

2. More waiting and experimental discussions enable children to develop their creativity or spontaneity for learning.
   更多的等待時間或實驗性的討論將會協助發展孩子的學習創造力與自發性。

Growing up in a small town or a rural area, children can become mentally and physically healthy by learning well, playing well and living in a children supporting environment.

在小鎮或郊區長大的孩子學得好、玩得好而且又在支持他們的環境中成長，因此他們在智能及體力上是健康的。

1. Growing up in a small town or rural area offers better chance for children to become mentally and physically healthy by learning well, playing well and living in a children friendly environment.

   小鎮或郊區的環境讓孩子學得好、玩得好，而且孩子在支持他們的環境中成長後，他們在智能及體力上是健康的。

2. Children can become mentally and physically healthy by learning well, playing well and living in a children friendly environment.

   孩子們學得好、玩得好，在支持他們的環境中成長後，他們在心智上和體能上會變得健康。

Children raised in the city have a great chance of learning social skills that can't be picked up while living suburban areas because people in big cities usually tend to live a life with close communications with others. Sure, we don't want our young ones to be exposed to any harm in big cities; however, it's still important for kids to get out and see the world and gain some valuable experiences along the way. The city offers a wide variety of entertainment and culture, from museums, parks, stadiums to concert halls. There are loads of festivals going on in the city. Getting around in the city is quite easy, thanks to the train systems, all night bus lines, streetcars and cabs. Most of my friends living in the city tend to ride bicycles because so many good things are usually not very far away.

單字小解

① **suburban** *adj.* 郊區的；鄉村的
② **be exposed to** *ph.* 暴露在
③ **museum** *n.* 博物館
④ **stadium** *n.* 體育場；體育活動中心
⑤ **loads of** *ph.* 大量的（量詞）
⑥ **festival** *n.* 節慶、慶典

Part
1

Part
2

Part
3

中文翻譯

　　在城市長大的孩子有絕佳機會磨練人際關係，這是鄉村生活無法提供的，因為城市的人們彼此間的溝通較密集。當然，我們並不想我們的孩子暴露在任何傷害中，然而，讓孩子出走去看世界，體驗有價值的生活經驗依然重要。城市提供娛樂及文化體驗的多樣性，舉凡博物館、公園、體育場到音樂廳都有。城市也有許多節慶活動。在城市到處走走很方便，這要感謝地鐵、夜線巴士、車輛及計程車。我大部分住城市的朋友都傾向騎自行車，因為許多好玩的僅在咫尺之間。

Unit 15
教育問題 2 Education Issues 2 (Children Education 2)

🅐 準備方向提示

1. 此類型題目焦點為自己本身想法、作風經驗以及價值觀感描述，平時可思考自己喜歡做什麼、為什麼有此選擇或者是與此有關的學習。

2. 累積描述正面價值觀感的詞彙（如 **confidence; brave; responsibility; righteous; royalty, ...**），可增強說明本身想法、作風經驗以及價值觀感的理由。

3. 可以多方學習勵志類英文電影，學習他／她們如何面對生活的壓力或如何將生活安排得更美好（如 *Good Will Hunting*），在選擇説明本身想法、作風經驗以及價值觀感時，可有些啟發式的腳本，作為自己對遇此題目觸類旁通的描述。

B 模擬題目 Track 57

Question: Do you agree or disagree with the following statement? Participating in team sports helps develop children's sense of cooperation. Give specific reasons to explain your choice.

你同意「孩子參加團隊體育活動有助於發展他們的團隊合作感」這樣的說法嗎？請詳述並解釋您的看法。

參考範文

　　I agree with the statement that participating in team sports helps develop children's sense of cooperation. There's no one miracle that can save it all, but taking one step every day. For instance, life skills must be directly taught to young children and be learned through participating in team sports. Kids can talk about the sport together and have a brainstorm to make the team better. That is to say that working together in a sports team encourages children's socialization. When kids participate in team sports, they learn to take responsibility from what goes wrong instead of blaming it on a teammate. People always say that they want a miracle. What is a miracle? It's time to grow up with children by joining their sport time, being there with them and seeing how team sports help children develop their confidence and sense of cooperation.

單字、片語說分明

① **sense of cooperation** *n.* 合作感
② **socialization** *n.* 社會化
③ **responsibility** *n.* 責任
④ **blame on** *ph.* 責備

⑤ **miracle** *n.* 奇蹟

⑥ **confidence** *n.* 信心

⑦ **cooperation** *n.* 合作

中文翻譯

我同意參與團隊運動可以發展孩子的團隊合作感。世界上並沒有解救所有一切的奇蹟，只有每天按部就班才算數。就像是生活技能必須直接傳授給年輕孩子，並從團體運動中學習。孩子們可以一同談論運動，且集思廣益思考如何使團隊有更好的發展。也就是說，團隊運動鼓勵孩子社交發展。孩子們參與團隊運動後，他們會學習為自己的錯誤負責，而不是責怪他人。人們常常說需要奇蹟。什麼是奇蹟呢？那就是陪著孩子參與他們的運動，看看團隊運動如何幫助孩子建立他們的信心及團隊合作感。

新托福口說參考範文解析與評點

托福口說答題拿分首要掌握以下要點

1. **What（內容資訊）**：本範文完全針對題目回答了所需的**內容資訊**。

2. **How（再解釋 1）**：文法上沒有錯誤，語意上可以理解，文章內有使用連接語詞（如 For instance; that's to say...）語意間內容本身也有承接，使聽者容易跟隨講者的話題內容。使用常用簡單明瞭的英文詞彙及句型片語，則能增加口語上的流暢度。

3. **Why（再解釋 2）**：本範文沒有離題，絕對針對題目回答，沒有答非所問。文章使用了個人經驗以及本身想法作風等的詞彙（**life skills; have a brainstorm; socialization; responsibility; confidence...**），清楚栩栩如生地描繪出本身想法、作風經驗以及價值觀感的結合。所描繪的情境先後皆有連貫關係，明顯連續指出二種不同的支持論點及理由。

> 在描述內容資訊時，本範文首先提出

1. I agree with the statement that participating in team sports helps develop children's sense of **cooperation**. → 開頭馬上不拖泥帶水的清楚提出立場。並再以自己本身想法、作風經驗以及價值觀感加強描述做此答案的原因 → There's no one miracle that can save it all, but taking one step every day. For instance, life skills must be directly taught to young children and be learned through participating in team sports. Kids can talk about the sport together and have a brainstorm to make the team better. That is to say that working together in a sports team encourages children's **socialization**.

2. 支持論點二、三再度以個人想法經驗及價值觀感，提出描述了具體例證及輔佐說明 → When kids participate in team sports, they learn to take **responsibility** from what goes wrong instead of **blaming** it **on** a teammate. People always say that they want a **miracle**. What is a miracle? It's time to grow up with children by joining their sport time, being there with them and seeing how team sports help children develop their **confidence** and sense of **cooperation**.

3. 此範文也從個人想法經驗作風方面、社群領域層面、以及心理層面不同方面點出回答者本身做此選擇的原因理由，並點出了以下個人做此選擇的原因：在對個人想法經驗作風方面（**life skills; have a brain storm...**）、社群領域層面（**responsibility; socialization...**）以及心理層面（**confidence; miracle...**）。

4. 結尾結論句的重申及巧妙的重新潤飾表示出答題者對題目的了解因此掌握良好 → What is a miracle? It's time to grow up with

children by joining their sport time, being there with them and seeing how team sports help children develop their **confidence** and sense of **cooperation**.

托福口說論述的架構組成單位

1. 開頭介紹（**Introduction**）：

   I agree with the statement that participating in team sports helps develop children's sense of **cooperation**.

2. 文章主體（**Body**）：

   A. 支持論點一（Supporting idea 1）：

   I. 支持句一（Supporting sentence 1）：

   There's no one miracle that can save it all, but taking one step every day.

   II. 支持句二（Supporting sentence 2）：

   For instance, life skills must be directly taught to young children and be learned through participating in team sports.

   III. 支持句三（Supporting sentence 3）：

   Kids can talk about the sport together and have a brainstorm to make the team better.

   IV. 支持句四（Supporting sentence 4）：

   That is to say that working together on a sports team encourages **socialization.**

   B. 支持論點二（Supporting idea 2）：

   I. 支持句一（Supporting sentence 1）：

   When kids participate in team sports, they learn to take **responsibility** from what goes wrong instead of

blaming it **on** a teammate.

II. 支持論點三（Supporting idea 3）：

People always say that they want a **miracle**. What is a miracle? It's time to grow up with children by joining their sport time...

3. 結尾結論（**Conclusion**）：

...being there with them and seeing how team sports help children develop their **confidence** and sense of **cooperation**.

此題目要求的是考生表達**自己本身想法、作風經驗以及價值觀**的描述能力，答案常常是因人而異，會因為考生的經驗及背景而選擇不同。**不過，訣竅在於累積不同活動經驗的描述，以此融入對自己生命及心靈成長的描述（如 responsibility; have a brainstorm; confidence and cooperation...）**。考試時適時運用這些描述並提供正面能量的詞彙，去說明做此選擇的原因。而掌握好這些要點， 就是考生在一定時間內快速整述自己本身想法、作風經驗、價值觀感，以及對自己的正面影響的綜合口語能力了。

🔧 新托福口說答題模板套用　🔊 Track 58

以上述短文為例，相關議題可依以下短文解析做變化，遇此類托福口說題目時可侃侃而談對題目迎刃而解。未劃底線的部分可不需更改，**劃底線**部分可替換為考生本身的經驗以及欲描述的項目。

開頭

1. I agree with the statement that participating in team sports helps develop children's sense of cooperation.

　→ 將劃底線的部分改為考生（您）自己本身想法、作風經驗以及價值觀感的描述。

→ I agree with the statement that <u>art and music bring vision to teenagers.</u>

主體

1. There's no one miracle that save it all but taking one step every ay. For instance, life skills must be directly taught to <u>young children</u> and be learned through <u>participating in team sports.</u> <u>Kids</u> can <u>talk about the sport together and have a brainstorm to make the team better.</u> That is to say that <u>working together on a sports team encourages socialization.</u>

→ 並描述簡短個人經驗的相關描述。將劃底線的部分改為考生（您）自己本身想法、作風經驗以及價值觀感。

→ There's no one miracle that save it all but taking one step every day. For instance, life skills must be directly taught to <u>teenagers</u> and be learned through <u>playing with music instruments or appreciating art works.</u> <u>Teenagers</u> can <u>share their ideas, talk about their talents together, and create their own works to bring out the best of them.</u> That is to say that <u>working together on art or music encourages socialization.</u>

2. When <u>kids participate in team sports,</u> they <u>learn to take responsibility from what goes wrong instead of blaming it on a teammate.</u>

→ 將劃底線的部分改為考生（您）自己本身想法、作風經驗以及價值觀感方面。

→ When <u>teenagers focus on music and art,</u> they <u>learn to take responsibility from what they are doing instead of fooling around or wasting time.</u>

3. People always say that they want a miracle. What is miracle? <u>Grow up with children by joining their sport time.</u>

→ 將劃底線的部分改為考生（您）**自己本身想法、作風經驗以及價值觀感**。

→ People always say that they want a miracle. What is miracle? <u>Grow up with our teenagers by joining their efforts in music and art.</u>

補充：

帶出重點或經典引言的萬用句：

People always say that they want a miracle. What is miracle? 接著放價值觀感的中心或經典引言.

（結尾）

之後再總結式或重新潤飾支持所提出的論點。

1. ...being there with them and <u>seeing how team sports help children develop their confidence and sense of cooperation.</u>

→ 將劃底線部分改成考生（您）**自己本身想法、作風經驗以及價值觀感**，最後結論句以不同方式重述重點句。

→ ...being there with them and seeing <u>how music and art transform teenagers to a better version of themselves and holding a good version of their own future.</u>

E 此類考題考前及應考時準備筆記要點

1. 具教育意義性質的詞彙

responsibility; commitment; perseverance; encouragement; optimistic; interpersonal skills; communicative skills...

2. 運動帶給人們心靈或生理方面正面影響的詞

Reenergize; relaxing; inspiring; peaceful time; excitement, keep fit; shape up; cheer up...

3. 運動類相關勵志性引言或詞彙（Quotes）

Train like an athlete, eat like a nutritionist, sleep like a baby, win like a champion.; Don't quit. Suffer now and live the rest of your life as a champion.; Fitness starts in your head. You must choose to eat clean, exercise regularly, and treat your body with respect...

 換句話說補一補 Track 59

There's no one miracle that save it all but taking one step every day.
世界上並沒有解救所有一切的奇蹟，只有每天按部就班才算數。

1. No single miracle can save it all but taking one step every day.
   沒有一個奇蹟可以解救一切，只有每天按部就班才算數。

2. Taking one step every day is the solution instead of waiting for miracles to happen.
   每天按部就班而非空等奇蹟，才是解決的方法。

That is to say that working together on a sports team encourages socialization.
也就是說，團隊運動鼓勵孩子社交發展。

1. Socialization can be encouraged by working together on a sports team.
   社交發展可透過團隊運動來激發。

2. A sports team encourages socialization by working together.
   團隊運動透過團結一致激發社交發展。

It's to grow up with children by joining their sport time, being there with them and seeing how team sports help children develop their confidence and sense of cooperation.
那就是陪著孩子參與他們的運動，看看團隊運動如何幫助孩子建立他們的信心及團隊合作感。

1. Miracles happen when you are with your children. Or to be specific, to see how team sports help children establish their confidence and sense of cooperation. Be there with them.
   奇蹟就在你陪伴孩子的時候發生。或者這麼說，想要知道團隊運動如何幫助你的孩子建立他們的信心和團隊合作感，就陪著他們吧。

2. Miracles will happen if you accompany your children. So just be there and see how team sports help children build their confidence and sense of cooperation.
   奇蹟就在你陪伴孩子的時候發生。所以就在那看看團隊運動如何幫助孩子建立他們的信心和團隊合作感吧。

Sports are one of the most common activities for people to get together and share in excitement. There's no feeling like when your heart's pumping and the crowd is cheering for your team to win. Children who play team sports and organized sports with others will have a good sense of responsibility, courage and commitment. Plus, they'll adopt strong interpersonal skills all while keeping fit and having a lot of fun. Team sports offer challenges, rewards and disappointment, which are all healthy life experiences. It's beneficial for children to develop relationships outside of home and school. Essentially, it's good to move out of our comfort zones and take on new challenges. Children are always learning and growing, so why not letting them have the chance to learn, grow and have fun together?

單字小解

① **excitement** *n.* 刺激、興奮

② **pumping** *adj.* 跳動、心跳

③ **organize** *v.* 組織

④ **responsibility** *n.* 責任

⑤ **commitment** *n.* 答應；承諾

⑥ **interpersonal** *adj.* 人際間的

⑦ **keep fit** *ph.* 保持矯健的體態

⑧ **disappointment** *n.* 失望

⑨ **essentially** *adv.* 其實而言；到底而言；實際而言；說實在的；實質而言

中文翻譯

　　運動是人們在一起享受愉悅的共同活動之一。沒有任何的感覺比得上當您運動時心跳加速，還有群眾為你的隊伍歡呼勝時。孩子參加運動團隊能夠培養責任感、勇氣，以及信守承諾。此外，孩子們能在維持矯健身軀及享受樂趣的同時，學習人際關係技巧。團隊運動提供挑戰、回饋以及失望，這些都是健康的經驗。讓孩子在學校及家庭之外有其他交友的機會，是有益的。其實，跳脫舒適圈接受新挑戰也是不錯的。孩子總是在成長，不如讓他們去學習、去成長並享受樂趣？

Unit 16
個人選擇【生活類】Personal Choice 1 - Entertainment

🅐 準備方向提示

1. 此類型題目焦點為對自己所偏好的活動或嗜好的描述，平時可思考自己喜歡做什麼、為什麼或者是與此有關的學習。

2. 累積描述正面心情的詞彙（bring me to heaven, refresh my mind, the luckiest person in the world...）等，可增強說明所偏好的活動或嗜好的理由。

3. 可以加入志工或海外遊學活動（長短期皆可），學習西方國家如何渡週末或長假期，或如何將生活安排的更美好惬意（volunteer, working holidays），了解西方文化後，在選擇活動描述方面，可有些啟發式腳本，作為自己對遇此題目觸類旁通的描述。

Question: When going on vacations, some people prefer to go camping in tents, others prefer to stay in hotels.

有些人喜歡露營搭帳篷度假，有些人喜歡待在旅館。

參考範文

When going on vacations, I prefer to go camping in tents instead of staying in hotels. First of all, I love S'mores. Just thinking about being surrounded by starry night sky and the warmth of campfire, I feel the camping fun already. With some marshmallows, a traditional nighttime campfire treat, I'm in heaven. Campfires are absolutely an obvious peak in camping. When the morning breaks, camping offers us a prime territory for some breathtaking moments of the sunrise. Nature is beautiful and just smells great and fresh. What's more fabulous is that camping gives the entire family a chance to have some true quality time together, whether it's playing sports, cooking or simply talking to each other without the usual distractions. Camping creates a peaceful state of mind. With family, a beautiful starry night and blazing fire, we've just got about everything we need in the world.

中文翻譯

　　當度假的時候，我喜歡搭帳棚露營而不是待在旅館。首先，我喜歡棉花糖夾心餅乾。只要想到被點點星空及營火圍繞，我已感受到露營樂趣。有了一些棉花糖，傳統的營火點心，我已心滿意足！營火無疑的是露營的顛峰。當清晨來臨時，營火地點就是觀賞日出的首席。大自然是如此美麗，如此芳香及清新。露營也給了家人間高品質的共處時刻。無論是談笑或烹食，都沒有日常的打擾。露營是一種心境，家人相聚，加上美麗星空及閃爍營火，我們是世界上最開心的一群。

單字、片語說分明

① **S'more** *n.* 棉花糖夾心餅乾

② **marshmallow** *n.* 棉花糖

③ **traditional** *adj.* 傳統的

④ **absolutely** *adv.* 絕對地

⑤ **obvious** *adj.* 明顯的

⑥ **fabulous** *adj.* 精采的

⑦ **entire** *adj.* 全部的、整個的

⑧ **quality time** *n.* 高品質的時光

⑨ **distraction** *n.* 分心

⑩ **blazing** *adj.* 炙燃的

新托福口說參考範文解析與評點

托福口說答題拿分首要掌握以下要點

1. **What（內容資訊）**：本範文完全針對題目回答了所需的**內容資訊**。

2. **How（再解釋 1）**：文法上沒有錯誤，語意上可以理解，文章內有使用連接語詞（如 **First of all; What's more...**）語意間內容本身也有承接，使聽者容易跟隨講者的話題內容。使用常用簡單明瞭的英文詞彙及句型片語，則能提升口語上的流暢度。

3. **Why（再解釋 2）**：本範文沒有離題，絕對針對題目回答，沒有答非所問。文章使用了個人新穎有趣的遊歷經驗的詞彙（**S'more; starry night; family quality time...**），清楚栩栩如生的描繪出自己興趣及經驗的結

合。所描繪的情境先後皆有連貫關係，明顯連續指出二種不同的支持論點
及理由。

> **在描述內容資訊時，本範文首先提出**

1. When going on vacations, I prefer to go camping in tents instead of staying in hotels. → 開頭馬上不拖泥帶水提出立場。

2. 並再以自己的親身遊歷及想法作風加強描述做此答案的原因 → First of all, I love S'mores. Just thinking about surrounded by starry night and the warmth of campfire, I feel the camping fun already. With some marshmallows, a traditional nighttime campfire treat, I'm in heaven. Campfires are absolutely an obvious peak in camping.

3. 支持論點二、三再度以個人經驗提出描述了具體例證及輔佐說明 → When the morning breaks, camping offers us a prime territory for some breathtaking moments of the sunrise. Nature is beautiful and just smells great and fresh. What's more fabulous is that camping gives the entire family a chance to have some true quality time together whether it's playing sports, cooking or simply talking to each other without the usual distractions.

4. 此範文也從個人有趣的遊歷經驗方面以及心理層面不同方面點出回答者本身做此選擇的原因理由，並點出了以下個人做此選擇的原因：在對個人有趣的遊歷經驗方面（**S'more; morning breaks...**）以及心理層面（**family quality time...**）。

5. 結尾結論句的重申及巧妙的重新潤飾表示出答題者對題目的了解，因此掌握良好 → Camping creates a peaceful state of mind. With family, a beautiful starry night and blazing fire, we've just got

about everything we need in the world.

托福口說論述的架構組成單位

1. 開頭介紹（**Introduction**）：

When going on vacations, I prefer to go camping in tents instead of staying in hotels.

2. 文章主體（**Body**）：

A. 支持論點一（Supporting idea 1）：

I. 支持句一（Supporting sentence 1）：

First of all, I love S'mores. Just thinking about surrounded by starry night and campfire warmth, I feel the camping fun already.

II. 支持句二（Supporting sentence 2）：

With some marshmallows, a traditional nighttime campfire treat, I'm in heaven.

III. 支持句三（Supporting sentence 3）：

Campfires are absolutely an obvious peak in camping.

B. 支持論點二（Supporting idea 2）：

I. 支持句一（Supporting sentence 1）：

When the morning breaks, camping offers us a prime territory for some breathtaking moments of the sunrise.

II. 支持句二（Supporting sentence 2）：

Nature is beautiful and just smells great and fresh.

C. 支持論點三（Supporting idea 3）：

I. 支持句一（Supporting sentence 1）：

What's more fabulous is that camping gives the entire family a chance to have some true quality time together, whether it's playing sports, cooking or simply talking to each other without the usual distractions.

3. 結尾結論（Conclusion）：

Camping creates a peaceful state of mind. With family, a beautiful starry night and blazing fire and we've just got about everything we need in the world.

此題目要求的是**考生表達對自己喜歡的活動的描述能力，答案常常是因人而異，會因為考生的經驗及背景而選擇不同**。不過，訣竅在於累積不同活動經驗的描述，以此融入對自己生命及心靈洗滌的描述（如 bring me peace; cool me down...），考試時適時運用這些描述提供自己正面能量的詞彙，去說明做此選擇的原因。而掌握好這些要點，就是考生在一定時間內快速整述自己喜歡的活動，以及這些活動對自己的正面影響的綜合口語能力了。

D 新托福口說答題模板套用　🎧 Track 62

以上述短文為例，相關議題可依以下短文解析做變化，遇此類托福口說題目時可侃侃而談對題目迎刃而解。未劃底線的部分可不需更改，**劃底線**部分可替換為考生本身的經驗以及欲描述的項目。

開頭

1. When going on vacations, I prefer to go camping in tents instead of staying in hotels.
   → 將劃底線的部分改為考生（您）**個人偏好的運動、娛樂或活動（根據題意）**的描述。
   → When going on vacations, I prefer to go visiting mother nature instead of doing indoor activities.

1. First of all, I love S'mores. Just thinking about surrounded by <u>starry night and campfire warmth</u>, I feel the <u>camping</u> fun already. With <u>some marshmallows, a traditional nighttime campfire treat</u>, I'm in heaven. <u>Campfires</u> are absolutely an obvious peak in <u>camping</u>.

   → 並描述簡短個人經驗的相關描述。將劃底線的部分改為考生（您）個人偏好的運動、娛樂或活動（根據題意）。

   → First of all, I love <u>ocean</u>. Just thinking about being surrounded by <u>beach sand and blue sky</u>, I feel the <u>beach</u> fun already. With <u>a cup of tropical pineapple cocktail, a traditional beach party treat</u>, I'm in heaven. <u>Campfires</u> are absolutely an obvious peak <u>when camping on the beach</u>.

2. When the morning breaks, <u>camping offers us a prime territory</u> for some breathtaking moments of the sunrice. Nature is beautiful and just smells great and fresh.

   → 將劃底線的部分改為考生（您）個人偏好的運動、娛樂或活動（根據題意）方面。

   → When the morning breaks, <u>visiting mother nature offers us a better chance</u> for some breathtaking moments of the sunrice. Nature is beautiful and just smells great and fresh.

3. What's more fabulous is that <u>camping</u> gives the entire family a chance to have some true quality time together, whether it's playing sports, cooking or simply talking to each other without the usual distractions.

   → 將劃底線的部分改為考生（您）個人偏好的運動、娛樂或活動（根據題意）。

   → What's more fabulous is that <u>visiting mother nature</u> gives the entire family a chance to have some true quality time together whether it's playing sports, cooking or simply talking to each other without the usual distractions.

結尾

　　之後再編述一項理由支持所提出的論點，並且間接指向了結尾結論句。

1. <u>Camping</u> creates a peaceful state of mind. With family, <u>a beautiful starry night and blazing fire</u> and we've just got about everything we need in the world.

   → 將劃現部分改成考生（您）個人偏好的運動、娛樂或活動（根據題意），最後結論句以不同方式重述重點句。

   → <u>Camping</u> creates a peaceful state of mind. With family, <u>beautiful beach sand and a charming sunset</u> and we've got just about everything we need in the world.

E 此類考題考前及應考時準備筆記要點

1. 不同的休閒活動

   hiking; mountain climbing; camping; yacht; sightseeing; photography; bicycling; kayaking...

2. 對個人有正面影響（心靈或生理方面）的詞彙

   bring me to heaven; cool down; fresh my mind; reenergize; relaxing; inspiring; peaceful time...

3. 不同活動的正反面描述詞彙

   starry night; close to Mother Nature; get away from electronic devises; breath the fresh air; bring family closer; quality time; air pollution; traffic; noises...

Just thinking about being surrounded by starry night and campfire warmth, I feel the camping fun already.

只要想到被點點星空及營火圍繞，我已感受到露營樂趣。

1. Just imagine being surrounded by starry night and campfire warmth, I feel the camping fun already.

   只要想到被點點星空及營火圍繞，我已感受到露營樂趣。

2. I feel I am actually camping already by just thinking about being surrounded by starry night and campfire warmth.

   我已感受到露營樂趣，只要想到被點點星空及營火圍繞。

With some marshmallows, a traditional nighttime campfire treat, I'm in heaven.

有了一些棉花糖，傳統的營火點心，我已心滿意足

1. It totally brings me to heaven just to have some marshmallows, a traditional nighttime campfire treat.

   有了美味傳統營火點心棉花糖，我已心滿意足。

2. It makes my day with some marshmallows, a traditional nighttime campfire treat.

   有了美味傳統營火點心棉花糖，我已心滿意足。

When the morning breaks, camping offers us a prime territory for some breathtaking moments of the sunrise.

當清晨來臨時，營火地點就是觀賞日出的首席。

1. When the morning breaks, camping gives us the best seat to enjoy some breathtaking moments of the sunrise.

   當清晨來臨時，營火地點就是觀賞日出的首席。

2. When the morning breaks, camping ensures us a prime territory for some breathtaking moments of the sunrise.

當清晨來臨時，營火地點就是觀賞日出的首席。

G 想想看還能怎麼答 🔊 Track 64

Ideally, I'd go with the camping. The Mother Nature is such a beautiful place and often has the best air quality. There are times when people go camping and garbage is left behind, but the situation has been improved. The hotel is often too formal to feel at ease and comfortable when we step out of our rooms. The camping offers a connection to the older days and simpler times and it's cheaper, too. A lot of restaurants can be found in the city near hotel, which are delicious, expensive, and often unhealthy. Food served by family, on the comtrary, is full of love and variety. It's even a great place to be when you want to reenergize your body and boost your spirit. At the end of the day, we all want peace and quiet and a nice place to rest our heads.

中文翻譯

我會以露營當作我的理想選擇。鄉村非常美麗也空氣清新。以前大家露營會遺留下垃圾，但這情況已有改善許多。旅館呢則讓人感覺到拘束不自在尤其是出旅館房門後。露營讓我們回到古早時代簡單花費少的生活方式。在旅館附近可以找到許多美味昂貴的餐廳，但那裡的食材通常並不健康的。露營的食物是家人烹煮了，豐富的食材裡面充滿了他們的愛。露營是讓您身心靈重新充電的好去處。在一天結束時，我們都需要和平、安靜的地方去歇息。

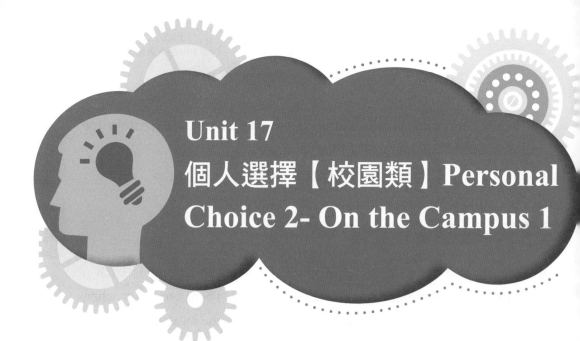

Unit 17
個人選擇【校園類】Personal Choice 2- On the Campus 1

A 準備方向提示

1. 此類型題目焦點為對自己的偏好（preferences）、生活習慣（life habits）或嗜好（habits）的描述，平時可思考自己喜歡做什麼、為什麼或者是與此有關的生活方式的選擇。

2. 練習托福聽力的情境式問題（campus conversations），可了解校園對話或海外求學可能會遇到的情境。

3. 累積校園對話詞彙（如 dormitory; final exam; a library, cafeteria; student union; international student office...），可增加口說內容的豐富性，同時提升切題度。

B 模擬題目 🔘 **Track 65**

Question: Would you rather have the university assign a student to share a room with you, or would you rather choose your own roommate? What do you think is better?

你會想要大學安排室友給你，還是由你自己選擇室友？

參考範文

I would rather choose my own roommate, absolutely. To share a space with someone every day is a big deal in life to me and that's exactly why I would rather choose my own roommate. Every day we have our own schedule, at the same time, we each also prefer certain lifestyles. For instance, the way we would like to decorate our room. What if my roommate holds totally different beliefs and goals I want to achieve? Maybe negotiation works. However, our minds might change when our roommate would like to have a party overnight while we are facing a huge examination the next day. Unless the belief and the lifestyle we possess are quite similar, thus we are able to cooperate well, I would rather have my roommates chosen by myself instead of randomly being assigned one.

中文翻譯

我絕對會想要選擇我自己的室友。對我來說每天和人共享一個空間是一件大事，所以我才會想要選擇自己的室友。我們每天都有自己的時程計劃，同時我們的生活生式也都各有偏好。就拿佈置我們的房間來說，要是我的信念和想要達成的目標和我完全不同怎麼辦？或許能靠溝通協調吧，但要是室友想要在我們隔天就要考試的晚上開整夜的派對，我們可能就會改變心意了。除非我們的信念和生活方式非

常相似，且能夠互相配合，否則我會希望我們能自己選擇自己的室友，而不是隨機分配室友。

單字、片語說分明

① **a big deal** *n.* 很重要的事
② **decorate** *v.* 佈置
③ **negotiation** *n.* 協調
④ **overnight** *adv.* 整夜
⑤ **possess** *v.* 擁有

新托福口說參考範文解析與評點

托福口說答題拿分首要掌握以下要點

1. **What**（內容資訊）：本範文完全針對題目回答了所需的內容資訊。

2. **How**（再解釋 1）：文法上沒有錯誤，語意上可以理解，文章內有使用連接語詞（如 For instance; however; unless... ），語意間內容本身也有承接，使聽者容易跟隨講者的話題內容。使用常用簡單明瞭的英文詞彙及句型片語，則能夠提升口語上的流暢度。

3. **Why**（再解釋 2）：本範文沒有離題，絕對針對題目回答，沒有答非所問。文章使用了個人經驗（如 the way to decorate the room; have a party; have an examination... ），清楚栩栩如生地描繪出自己的習慣及經驗，切題度高，且所描繪的情境先後皆有連貫關係，明顯連續指出二種不同的支持論點及理由。

> **在描述內容資訊時，本範文首先提出**

1. I would rather choose my own roommate, absolutely. → 開頭馬上不拖泥帶水的點出立場。

2. 並再以自己的想法、經驗或習慣方式加強描述做此答案的原因 → To share a space with someone every day is **a big deal** in life to me and that's exactly why I would rather choose my own roommate. Every day we have our own schedule, at the same time, we each also prefer certain lifestyles.

3. 支持論點二再度以個人經驗提出描述了具體例證及輔佐說明 → What if my roommate holds totally different beliefs and goals I want to achieve? Maybe **negotiation** works. However, our minds might change when our roommate would like to have a party **overnight** while we are facing a huge examination the next day.

4. 此範文也從個人想法及生活習慣方面以及心理層面不同方面點出回答者本身做此選擇的原因理由，並點出了以下個人做此選擇的原因：在對個人想法及生活習慣方面（**schedule, room decoration...**）以及心理層面（**hold totally different beliefs and goals...**）。

5. 結尾結論句結合上述理由並重申及巧妙的重新潤飾表示出答題者對題目的了解，因此掌握良好 → Unless the belief and the lifestyle we **possess** are quite similar, thus we are able to cooperate well, I would rather have my roommates chosen by myself instead of randomly being assigned one.

托福口說論述的架構組成單位

1. 開頭介紹（**Introduction**）：

   I would rather choose my own roommate, absolutely.

2. 文章主體（**Body**）：

   A. 支持論點一（Supporting idea 1）：

   I.　支持句一（Supporting sentence 1）：

   To share a space with someone every day is **a big deal** in life to me and that's exactly why I would rather choose my own roommate.

   II.　支持句二（Supporting sentence 2）：

   Every day we have our own schedule, at the same time, we each also prefer certain lifestyles.

   III. 支持句三（Supporting sentence 3）：

   For instance, the way we would like to **decorate** our room.

   B. 支持論點二（Supporting idea 2）：

   I.　支持句一（Supporting sentence 1）：

   What if my roommate holds totally different beliefs and goals I want to achieve? Maybe **negotiation** works.

   II.　支持句二（Supporting sentence 2）：

   However, our minds might change when our roommate would like to have a party **overnight** while we are facing a huge examination next day.

   C. 結尾結論（**Conclusion**）：

   Unless the belief and the lifestyle we **possess** are quite similar, thus we are able to cooperate well, I would rather have my roommates chosen by myself instead of randomly being assigned one.

　　此題目要求的是考生表達對自己生活習慣、偏好或想法的描述能力。題材一樣，會因為個人生活習慣、偏好或想法的差異而有不同的答案組合。**建議可以在練習托福聽力或閱讀的考古題時，特別注意校園對話的部份**，像是有到圖書館、地下餐廳、學生會辦、國際學生會館或宿舍交誼廳等等各式各樣不同的**校園情境**，先聽取或模仿情境對話，學習其中的情境及應對進退，作為此類托福口說題目的啟發性腳本，再加以統整自己的想法及風格。掌握好這些步驟後，遇此試題便能發揮考生（您）在一定的時間內，快速統整的綜合整述能力！

🔩 新托福口說答題模板套用 ⏺ Track 66

　　以上述短文為例，相關議題可依以下短文解析做變化，遇此類托福口說題目時可侃侃而談對題目迎刃而解。未劃底線的部分可不需更改，**劃底線**部分可替換為考生本身的經驗以及欲描述的項目。

開頭

1. I would rather choose my own <u>roommate</u>, absolutely.
   → 將劃底線的部分改為考生（您）**所偏好的處事風格或生活選擇（根據題意）**。
   → I would rather choose my own <u>group members</u>, absolutely.

主體

1. Every day we have our own schedule, at the same time, we each also prefer certain <u>lifestyles</u>. For instance, the way we would like to <u>decorate our room</u>.
   → 將劃底線的部分給為考生（您）**所偏好的處事風格或生活選擇（根據題意）**與相關的敘述。

→ Every day we have our own schedule, at the same time, we each also prefer certain <u>way of thinking</u>. For instance, the way we would like to <u>present our papers or express our ideas</u>.

2. What if my <u>roommate</u> holds totally different beliefs and goals I want to achieve? Maybe negotiation works. However, our minds might change when our <u>roommate</u> would like to have a party overnight while we are facing a huge <u>examination</u> the next day.

→ 將劃底線的部分改為考生（您）**所偏好的處事風格、生活選擇（根據題意）**方面。

→ What if our <u>group members</u> hold totally different beliefs and goals they want to achieve? Maybe negotiation works. However, our minds might change when our <u>group members</u> would like to have a party overnight while we are facing a huge <u>presentation</u> the next day.

結尾

編述一項理由支持所提出的論點，之後再總結式或重新潤飾支持所提出的論點。

1. Unless <u>the belief and the lifestyle</u> we possess are quite similar, thus we are able to cooperate well, I would rather have my <u>roommates</u> chosen by myself instead of randomly being assigned one.

→ 將劃底線的部分改為考生（您）**所偏好的處事風格或生活選擇（根據題意）**的描述。最後結論句以不同方式重述重點句。

→ Unless <u>the belief and goal</u> we possess are quite similar, thus we are able to cooperate well, I would rather have my <u>group members</u> chosen by myself instead of randomly being assigned one.

E 此類考題考前及應考時準備筆記要點

1. 美國日常生活用語

   I need to do laundry; **go to** cafeteria; fitness center; front desk; **go to meet** the dormitory superintendent; the administrative building is in the campus; **go** grocery shopping; **where to apply for** the free bus service...

2. 美國校園用語

   Supervisor; photo ID; orientation; teaching demonstration; lab（laboratory）; tutor; miscellaneous expenses; semester; database...

3. 學術討論用語

   supervisor; term paper; comprehension test; final exam; presentation; lecture; conference...

F 換句話說補一補　Track 67

I would rather choose my own roommates, absolutely.
我絕對會想要選擇我自己的室友。

1. Choosing my own roommate is absolutely my first priority.
   選擇自己的室友絕對是我第一優先的決定。

2. I prefer to choose my own roommates for sure.
   我當然是偏好選擇自己的室友。

What if my roommate holds totally different beliefs and goals I want to achieve? Maybe negotiation works.
要是我的信念和想要達成的目標和我完全不同怎麼辦？或許能靠溝通協調吧。

1. What if my roommate holds completely different beliefs and goals I possess? I doubt that negotiation works.
   要是我和室友的信念和目標完全不同怎麼辦？協調溝通不見得有用。
2. What if my roommate has an entirely different idea of beliefs and goals? The negotiation works?
   要是我室友對信念和目標有不同的想法怎麼辦？協調有用嗎？

Every day we have our own schedule, at the same time, we each also prefer different lifestyles.
我們每天都有自己的時程計劃，同時我們的生活生式也都各有偏好。

1. We have our own schedule each day. Also, we each have a preference for certain lifestyles.
   我們每天都有自己的時間安排，而且我們的生活方式也各有偏好。
2. Every day we own our schedule and have a preference for certain lifestyles.
   我們自己每天都有時間安排，對生活方式也各有偏好。

想想看還能怎麼答 Track 68

    In many ways, regardless of your choice, roommates can be troublesome. At times, we all get into uncomfortable interactions with people, whether family, friends, or acquaintances. Now, if the choice is mine, I will surely conduct interviews with candidates to prescreen for the most appropriate roommate. It's not easy to simply judge a person's entire character and life experience or future solely in a 20 minute chat over a medium cup of Starbuck's pricey coffee; however, it's possible to understand in that short time whether the two of you click or not. During the pre-screening, I'd be sure to ask some real simple, yet necessary questions that will reveal some clear truths about the potential candidates. For example, cleanliness is one of concerns when it comes to living with people. Each person has his or her own idea of what cleanness is. Anyway, I would rather have my roommates chosen by ourselves instead of randomly being assigned one.

單字小解

① **troublesome** *adj.* 麻煩的
② **at times** *adv.* 有時候
③ **uncomfortable** *adj.* 不舒服
④ **conduct** *v.* 進行
⑤ **candidate** *n.* 候選人
⑥ **prescreen** *v.* 預選
⑦ **pricey** *adj.* 昂貴的
⑧ **click** *v.* 合得來
⑨ **potential** *adj.* 很有潛力的
⑩ **cleanliness** *n.* 整潔

中文翻譯

　　先不管這不是你的選擇，室友在各個方面都很麻煩。有時我們和他人的互動會不自在，不管對方是家人或是朋友。若要我現在選擇，我一定會私下面談可能的人選，篩檢後選出最適合的室友。用短短 20 分鐘喝一杯星巴克中杯咖啡的時間就要看出一個人的個性、判斷他們的生活經驗或未來，是不容易的，但至少可以看出你們兩個人合不合的來。在篩檢的過程中，我會問一些簡單但必要的問題，而這些問題會清楚地透露出可能人選的事實。舉例來說整潔度是和人同住時會關心的其中一點。而每個人對整潔的定義都不同。

Unit 18
個人選擇【校園類】Personal Choice 3- On the Campus 2

A 準備方向提示

1. 此類型題目焦點為考生個人價值觀點的描述，平時閱讀有深度的英文文章（如 Times; newspapers），思考自己對事物的看法及選擇、為什麼有此或者是與此有關的知識攝取。

2. 累積智慧型諺語（proverbs, wisdom quotes），可增強說明所所選擇的價值觀感的理由。

3. 可以多方聽聽名人演講（TED Talk），學習他／她們如何面對職場生涯的抉擇及思考點，日後在選擇價值觀感時，可有些啟發式的腳本，作為自己對遇此題目觸類旁通的描述。

B 模擬題目 Track 69

Part 1

Question: Do you agree or disagree with the following statement? It's a waste of time for university students to take courses outside their major fields. Use specific reasons and examples in your answer.
你認同「修外系課對大學生來説是浪費時間」的這種説法嗎？請詳述並舉例來支持您的看法。

Part 2

參考範文

Part 3

I disagree with the statement that it's a waste of time for university students to take courses outside their major fields. My reasons will be the following. Firstly, there always have new knowledge or skills for us to gain in life. Believe it or not, we can never have enough when it comes to new knowledge or skills. So we should keep humble and learn all the time. Secondly, the more we know, the more opportunities for us to have a bright future. I believe that the universe promises those who prepare the most a good future and chances. Last but not least, university education is simply a very beginning of life and career, so it's better to equip ourselves as much as possible before we entering the big jungle of the real world. Taking more courses other than our major is actually a key to success.

中文翻譯

我不同意修主修以外的課是浪費時間的説法。生活的知識及經驗永遠不嫌多。不管你相信與否，經驗與知識永遠都不夠。我的理由如下。首先，我們應該要保持謙虛及學習。再者，我們懂得越多，我們會有更的機會迎向璀璨的未來。我相信宇宙也應許準備最好的人更好的未來及機會。最後也很重要的是，大學教育只是生活

及職場的開端,所以在我們真正進入都市叢林之前,最好是將自己調整到最佳狀態。修主修以外的課正是通往成功的關鍵。

單字、片語說分明

① **humble** *adj.* 謙虛
② **bright** *adj.* 明亮的、聰明的
③ **jungle** *n.* 叢林
④ **legacy** *n.* 傳統、文物遺產
⑤ **artistic aroma** *n.* 藝術氣息、藝術氣氛

C 新托福口說參考範文解析與評點

托福口說答題拿分首要掌握以下要點

1. **What(內容資訊)**:本範文完全針對題目回答了所需的**內容資訊**。

2. **How(再解釋 1)**:文法上沒有錯誤,語意上可以理解,**文章內有使用連接語詞(如 Firstly; secondly; last but least...)**,語意間內容本身也有承接,使聽者容易跟隨講者的話題內容。使用常用簡單明瞭的英文詞彙及句型片語,則能夠提升口語上的流暢度。

3. **Why(再解釋 2)**:本範文沒有離題,絕對針對題目回答,沒有答非所問。文章使用了個人價值觀感描述(**good chance; beginning of career...**),所描繪的情境先後皆有連貫關係,明顯連續指出三種不同的支持論點及理由。

在描述內容資訊時，本範文首先提出

1. I disagree with the statement that it's a waste of time for university students to take courses outside their major fields. → 開頭馬上不拖泥帶水提出立場。

2. 並再以自己的價值觀點及想法作風加強描述做此答案的原因 → Firstly, there always have new knowledge or skills for us to gain in life. Believe it or not, we can never have enough when it comes to new knowledge or skills. So we should keep **humble** and learn all the time.

3. 支持論點二、三再度以個人的價值觀點及想法作風提出描述了具體例證及輔佐說明 → Secondly, the more we know, the more opportunities for us to have a bright future. I believe that the universe promises those who prepare the most a good future and chances. Last but not least, university education is simply a very beginning of life and career, so it's better to equip ourselves as much as possible before we entering the big jungle of the real world.

4. 結尾結論句的重申及巧妙的重新潤飾表示出答題者對題目的了解，因此掌握良好 → Taking more courses other than our major is actually a key to success.

托福口說論述的架構組成單位

1. 開頭介紹（**Introduction**）：

I disagree with the statement that it's a waste of time for university students to take courses outside their major fields. My reasons will be the following.

2. 文章主體（**Body**）：

A. 支持論點一（Supporting idea 1）：

I. 支持句一（Supporting sentence 1）：

Firstly, there always have knowledge or skills for us to gain in life.

II. 支持句二（Supporting sentence 2）：

Believe it or not, we can never have enough when it comes to new knowledge or skills.

III. 支持句三（Supporting sentence 3）：

So we should keep humble and learn all the time.

B. 支持論點二（Supporting idea 2）：

I. 支持句一（Supporting sentence 1）：

Secondly, the more we know, the more opportunities for us to have a **bright** future.

II. 支持句二（Supporting sentence 2）：

I believe that the universe promises those who prepare the most a good future and chances.

C. 支持論點三（Supporting idea 3）：

I. 支持句一（Supporting sentence 1）：

Last but not least, university education is simply a very beginning of life and career, so it's better to equip ourselves as much as possible before we entering the big

jungle of the real world.

D. 結尾結論（**Conclusion**）：

　　　　Taking more courses other than our major is actually a key to success.

　　此題目要求的是考生表達自己對大學生是否可多學習主科以外相關課題，其實比較傾向的答案會是鼓勵多攝取新知及新經驗。訣竅在於累積不同正面積極理由的描述，以此融入對自己生命及心靈昇華的描述（如 **equip us; get us ready; upgrade our life; enhance our depth in life...**），考試時要能適時運用這些描述提供自己正面能量的詞彙，去說明做此選擇的原因。而掌握好這些要點，就是考生在一定時間內快速整述自己所採取的立場價值觀感，以及對自己的正面影響的綜合口語能力了。

🔧 新托福口說答題模板套用　🔵 Track 70

　　以上述短文為例，相關議題可依以下短文解析做變化，遇此類托福口說題目時可侃侃而談對題目迎刃而解。未劃底線的部分可不需更改，**劃底線**部分可替換為考生本身的經驗以及欲描述的項目。

開頭

1. I disagree with the statement that <u>it's a waste of time for university students to take courses outside their major fields</u>. My reasons will be the following.

→ 將劃底線的部分改為考生（您）**個人價值觀感或看法（根據題意）**的描述。

→ I disagree with the statement <u>that it's a waste of time for teenagers to take leisure activities and just focus on their studies.</u> My reasons will be the following.

1. Last but not least, <u>university education is simply a very beginning of life and career</u>, so it's better to equip ourselves as much as possible before we entering the big jungle of the real world.

   → 將劃底線的部分改為考生（您）個人價值觀感或看法（根據題意）方面。

   → Last but not least, <u>studying is simply one page of our life</u> , so it's better to equip ourselves as much as possible before we enter the big jungle of the real world.

結尾

結尾句結論句再綜合潤飾個人價值觀感的立場。

1. <u>Taking more courses other than our major</u> is actually a key to <u>success</u>.

   → 將劃底線的部分改為考生（您）個人價值觀感或看法（根據題意）方面，最後結論句以不同方式重述重點句。

   → <u>Taking time on leisure activities other than our studies</u> is actually a key to success and <u>healthy body and life</u>.

   補充：

   其實改成 leisure activities 時，可以增加運動對身心靈方面都有健康正面影響的理由論述喔，這樣可使文章更有說服力、增加文章內容深度。

此類考題考前及應考時準備筆記要點

1. 不同的休閒活動

hiking, mountain climbing, camping, yacht, sightseeing, photography, bicycling, kayaking....

2. 對個人有正面影響（心靈或生理方面）的詞彙

bring me to heaven, cool down, fresh my mind, reenergize, relaxing, inspiring, peaceful time...

3. 累積智慧型諺語

better late than never; your thoughts control your life; learning is a treasure that will follow its owner everywhere he who walks with integrity walks securely...

F 換句話說補一補　Track 71

My reasons will be the following.
我的理由如下。

1. The following are my reasons.
   以下是我的理由。

2. Let me address the following as my reasons.
   我的理由如下。

I believe that the universe promises those who prepare the most a good future and chance.
我相信宇宙也應許準備最好的人更好的未來及機會。

1. I believe in universe because it guarantees those who prepare the most a good future and better chances.
   我對宇宙懷有信念，因為它應許準備好的人有更好的未來和機會。

2. We should hold a firm belief that universe promises those who prepare the most a good future and chance.
   我們要相信宇宙會讓準備好的人有更好的未來和機會。

Taking more courses other than our major is actually a key to success.
修主修以外的課正是通往成功的關鍵。

1. I believe that it is a key to success by taking more classes other than our major.
   我覺得通往成功的關鍵就是修主修以外的課。

2. Taking more courses other than our major certainly ensures us to reach success.
   修主修以外的課可引領我們前往成功的道路。

 **G** 想想看還能怎麼答 Track 72

Knowledge empowers us to shape the situation. Ignorance empowers the situation to shape us. I feel it is a matter of our choices, whether or not we would like to create more diversities and opportunities after we graduate from university. I still intend to say that it won't be a waste of time for university students to take courses outside their major fields. Take students whose major is science or business management for instance, if they can also study a foreign language, firstly, they can broaden their academic horizon. Secondly, after they graduate, a foreign language might bring them an opportunity to the market in a foreign country and contribute to the society what they have learned. Or perhaps they could also combine their foreign language with marketing strategies, so they can create another career for themselves and for people who need jobs.

Part
1

Part
2

Part
3

單字小解

① **empower** *v.* 使充滿能量

② **ignorance** *n.* 無知

③ **diversity** *n.* 多樣性

④ **take...for instance** *ph.* 以……為例

⑤ **academic** *adj.* 學術的

⑥ **horizon** *n.* 地平線、眼界

⑦ **contribute to** *ph.* 貢獻

⑧ **marketing strategy** *ph.* 商業策略

中文翻譯

　　知識讓我們去塑造局勢。無知讓局勢改變我們。我認為是否要在畢業後創造多元性和機會是我們的選擇。我會傾向修主修以外的課對大學生而言並非是浪費時間。就拿主修是科學類科或商業類科的為例，假如他們可以學習外國語言，他們在學術上可以開闊視野。再者，在他們畢業之後，外國語文可以讓他們在其他國家發展他們的專業，又能在社會貢獻所學。或者，他們還能將語言結合商業知識，為他們自己及他人創造商業新機。

PART 3
口說活用篇

Unit 19
校園生活敘述與討論
Campus Talks

A 準備方向提示

1. 此類型題目焦點為對時間、人物互動、事件、節慶或活動（**Time; event; activity; festival; people; fair**）描述的敏感度及反應能力。

2. 專注於對話內容的時間點或事件及參與的人物，結合聽力內容後快速重點整述（**conversation; interaction vs information**）。

3. 配合前述相關校園口說題組的技巧，了解校園中（**campus life conversation**）可能會有哪些狀況，訓練對聽力內容及時間表結合的口語表述能力。

Listen to the following conversation carefully.

請仔細聽以下的對話。

Question: What is this campus conversation mainly talking about? In order to answer the question appropriately, please address examples or evidences from the conversation as more as possible.

試問此校園對話的主要內容為何？請簡短的以文章及聽力內容中的具體證據及範例陳述出來。

Raj and Miranda are talking about an Autumn Sport Festival. This sport festival sounds big in that the school will be closing for three days just for that. Raj is interested in joining. After hearing Raj's words, Miranda is interested in going too. She would like to have some resort vacation package or music center tickets. While if they would like to join the competition, they will have to invite more people to join their team, and Miranda will be going to check with her cousin and see whether or not he could join them. Raj will also be going to register for a team. In order to have a better understanding and preparation for this event, Raj suggests that everybody should go to the festival meeting so they can know what could be those requirements and regulations. The meeting will be held on Friday, May 5.

中文翻譯

Raj 及 Miranda 正討論著秋季運動節。此活動似乎很盛大，因為校園將為此活動停課三天。Raj 希望可以參加競賽。經過 Raj 的說明，Miranda 也希望可以加入。Miranda 希望可以獲得度假勝地的招待券。假如他們真想參加，那他們必須邀請更多人加入他們的團隊，因此 Miranda 想詢問她的堂哥是否能加入。Raj 則負責登入團隊競賽。為了對比賽要求及規則有更多了解，Raj 希望大家都可以參加競賽說明會。競賽說明會將在五月五號舉行。

單字、片語說分明

① **festival** *n.* 節慶
② **package** *n.* 方案；包裝
③ **preparation** *n.* 準備
④ **requirement** *n.* 要求、必備條件
⑤ **regulation** *n.* 規定、規範

C 新托福口說參考範文解析與評點

托福口說答題拿分首要掌握以下要點

1. **What**（內容資訊）：本範文完全針對題目回答了所需的內容資訊。

2. **How**（再解釋 1）：文法上沒有錯誤，語意上可以理解。

3. **Why**（再解釋 2）：本範文沒有離題，絕對針對題目回答，沒有答非所問。文章針對所提供對話的內容及聽力內容加以整理論述。

D 此類考題考前及應考時準備筆記要點

1. 校園大小事
   astray dogs, cup cake, caroling, student night, orientation, club fair, dormitory life...

2. 不同的校園活動主題

job fair, club fair, international student fair, culture fair, renaissance festival, grandpa and grandmom day, parents day, music festival, international student festival, Chinese culture fair, video game festival, off-campus housing fair...

3. 不同校園場景詞彙

main campus, cafeteria, international student office, dormitory, laundry room, reading room, auditorium, conference room, administration building, canteen, lounge...

 E 換句話說補一補 Track 75

This sport festival sounds big in that the school will be closed for three days just for that.
此秋季運動季活動似乎很盛大，因為校園將為此活動停課三天。

1. This sport festival seems to be huge and the school will be closed for three days just for that.
   此秋季運動季活動似乎很盛大，因為校園將為此活動停課三天。

2. This sport festival sounds big because the school will have to be closed for three days just for that.
   此秋季運動季活動似乎很盛大，因為校園將為此活動停課三天。

While if they would like to join the competition, they will have to invite more people to join their team, and Miranda will be going to check with her cousin and see whether or not he could join them.
假如他們真想參加，那他們必須邀請更多人加入他們的團隊，因此 Miranda 將問問她的堂哥是否能加入。

1. If they are planning to join the competition, they will have to invite more people to join their team, and Miranda will talk to her cousin and see whether or not he would like to join them too.
   假如他們真想參加，那他們必須邀請更多人加入他們的團隊，因此 Miranda 想要問問她的堂哥能否加入。

2. To join the competition, they will have to invite more people to join their team, and Miranda will go to her cousin and see whether or not he is interested in joining them.
   假如他們真想參加，那他們必須邀請更多人加入他們的團隊，因此 Miranda 想要問問她的堂哥能否加入。

The meeting will be held on Friday, May 5.
競賽說明會將在五月五號舉行。

1. The meeting will take place on Friday, May 5.
   競賽說明會將在五月五號舉行。

2. They will have a meeting on Friday, May 5.
   競賽說明會將在五月五號舉行。

F 錄音原文

校園對話內容 Dialogue

Raj met Miranda on their way to campus cafeteria in front of Kirkland Hall.
Raj 在去學校餐廳的途中遇見 Miranda，兩人站在 Kirkland Hall 前。

Raj: Did you read the campus **announcement** on the **bulletin** in front of the student office this morning?

Part 1

Part 2

Part 3

Raj：妳有看見今天早上學生事務處外的校園公告嗎？

Miranda: Which new announcement are you talking about? President selection? The Autumn Sport Festival that everybody is going to be off the school in the afternoon from Tuesday to Friday for this four days thing?

Miranda：是哪個新公告呢？學生會長選舉？還是學校會有四天、星期二到星期五停課的秋季校園運動會？

Raj: Yeah, sounds exciting, isn't it? Do you have any interest in this one? Or any friends you know may be interested in it?

Raj：是的，很振奮人心吧！妳想參加嗎？或有認識的朋友想一起參加嗎？

Miranda: Hmmmm...let me see. I think my cousin from Engineering Department may be interested in it too. However, he may have a test to prepare for on the exact same week Monday. I could check with him to see whether he's going to join our team or not.

Miranda：嗯我想想……我想我工程學系的堂哥應該也會想參加。不過他那個禮拜的星期一會有一個測驗。我會問問他有沒有興趣加入我們的團隊。

Raj: There will be a lot of prizes, such as brand new **laptops** with booming **wireless speakers**, a package of two nights in GreenBay Resort, wait wait, there's more, or four free tickets to the music festival that just opened this week. Man... they even have movie tickets...cell phones...

Raj：有許多獎項喔。如全新無線音箱筆電、兩天的名勝地旅遊招待、還有四張免費的音樂季入場券，還有電影票、手機……等等。

Miranda: Wow, that sounds so **tempting**, how do we join it? Are we joining it? I really want those tickets to GreenBay Resort. How do we join it? Do we register? Where can we go to register?

Miranda：聽起來太誘人了。如何參加呢？我們會參加嗎？我真的很想贏得 Green Bay 勝地免費招待。怎麼樣登記參賽呢？

Raj: Great! I'll take care of the registration. Now all we need to do for this new baby is to think of a team name and some members we are interested in inviting.

Raj：我會負責登記參賽。現在我需要大家一同想想隊名以及邀請更多的隊友。

Miranda: Alright! I'll check with my cousin tonight after he returns from his part-time job at the library. I'll go to the office and grab a flyer too.

Miranda：好，我今晚在我堂哥從圖書館打工回來後問問他。我也會去拿幾張活動宣傳單。

Raj: If you guys agree with the idea, the **luncheon** meeting of the whole Autumn Sport Festival details, **policies** and **regulations** will be held at noon on this Friday, May 5, in the Hall of Prentiss-Lucas. Please also let your cousin know this incoming luncheon meeting and see whether or not he can set a time for it too. I hope we all can be there to know what we are going to do to come to a decision.

Raj：假如你們同意，整個活動細則或規範的午餐說明會將會在五月五號的星期五於 Prentiss-Lucas 舉行。請也告知妳堂哥這消息吧！希望大家屆時都可以參加並一塊討論。

Miranda: Sounds great. So I guess we'll discuss it again later tonight online?
Miranda：好的，那晚上線上繼續討論囉！

Raj: Yap, let's do it!
Raj：好的，就這麼決定。

Miranda: Se'ya.
Miranda：再見。

Raj: Ok, take care.
Raj：保重。

單字小解

① **announcement** *n.* 公告
② **bulletin** *n.* 布告欄
③ **laptop** *n.* 筆電
④ **wireless** *adj.* 無線的
⑤ **speaker** *n.* 播放器
⑥ **tempting** *adj.* 誘人的
⑦ **luncheon** *n.* 午餐
⑧ **policy** *n.* 政策
⑨ **regulation** *n.* 規則

Unit 20
課堂內容敘述與討論【文科】
Lecture Descriptions 1

A 準備方向提示

1. 此類型題目焦點為測驗考生對課堂討論（Classroom discussion and interaction）的了解程度以及回答互動時的反應能力。

2. 聽取上課短文後，依據自己所寫快速筆記（如果沒有做筆記習慣也可，只要平時有訓練好英文資訊聽取後的快速整述能力即可），做快速重點整述。

3. 配合前述相關校園口說題組的技巧，焦點再不同科系的課堂講解或知識的吸取，了解不同科系的課堂討論（academic conversation）中可能會有哪些狀況，訓練對聽力內容快速整理的口語表述能力。

 Track 76

Listen to the following lecture carefully.

請仔細聽接下來課堂的內容。

Question: What is the classroom discussion mainly talking about? Please use specific evidences or examples from the lecture to briefly explain and summarize it.

試問此課堂學術討論的主要內容為何？請列舉課堂中的具體實例簡述課堂內容。

 Track 77

　　This literature discussion starts from one of the narrative ways of writing a novel, symbolism. Professor hasn't given the definition to the relation between symbols and many other social terms, such as cultures, communities or societies. At the same time, he indicates that knowing cultures, communities or societies is a critical key to understand any possible symbolic meanings. Anything can be symbolic or metaphorical as long as readers capture the implied concept. Thus, words in a broad sense of symbolism are symbols too. Virginia Woolf's *To the Lighthouse* later is brought up as an example to support professor's point. They start with the symbolic meaning of a lighthouse. This is a good beginning because the lighthouse implies both spiritual strength and physical guidance to those who are traveling by sea. Professor indicates that authors use symbolic ways to indirectly express some certain points which are argumentative or delicate.

中文翻譯

　　此文學課堂首先談小說撰寫的手法之一，象徵手法。教授並未對所謂的符號以及其他社會科學學術名詞例如：文化、社群或社會等的關係下任何定義。他也指出了解文化、社群及社會是了解潛在符號象徵意義的關鍵，只要讀者可以接收到隱涵的概念，任何物件都可以是象徵性或隱寓性的。也因此，廣義而言，文字也是象徵性符號。維吉尼亞吳爾孚的《燈塔行》被提出來解釋及佐證教授的論點。後來開始探討燈塔的象徵性，這是一個很好的開始，因為燈塔象徵的是航海人精神上的力量以及身體力行的指引。教授指出作者使用象徵性的手法間接地表達某些具爭議性或敏感的議題。

單字、片語說分明

① **critical** *adj.* 批判性的

② **metaphorical** *adj.* 隱喻性的

③ **symbolic** *adj.* 象徵性的

④ **capture** *v.* 取得、獲得

⑤ **concept** *n.* 概念、觀念

⑥ **bring up** *v.* 提出

⑦ **imply** *v.* 暗指、暗示

⑧ **physical** *adj.* 實體的

⑨ **argumentative** *adj.* 具爭議性的

⑩ **delicate** *adj.* 敏感的

C 新托福口說參考範文解析與評點

> 托福口說答題拿分首要掌握以下要點

1. **What**（內容資訊）：本範文完全針對題目回答了所需的**內容資訊**。

2. **How**（再解釋 1）：文法上沒有錯誤，語意上可以理解。

3. **Why**（再解釋 2）：本範文沒有離題，絕對針對題目回答，沒有答非所問。文章針對所提供專業課程的聽力內容加以整理論述。

D 此類考題考前及應考時準備筆記要點

1. 不同學術領域專業課程了解

   hololens, engineering, biomolecular, economics, statistics, business administration...

2. 對文史哲學議題的接觸

   feminism, Greek mythology, Renaissance, Hamilton, Divina Commedia, Cervantes, World Recession...

3. 開頭介紹句

   This presentation mainly speaks the idea of...

   This lecture leads students to talk about...

   The male student / female student addresses that...

   The professor also wants to explain.... add a certain idea of...

Anything can be symbolic or metaphorical as long as readers capture the implied concept.
任何物件都可以是象徵性或隱寓性的，只要讀者可以接收到隱含的概念。

1. We can say something is symbolic or metaphorical when readers capture the message from the authors.
   只要讀者可以接收到作者的隱含概念，我們可以說那些都是象徵性或隱寓性的事物。

2. As long as readers capture the implied meaning, anything works symbolically or metaphorically.
   只要讀者可以接收到隱含的概念，任何事物都可以是象徵性或隱寓性的。

Thus, words in a broad sense of symbolism are symbols too.
也因此，廣義而言，文字也是象徵性符號。

1. As a matter of fact, in a broad sense of symbolism, words are symbols too.
   其實，廣義而言，文字也是象徵性符號。

2. Therefore, broadly speaking, words are symbol as well.
   也因此，廣義而言，文字也是象徵性符號。

Professor indicates that authors use symbolic ways to indirectly express a certain point which is argumentative or delicate.
教授指出作者使用了象徵性手法間接地表達某些爭議性或敏感的議題。

1. Professor addressed that an argumentative or delicate message is indirectly expressed through symbolism.
   教授指出象徵性手法用來間接地表達某些爭議性或敏感的議題。

2. The argumentative or delicate point of view is indirectly expressed via a symbolic way from professor's lecture.
某些爭議性或敏感的議題透過象徵的方式間接地表達出來。

錄音原文

Professor

First of all, what is symbolism?

教授

首先，什麼是象徵主義？

Female Student

Something we can show some ideas, feelings, emotions or images by words or designs?

女學生

那些能用文字或設計表達的概念、感受、情緒或圖像嗎？

Male Student

I feel that any artistic methods of revealing ideas or truths. That can be symbolism.

男學生

我想應該是任何能表達概念或真相，富有美感的方式吧。那就是象徵主義。

Professor

We are definitely on the right track. In order to get the picture clear, we should know that different cultures, communities and societies contribute to this entire conversation as well. Any figures, characters, objects, colors,

or words are used to represent abstract ideas, concepts or meanings. And symbols can show readers a certain concept through some designs, images, or words. A symbol is anything else in the broadest sense. Words are thus symbols too. A dove could probably give you some association with peace, an eagle with **heroic endeavors**, or a rising sun with hope? Why? Let's wait till the answer show up itself. For now, are we all agreeing that perhaps using symbols allows authors to express themselves indirectly on certain **controversial** or delicate matters? Today we're going to discuss Virginia Woolf's *To the Lighthouse* and her writing style.

教授

我們這些想法都沒錯。為了能更清楚這個概念，我們要知道這和不同的文化、社群和社會也有很密切的關係。形象、角色、事物、色彩用來傳達抽象的概念或意義；象徵則透過某些設計、圖像或是文字將概念展現給讀者。廣義的來說，象徵可以是任何事物，文字也可以是象徵。鴿子會讓你聯想到和平；老鷹和英勇的事蹟連結在一起，還有朝陽代表希望？為什麼呢？這個答案在稍後課程將會不言而證。現在，我們都同意象徵手法讓作者可以間接地表達具爭議或敏感的議題了嗎？今天我們將探討維吉尼亞吳爾孚女士的《燈塔行》，及她的寫作風格。

Male Student

The stream of consciousness? Poetic presentational techniques too.

男學生

意識流？還有詩意的呈現技巧？

Professor

That's correct. A special form of the interior monologue. A formal use of silence in literature. She uses a variety of techniques including images and metaphors to fulfill her poetic fictions with **psychological** sense.

男教授

沒錯。還有內在獨白這個獨特的風格；這也是文學中表達沉默的正統方式。她使用了多種技巧，包括影像還有暗喻去完成她詩境小說的心理層面。

Male Student

Her other novel, *Mrs. Dalloway*?

男學生

那麼她的另外一部小説《達洛維夫人》呢？

Female Student

I feel they both represent different types of **stream of consciousness.** Crossover?

女學生

我覺得他們各代表不同意識流手法。交叉性質的意識流手法？

Professor

They all represent different kinds of stream of consciousness. In stream of consciousness, the speaker's thought processes are often depicted as overheard in the mind or addressed to himself or herself. Monologue and metaphorically. The lighthouse stands alone and tall no matter how rainy, stormy, cloudy, bright or dark the weather is. It is a spiritual **hermit** guiding all those who are traveling by sea.

教授

它們都代表不同的意識流手法。在意識流裡，講者的想法通常會以獨白式及隱寓性地的方式，在腦海裡描述或向自己表述。無論是風或是雨、明亮或黑暗，燈塔總是獨自佇立著。它就像是精神上的隱士，引領著所有航海人的生活。

Female Student

Mrs. Caroline Ramsay stands as a guiding star for other family members. She is also the spiritual bridge among those whom she cares about and loves.

女學生

卡洛琳萊絲女士指引其他的家庭成員。她也是她所愛的人的精神橋樑。

Male Student

The Lighthouse is a symbol of spiritual **strength**.

男學生

燈塔象徵著精神層面上的力量。

Professor

Different **critics** have explained this symbol in a lot of different ways. For instance, one of them is symbolized like truths that **triumph over** darkness. Still critics are **interpreting** those symbols in many other ways.

教授

不同的評論曾經對此做不同的分析,譬如,其中之一就是真相有超越黑暗的象徵。許多評論依然持續對這些象徵有不同的解釋。

單字小解

① **heroic** *adj.* 英勇的

② **endeavor** *n.* 事蹟

③ **indirectly** *adv.* 間接地

④ **psychological** *adj.* 心理學的

⑤ **stream of consciousness** *ph.* 意識流

⑥ **hermit** *n.* 隱士

⑦ **strength** *n.* 力量

⑧ **critic** *n.* 評論者

⑨ **triumph over** *ph.* 戰勝

Unit 21
課堂內容敘述與討論【理科】
Lecture Descriptions 2

⚙ 準備方向提示

1. 此類型題目焦點為測驗考生對課堂討論（Classroom discussion and interaction）的了解程度以及回答互動時的反應能力。

2. 聽取上課短文後，依據自己所寫快速筆記（如果沒有做筆記習慣也可，只要平時有訓練好英文資訊聽取後的快速整述能力即可），做快速重點整述。

3. 配合前述相關校園口説題組的技巧，焦點再不同科系的課堂講解或知識的吸取，了解不同科系的課堂討論（academic conversation）中可能會有哪些狀況，訓練對聽力內容快速整理的口語表述能力。

B 模擬題目 Track 79

Listen to the following lecture carefully.
請仔細聽接下來課堂的內容。

Question: What is this lecture mainly about? Please briefly summarize it with the idea.

這堂課的主旨是什麼？請概括說明。

參考範文 Track 80

　　The professor mentions about water resources and how we in the western countries tend to use more than our fair share of the world's fresh water supply. He also talks about how we can easily conserve water and save money by collecting rainwater wherever it's legal. One statistics he shares is that the developed world uses around 13,000 gallons of water to flush just 165 gallons of waste, per person, annually. He states that the average household in the west could collect around 18,000 gallons of rainwater each year. He took the time to discuss a new piece of technology called a Janicki Omniprocessor that can boil sewer sludge and convert it into ash, electricity and most importantly, the cleanest drinking water known to man. Moreover, this will be a money-making industry that will provide safe sanitation for over 2.5 billion people in developing countries across the globe.

中文翻譯

　　教授提及水資源的問題以及在西方社會的我們使用過多的新鮮水資源。他也告知我們如何在合法的情況下保存水以及為何收集雨水的方法。有一項統計資料顯示，已發展國家每人每年使用了 13000 加崙的水沖去 165 加崙的廢棄物。他也說

明一般家庭每年可收集 18000 加崙的雨水。他也花時間討論了 Janicki 新科技壓縮器，此機器可將汙泥煮沸並其轉成灰燼或電力以及眾人皆知的乾淨水。此外，這會是個賺錢的工業，也可以提供安全衛生給全球發展中國家將近 2.5 億人的福祉。

單字、片語說分明

① boil *v.* 煮沸
② sewer *n.* 下水道
③ sludge *n.* 汙泥
④ convert *v.* 轉換
⑤ ash *n.* 灰燼

C 新托福口說參考範文解析與評點

托福口說答題拿分首要掌握以下要點

1. **What**（內容資訊）：本範文完全針對題目回答了所需的內容資訊。

2. **How**（再解釋 1）：文法上沒有錯誤，語意上可以理解。

3. **Why**（再解釋 2）：本範文沒有離題，絕對針對題目回答，沒有答非所問。文章針對所提供專業課程的聽力內容加以整理論述。

D 此類考題考前及應考時準備筆記要點

1. 不同學術領域專業課程了解

hololens, engineering, biomolecular, economics, statistics, business administration...

2. 對工科議題的接觸

   energy saving, nanotechnology, biomedical, Information Engineering, telecommunication, artificial intelligence...

3. 各式連接語詞

   what's more, in addition, moreover, as a matter of fact, therefore, in other words, that is to say, accordingly...

🅔 換句話說補一補　🎧 Track 81

One statistic he shared was that the developed world uses around 13,000 gallons of water to flush just 165 gallons of waste, per person, annually.
研究顯示已發展國家的每人每年會使用 13,000 加崙的水沖馬桶，只為沖掉 165 加崙的排泄物。

1. The professor shared a statistic that says, annually, the average person in the developed countries uses 13,000 gallons of water to flush a mere 165 gallons of waste.
   教授分享了一份數據，其上顯示已發展國家的每人人每年會使用 13,000 加崙的水沖馬桶，只為沖掉 165 加崙的排泄物。

2. The average individual in the developed world produces 165 gallons of waste, but uses 13,000 gallons of water to flush it away.
   已發展國家中的每人平均會產生 165 加崙的排泄物，但卻用了 13,000 加崙的水來沖洗這些廢棄物。

He also talked about how we can easily conserve water and save money by collecting rainwater wherever it's legal.
他也談到合法收集雨水以省水和省錢的方式。

1. The professor recommends collecting rainwater, wherever legal, as a means of saving money and water.
   教授建議合法收集雨水的方式來做為省錢和省水的方法。

2. We can easily conserve water and save money simply by collecting rainwater where it's legal, according to the professor.

根據教授的説法，我們可以透過合法收集雨水的方式輕鬆省水和省錢。

Moreover, this will be a money-making industry that will provides safe sanitation for over 2.5 billion people in developing countries across the globe.

此外，這會是個賺錢的工業，也可以提供安全衛生給全球發展中國家將近 2.5 億人的福祉。

1. More than 2.5 billion people around the world don't have access to safe sanitation, so this will also be a money-making industry.

全球約有 2.5 億的人沒有安全衛生系統，所以這將會是一個賺錢的工業。

2. In addition, the number of people in developing countries around the world without safe sanitation is over 2.5 billion, so this will surely be a lucrative industry.

此外，無法取得安全衛生系統的人口約有 2.5 億人以上，所以這絕對是一個非常有賺頭的行業。

錄音原文

Male Student

Sir, last week, you promised we'd have a "unique" discussion.

男學生

老師，上週您有提到今天會有一個很獨特的話題？

Professor

You're right. I haven't forgotten about it. I have a question to ask you. Who has heard of graywater?

教授

是的，我記得，現在有個問題給你們，什麼是灰水？

Female student

That's reused water from your sink or bathtub.

女學生

是我們洗手臺或浴缸裡用過的水。

Professor

Precisely. It's water that has already been used. Now, we all know that water is a valuable resource. In the western world, we tend to use more than what's necessary. Some may even say we use more than our fair share. We all know that water conservation can help to save money and the environment. For example, we could **reroute** our **drainage pipes** from our sinks to a collection tank outside and this water could be used to water our garden or plants around the house. Just don't go drinking it. We could also use our sink water to flush the toilet. A study shows that the developed world tends to use 13,000 gallons of water to flush only 165 gallons of waste each year, per person. It's probably **in our best interest** to reroute our sink pipes to our toilet tanks. By that way we don't have to continue using clean water to flush our toilets. Lastly, though catching rainwater is illegal in some parts, if it is accepted, by simply placing a **barrel** at the bottom of your **downspout**, we could collect around 18,000 gallons of water annually. This may make your sprinkler obsolete.

教授

正是。就是已經用過的水。現在，我們都知道水是重要的資源，而我們西方國家似乎太常浪費這種資源了。也就是說我們使用過多。我們也了解儲水能幫助我們省錢及保護環境。例如，我們可以重新牽引我們的排水管，以便收集洗手臺的水去灌溉花園或房子周圍的植物，但不要當飲用水喝掉。我們也可以用洗手臺的水沖廁所。研究顯示已發展國家的每人每年會使用 13,000 加崙的水沖馬桶，只為沖掉 165 加崙的排泄物。最好還是重新牽引我們洗手臺的管子到廁所和浴缸，這樣我們就不用乾淨的水去沖廁所。近年來，儘管收集雨水在某些地區並不合法，但在合法可接受的地區，你可在排水管下方放一個桶子，這麼做每年可以收集到 18,000 加崙的水，您的連蓬頭也可擱置一旁啦。

Female Student

My family has begun collecting rainwater and my father often manually scoops water from the sink after washing dishes to water the plants in the back.

女學生

我的家人已經開始收集雨水，我父親也自己將洗完碗的水舀到後院灌溉花園。

Professor

Did you know that over 2.5 billion people are without access to safe water? The **water sanitation systems** used in the developed world cannot work in the developing world, as things stand today, so something innovative and simple has to happen. Now, here's where it gets interesting. **Sewer sludge** is being converted into ash, electricity and clean drinking water through a device called a Janicki Omniprocessor. The unit **boils** sewer sludge and separates the water vapour from the solids. The solids are dried and run through an extreme fire which creates high pressure, high temperature steam that then helps to drive the generator that creates electricity. The electricity created is used to power the processor, while excess electricity can be sent back into the community. The water vapour that is created during the boiling process runs through a cleaning system, creating the cleanest, purest water known to man. There are business opportunities arising in the collection and selling of sludge, as well as the purchase of the ash, electricity and water that the processor produces.

教授

你知道有超過 25 億人無法取得安全衛生的飲用水。已開發國家使用的飲水衛生系統無法在開發中國家使用，所以必須要有些新穎簡單的發明。這就是最有趣的地方。Janicki 處理器將下水道污泥轉換成灰、電力和乾淨的水的裝置。此裝置燃燒下水道污泥也將水蒸汽從固體中分開。乾燥後的固體接著通過大火，進而產生高壓及高溫，進而協助發電機製造電力。製造的電力將協助處理機運作，過剩的電力可以再送回社區。水蒸氣在煮沸的過程中通過濾淨器製造出最乾淨純淨的水。污水泥是一個生意契機，跟購買處理器所製作的灰燼、電力及水也是一樣。

Male Student

It's a dirty job, but somebody's gotta do it.

男學生

這是不討人喜歡的工作，但還是得有人做。

單字小解

① **reroute** *v.* 重新改道

② **drainage pipe** *n.* 排水管

③ **in our best interest** *ph.* 對我們最有利

④ **barrel** *n.* 桶

⑤ **downspout** *n.* 排水管

⑥ **sewer sludge** *n.* 汙泥

⑦ **water sanitation system** *n.* 淨水系統

⑧ **boil** *v.* 煮沸

Unit 22
課堂內容敘述與討論【工科】
Lecture Descriptions 3

A 準備方向提示

1. 此類型題目焦點為測驗考生對課堂討論（Classroom discussion and interaction）的了解程度以及回答互動時的反應能力。

2. 聽取上課短文後，依據自己所寫快速筆記（如果沒有做筆記習慣也可，只要平時有訓練好英文資訊聽取後的快速整述能力即可），做快速重點整述。

3. 配合前述相關校園口說題組的技巧，焦點再不同科系的課堂講解或知識的吸取，了解不同科系的課堂討論（academic conversation）中可能會有哪些狀況，訓練對聽力內容快速整理的口語表述能力。

模擬題目　Track 82

Listen to the following lecture carefully.

請仔細聽下列課堂內容。

Question: What is the classroom discussion mainly talking about? Please use specific evidences or examples from the lecture to briefly explain and summarize it.

試問此課堂學術討論的主要內容為何？請列舉課堂中的具體實例簡述課堂內容。

參考範文　Track 83

The professor started with a question like *what is real?* Both students gave good answers, such as a thought is real and anything we can touch is real. Then the professor guides the discussion toward what technology can do to. Technology can bring something unreal to be visualized. For example, cell phones were just considered to make some phone calls; however, cell phones are also working as personal portable laptops. What's more, cell phones nowadays are more than just a physical communication tool. Our brains are our sensory organs delivering information from the external world. To be specific, everything we see, hear, feel, or taste is an interpretation of outside world. This is what we called "reality". Virtual reality grants the possibility of walking into the constructs of the imagination without losing meanings or intent.

中文翻譯

　　教授以「什麼是真實」的問題為課堂開頭。兩位學生的回應都不錯，思想是真實的，我們可以觸及的皆為真實。之後教授又把討論引向科技可以做什麼。科技可以將不真實視覺化。例如說，手機可以用來打電話，然而，手機也可以是個人隨身攜帶式電腦，也就是說，現今的手機不僅限於溝通工具。我們的腦就是感官器官，負責傳遞來自外界的資訊，這就是真實。除此之外，網路是另一個人們將想像付諸於現實生活的突破性科技發明。這就是虛擬實境，並讓想像不至於失去意義或目的。

單字、片語說分明

① **technology** *n.* 科技
② **portable** *adj.* 可攜帶的
③ **interpretation** *n.* 釋義、解釋
④ **technological** *adj.* 科技的
⑤ **breakthrough** *n.* 突破
⑥ **construct** *n.* 建設、建構
⑦ **intent** *n.* 目的、目標

C 新托福口說參考範文解析與評點

托福口說答題拿分首要掌握以下要點

1. **What**（內容資訊）：本範文完全針對題目回答了所需的內容資訊。

2. **How**（再解釋 1）：文法上沒有錯誤，語意上可以理解。

3. **Why**（再解釋 2）：本範文沒有離題，絕對針對題目回答，沒有答非所問。文章針對所提供專業課程的聽力內容加以整理論述。

⚙D 此類考題考前及應考時準備筆記要點

1. 不同學術領域專業課程了解

   hololens, engineering, biomolecular, economics, statistics, business administration...

2. 對工科議題的接觸

   energy saving, nanotechnology, biomedical, Information Engineering, telecommunication, artificial intelligence...

3. 各式連接語詞

   what's more, in addition, moreover, as a matter of fact, therefore, in other words, that is to say, accordingly, ...

⚙E 換句話說補一補　💿 Track 84

Both students gave good answer, such as a thought is real and anything we can touch is real.

兩位學生的回答都不錯，例如：思想是真實的，我們可以觸及的皆為真實。

1. Take both students' answers for instance, a thought is real and anything we can touch is real.

   以兩位學生的回答為例，思想是真實的，我們可以觸及的皆為真實。

2. For instance, a thought is real and anything we can touch is real, which are both good answers from students.

   例如，思想是真實的，我們可以觸及的皆為真實，這些都是不錯的答案。

What's more, cell phones nowadays are more than just a physical communication tool.

再者，現今手機不僅限於溝通工具。

1. Additionally, cell phones are currently more than just a physical communication tool.

   除此之外，現今的手機不僅限於溝通工具。

2. Also, cell phones work more than just a physical communication tool.

   再者，現今手機不僅限於溝通工具。

To be specific, everything we see, hear, feel, or taste is an interpretation of outside world. This is what we called "reality".

這麼說好了，我們所見、所聞、所感受、所品嚐的都是對外界的理解。這就是我們所說的「現實」。

1. Or I would like to explain it in this way: reality is established by the ways we understand the external world through seeing, hearing, feeling or tasting.

   又或者這麼解釋：我們透過看、聽、感受或品嚐來理解外界，並建構現實。

2. We think what we see, hear, feel, or taste in the outside world is reality.

   我們認為我們在外界所看、所聽、所感受或品嚐的即為現實。

F 錄音原文

Professor

Let's begin with a question. What is real?

教授

讓我們就以什麼是真實這個問題開始吧。

Part
1

Part
2

Part
3

Female Student

Anything you can see or touch is real.

女學生

所有可碰觸的都是真實。

Male Student

My thoughts are reality.

男學生

我的思想是真實。

Professor

I think we're getting somewhere. Today we're going to discuss VR or virtual reality. It had a tough beginning since most people doubted the concept of **alternative existence**. Technology just wasn't able to allow creators to bring their **witty** ideas to **physical** existence. The technology just wasn't good enough for them to **justify** the idea. Virtual reality eventually began to show its potential in the **military** where inventors and their projects received **funding** to produce simulators for training purposes. Then there was another technological breakthrough most tech geniuses focused on instead. Can you name it?

教授

都是很好的答案。今天我們要討論的就是虛擬實境。這個概念最初不是很多人接受，大部分人對多重存在有異議。過去的科技上無法讓發明者去呈現他們對實際存在的聰明論點。科技就是無法讓他們辯證這些點子。後來虛擬實境逐漸在軍事方面嶄露頭角，發明者在此領域獲取基金為訓練研發虛擬實境。接著又有一科技突破讓科技菁英再度投入，猜看看為何？

Male Student

Oh, surely the Internet.

男學生

喔，當然是網路。

Professor

Bingo. In most other cases, the **phenomenon** we now know as the Internet took the center stage and the VR industry pretty much closed up shop. The Internet represented a promising technological revolution that allowed everybody to engage at a low cost. Meanwhile the average mind just couldn't grasp the concept of virtual reality, nor could they see how it could be **implemented**. For example, what did you think the use of cell phones to be?

教授

是的！大部分的情況，目前就是網路大大超越虛擬實境工業，獨占鰲頭。網路這種前瞻性科技革命，讓大家以最低成本就可投入。大部分的人還是無法了解虛擬實境的概念，也不知道如何實行這樣的概念。例如，你們認為手機還可以怎麼用？

Male Student

Nothing more than making calls while away from home.

男學生

遠離家時可打電話回家。

Female Student

I don't think anybody really thought cell phones would be so much like computers.

女學生

我不覺得以前人有想過手機可以是電腦。

Professor

Back to the subject of what 'real' is. If you're talking about what you can hear, what you can smell, taste and feel, then real is simply electrical signals interpreted by your brain. If you see a vision of you graduating with honours or you see yourself driving a nice car in the future, that is real. The thought of your favourite muffins makes your hungry because the thought is real. Everything we experience in life can be reduced to electrical activity stimulating our brains as our sensory organs deliver information about the external world. This is essentially "reality". In other words, the brain is reality. Everything you see, hear, feel, taste and smell is an interpretation of what's *outside*, and created entirely *inside* your head. It's our personal perceptions that determine the properties of characteristics like taste, colour, and smell. Our brains act as a filter to help give us build our own understanding of what is real. With this understanding, would you consider VR to be useful?

教授

回到之前的話題，到底什麼是真實？假如你覺得真實是可以聽到、聞到、嚐得到或感覺到的，那麼真實對你只是傳達到你腦袋的電波。假如你預見你以最高榮譽畢業或未來開名車，那就是真實。一想到你最愛的馬芬蛋糕讓你飢餓，因為這個想法是真的。透過感覺器官傳達外部的資訊，任何生活中的體驗都可以是刺激你腦波的電波。這就是真實中的真實。換言之，你腦中的就是真實。所以外在都只是一種轉譯，進而創造了你的內在構思。是我們個人的接收決定了味覺及顏色。我們的頭腦像是過濾器，幫我們決定什麼是真實。如此解釋，你們覺得虛擬實境是否有用？

Female Student

I'm not sure how it wouldn't be. I mean, a lot of things are useful, but not always necessary.

女學生

我不覺得沒用，很多東西都很有用，但我們不一定需要。

Professor

Virtual reality grants us the possibility of walking into the **constructs** of the imagination without losing meanings or intent. Our words can sometimes be lost in translation, as each of us perceives things differently. Words are often an inefficient method of **relaying** intent. VR holds the promise of allowing us to literally show one another what we mean rather than just describing it with **crude verbal approximations**. The limitation of words is that their meanings are only as detailed as the readers or listeners choose. For this reason virtual reality offers the possibility of evolving our communication into a kind of **telepathy,** ultimately bridging the gap between our **discrete** imaginations.

教授

虛擬實境讓我們有機會創造想像，同時也保留意義及目的。我們的想法會失意，因為我們每個人解釋事物的角度都不同。文字有時無法傳達意義。虛擬實境讓我們不必僅僅以口頭元素描述，就能真實地將我們想法傳達給對方。文字也是有限制的，讀者或聽者往往只選擇他們想聽的。也就是這樣，虛擬實境讓我們的溝通有機會進階到心電感應，進而連結我們片段的想像。

單字小解

① **alternative** *adj.* 其他的；另類的

② **witty** *adj.* 機智的

③ **physical** *adj.* 具體的

④ **justify** *v.* 解釋

⑤ **military** *n.* 軍隊

⑥ **funding** *n.* 基金

⑦ **phenomenon** *n.* 現象

⑧ **implement** *v.* 執行

⑨ **crude** *adj.* 粗糙的

⑩ **verbal** *adj.* 語言上的

⑪ **approximation** *n.* 現象

⑫ **telepathy** *n.* 心電感應

⑬ **discrete** *adj.* 分離的

Unit 23
公告描述與討論 1
Notice Descriptions 1

A 準備方向提示

1. 此類型題目焦點為對時間事件（Time and event）描述的敏感度及反應能力。

2. 快速瀏覽提供的傳單內容（flyer's information），結合聽力內容後快速重點整述。

3. 配合前述相關校園口說題組的技巧，了解校園中可能會有哪些狀況，訓練對聽力內容及時間表結合的口語表述能力。

 Track 85

Please read the notice carefully first and then listen to the following conversation about this notice.

請先仔細看公告內容，並聽以下和公告有關的對話。

Lemay Hall

This is to inform all students who live at the main campus that tomorrow morning, November 1, service work will be performed on the building fire alarm system between the hours of 9:00 and 11:00. As part of this procedure, it will be essential to test the alarm and you may hear it go off three or four times in the course of the morning. Do not panic or be concerned when you hear the alarm go off. It is part of the normal service routine. So if you have any questions concerning this event, please reach us by the following contact information:

676-555-3334
superservice@gmail.com
Kirkwood Hall

Thank you for your patience.

Question: What is the notice about? And what are the two students talking about in the conversation?

試問公告的主旨，以及兩位學生的談話內容。

Track 86

This is a dormitory notice posted at Lemay Hall regarding the fire alarm system drill. It suggests students to stay calm and cool while the building alarm system testing goes on November 1. It is a regular maintenance process, so students certainly don't have to panic when hearing the alarm system go on and off more than three times. This alarm system testing is going to happen at dormitory buildings instead of main campus. The female student will go to main campus for class at ten a.m., and by then the alarm system testing will have been going on for one hour. The male student will go to main campus for breakfast from 8 a.m. Sounds like he won't be affected too much by the alarm system testing. The female student feels that she's not paying attention to the dormitory notices for some time, so she didn't even know what's going on about dormitory news.

中文翻譯

此篇為 Lemay Hall 宿舍有關消防警報器維護例行程序的公告。公告建議學生在 11 月 1 號大樓火警維護例行程序時，需維持冷靜。由於這只是例行的維護程序，所以當學生聽到三～四次的火災警鈴聲時並不必驚慌。這項消防警報器維護例行程序將只在宿舍大樓而不是主校園區進行。女學生說她在十點的時候會到主校園，屆時火警維護例行程序就已經進行了一小時。男學生說他八點會在主校園的餐館吃早餐，聽起來他也不大受到影響。女學生認為她太久沒有注意宿舍公告了，因此有許多宿舍消息她都不知道。

單字、片語說分明

① **dormitory** *n.* 宿舍

② **regarding** *prep.* 有關、關於

③ **drill** *n.* 訓練；重複不斷的演練或練習

④ **maintenance** *n.* 維護、維修

⑤ **pay attention to** *ph.* 注意到

C 新托福口說參考範文解析與評點

托福口說答題拿分首要掌握以下要點

1. **What**（內容資訊）：本範文完全針對題目回答了所需的內容資訊。

2. **How**（再解釋 1）：文法上沒有錯誤，語意上可以理解。

3. **Why**（再解釋 2）：本範文沒有離題，絕對針對題目回答，沒有答非所問。文章針對所提供 單或公告的內容及聽力內容加以整理論述。

D 此類考題考前及應考時準備筆記要點

1. 校園大小事

astray dogs, cupcake, caroling, student night, orientation, club fair, dormitory life...

2. 相關引述傳單或公告開頭語

This is a post regarding; A dormitory / office / library post mentioned that; I got some news from the flyer saying that...

3. 不同校園場景詞彙

main campus, cafeteria, international student office, dormitory, laundry room, reading room, auditorium, conference room, administration building, canteen, lounge...

E 換句話說補一補 Track 87

This is a dormitory notice posted at Lemay Hall regarding the fire alarm system drill.

此篇為 Lemay Hall 宿舍有關消防警報器維護例行程序的公告。

1. A dormitory notice was posted at Lemay Hall talking about the fire alarm system drill.

   此篇為 Lemay Hall 宿舍有關消防警報器維護例行程序的公告。

2. A note posted at Lemay Hall's dormitory is warning about the fire alarm system drill.

   貼在 Lemay Hall 宿舍的公告和消防警報器維護例行程序有關。

This alarm system testing is going to happen at dormitory building instead of main campus.

這項消防警報器維護例行程序只會在宿舍大樓而不是主校園區進行。

1. The alarm system testing will happen at dormitory building instead of main campus.

   這項消防警報器維護例行程序將只在宿舍大樓發生，而不是主校園區。

2. The alarm system testing is going to happen at dormitory building rather than the main campus.

   這項消防警報器維護例行程序將只在宿舍大樓發生，而不是主校園區。

The female student feels that she's not paying attention to the dormitory notices for some time, so she didn't even know what's going on about dormitory news.

女學生認為她太久沒有注意宿舍公告，因此有許多宿舍消息都不知道。

1. Due to the lack of attention of the dormitory notice for some time, the female student feels that she doesn't have any idea of what news is

happening at dormitory.

因為太久沒有注意宿舍公告，因此女學生覺得有許多宿舍公告她都不知道。

2. Lacking of attention to the dormitory notice for some time, the female student feels that she's been left behind of the news at dormitory.

因為太久沒有注意宿舍公告，因此女學生覺得有許多宿舍公告她都不知道。

🔧 錄音原文

傳單或公告相關對話內容 Dialogue

Male Student

Did you see the notice posted on students' dormitory Lemay Hall?

男學生

你有看到 Lemay Hall 學生宿舍的公告嗎？

Female Student

Not yet. What is that about?

女學生

沒耶，是有關什麼？

Male Student

It's about the building fire alarm system. Due to the **regular** maintenance, the building fire alarm system will be off three or four times during our morning session. I think it says the time between nine a.m. to eleven a.m.

男學生

是有關校園建築物的消防警報系統。為了進行例行維護程序，校園建築物的警報器會在我們九點到十一點於主校園上課時，有三～四次的響鈴聲。

Female Student

Oh wow. And when that will be?

女學生

是何時呢？

Male Student

On November 1. It suggests that while hearing the alarm going on and off for more than three times, all we have to do is to be calm and cool, don't **panic**. This is part of the testing process.

男學生

在 11 月 1 號，校方要我們在警鈴響起時保持冷靜。這只是例行演練過程。

Female Student

November 1? That's tomorrow. I've been not paying attention to dormitory notices for awhile. If that's tomorrow...let me see...my first class starts at ten ten. So by the time I get to classroom, the building alarm system testing should probably have been going on for one hour.

女學生

11 月 1 號不就是明天？我已經好一陣子沒有注意到宿舍公告了。明天我的第一堂課在十點。所以當我到校園上課時，火警預演已經開始 1 個小時了。

Male Student

The building alarm system testing is at Lemay Hall, so perhaps Pillsbury Hall in the main campus should be fine. I'll be at the main campus for breakfast when the cafeteria is open at 8 a.m. Main campus' alarm system maintenance process should take place the week after.

男學生

火警預演主要是在 Lemay Hall，在主校園區的 Pillsbury Hall 應該還好不

Part
1

Part
2

Part
3

致受影響。明早八點我就會到主校園區的學生餐廳用早餐了。主校園的消防預演應該會是在一週之後進行。

Female Student
Gotcha.
女學生
原來如此,了解。

中文翻譯

Lemay 大廳

　　這是給住在主校園的學生的通知。明天早上(11 月 1 日)的早上 9 點到 11 點,會實施大樓消防系統的測試。過程中會測試警報器,整個早上可能會有三到四次的響鈴聲,若聽到請勿驚慌,這只是測試。關於這項測試若有任何問題,請透過下列方式聯絡我們:

電話:676-555-3334
E-mail: superservice@gmail.com
Kirkwood 大樓

感謝您的耐心。

單字小解

① **regular** *adj.* 一般的
② **panic** *adj.* 驚慌的

Unit 24
公告描述與討論 2
Notice Descriptions 2

A 準備方向提示

1. 此類型題目焦點為對時間或緊急改變事件描述的敏感度及反應能力。

2. 快速瀏覽提供的閱讀資料，結合聽力內容後快速重點整述。

3. 配合前述相關校園口說題組的技巧，了解校園中可能會有哪些狀況，訓練對聽力內容及時間表結合的口語表述能力。

  **Track 88**

Please read the notice carefully first and then listen to the following conversation about this notice.

請先仔細看公告內容，並聽以下和公告有關的對話。

> ### Attention!
>
> We regret that due to problems with the AC system in the auditorium, tonight's speech by Frank Jackson entitled "Music is my life and an art." has been canceled. We are sorry for any inconvenience this may cause.
>
> The auditorium should reopen by Monday and our monthly lecture series will resume next Tuesday at 6:00 P.M. with what promises to be an excellent experience shared by Ashely Smith about her incredible adventure up the Alps.
>
> Join us then!

Question: What are this notice and the two students' conversation mainly about? Please briefly summarize it with evidences or examples.

請舉例並概述公告的主旨以及兩位學生的談話內容。

This is an auditorium temporary shut down notice due to AC system problem. The male student was planning to go to a speech entitled *Music is my life and an art.* He had been expecting to go to Frank Jackson's speech. The female student kindly offered another idea for the night, which is going to the Final NBA game. The male student is wondering how she can still have the ticket for such a popular NBA game. The female student reveals that the secret of getting the ticket is to ask her uncle Bob who is working for the team. At the same time, even though tonight's speech will be canceled, the monthly lecture series will resume next Tuesday at 6:00 P.M. with what promises to be an excellent experience shared by Ashely Smith about her incredible adventure up the Alps.

中文翻譯

這是禮堂因冷氣維修而暫時關閉的通知。這位男學生本來計畫要去聽 Frank Jackson 的演講，題目是《音樂是我的生命也是藝術》。女學生則體貼提供去看 NBA 冠軍賽的主意。男學生則是非常好奇女學生如何可以拿到最受歡迎的 NBA 冠軍賽門票。女學生於是揭露了拿到 NBA 票的秘密在於透過她在 NBA 裡工作的叔叔 Bob。儘管今天的演講會被取消，下週二晚上六點系列演講活動又會恢復正常。保證會有 Ashely Smith 在阿爾卑斯山的驚人探險分享，精彩可期。

> **單字、片語說分明**

① **auditorium** *n.* 禮堂；會議廳

② **temporary** *adj.* 暫時的、短暫的

③ **shut down** *ph.* 關閉

④ **promise** *v.* 承諾、答應

⑤ **incredible** *adj.* 不可置信的

⑥ **adventure** *n.* 冒險、探索

新托福口說參考範文解析與評點

> **托福口說答題拿分首要掌握以下要點**

1. **What（內容資訊）**：本範文完全針對題目回答了所需的**內容資訊**。

2. **How（再解釋 1）**：文法上沒有錯誤，語意上可以理解。

3. **Why（再解釋 2）**：本範文沒有離題，絕對針對題目回答，沒有答非所問。文章針對所提供更新公告時間文章的內容及對話聽力內容加以整理論述。

D 此類考題考前及應考時準備筆記要點

1. 不同的休閒活動主題

   hiking, mountain climbing, listen to music, reading, photography, bicycling, watch TV, mediation...

2. 形容對活動感覺正面或負面的詞彙

   正面：

   excellent, incredible, irreplaceable, extraordinary, exceedingly amazing, successful, inspiring, peaceful, cool down, fresh my mind, reenergize, bring someone new idea, runner's high, relaxing, inspiring, peaceful time, spectacular...

   負面：

   terrible, troublesome, ridiculous, suck, bring/drag one down, ruin one's day, break one's heart, feeling down, ...

3. 描述相關休閒活動經驗的詞彙

   experience, adventure, exploration, challenge, excitement, extreme sport, view, vision, journey, tour...

換句話說補一補 🔵 Track 90

This is an auditorium temporary shut down notice due to AC system problem.
這是禮堂因為冷氣維修而暫時關閉的通知。

1. Due to AC system problem, a temporary auditorium shut down occurs.
   禮堂因冷氣維修將暫時關閉。
2. Owing to the AC system problem, the auditorium will have a temporary shut down.
   因為冷氣維修，禮堂將暫時關閉。

The female student kindly offers another idea for the night, which is going to the Final NBA game.
女學生則體貼地提供去看 NBA 冠軍賽的主意。

1. The female student nicely offers the NBA's final game as another brilliant idea.
   女學生則體貼提供去看 NBA 冠軍賽的絕佳主意。
2. The female student sweetly brings up the NBA's final game as another great option for the night.
   女學生則體貼提供去看 NBA 冠軍賽的好主意。

At the same time, even though tonight's speech will be canceled, the monthly lecture series will resume next Tuesday at 6:00 P.M. with what promises to be an excellent experience shared by Ashely Smith about her incredible adventure up the Alps.

同時，儘管今天的演講會被取消，下週二晚上六點系列演講活動又會恢復正常。保證會有 Ashely Smith 在阿爾卑斯山的驚人探險分享，精彩可期。

1. Also, the monthly lecture series will resume next Tuesday at 6:00 P.M. with what highly suggests to be an incredible journey shared by Ashely Smith about her astonishing exploration up the Alps.

   同時，儘管今天的演講會被取消，下週二晚上六點系列演講活動又會恢復正常。保證會有 Ashely Smith 在阿爾卑斯山的驚人探險分享，精彩可期。

2. Meanwhile, Ashely Smith's exceedingly amazing speaking about her adventure up the Alps. next Tuesday at 6:00 P.M. guarantees a quality restart of monthly lecture even though tonight's speech will no longer be held.

   同時，儘管今晚的演講取消了，但下週二晚上六點的演講活動系列就會恢復正常，Ashely Smith 將在那天率先分享她在阿爾卑斯山的驚奇旅程，保證精彩。

Part
1

Part
2

Part
3

錄音原文

Male Student

Oh no, the speech I plan to go to is **canceled**. I gave two movie tickets to Carson so I can go to listen to the speech of Frank Jackson tonight.

男學生

噢不，我想要聽的演講取消了。我給了兩張票給 Carson 才換到今晚 Frank Jackson 的演講。

Female Student

I'm sorry. My roommate and I will go to **Warriors** and **Cavaliers**' NBA final tonight. If you would like to join us, perhaps we can ask uncle Bob for another ticket?

女學生

不好意思耶，我和室友今天晚上要去看勇士對騎士的 NBA 決賽，如果你也想去，或許我們可以去問問 Bob 叔叔還有沒有票。

Male Student

Shut up! That's the final. How can he still get tickets today?

男學生

怎麼可能，這是決賽耶，他怎麼可能還有票！

Female Student

He works for the team. There's always someone who cancels tickets at the last minute or would like to give tickets away or something.

女學生

他在球隊工作呀，而且總是有人會在最後一分鐘取消球票，或是想要把球票送人之類的。

Male Student

Thank you so much for your kindness. When can I know whether or not I get the ticket to go to?

男學生

你人真好，太感謝你了。那我要怎麼知道我能不能拿到票？

Female Student

I will **text** you around three o'clock this afternoon. Btw, I heard that there's a speech coming next week at 6:00 p.m. This speech will be by Ashely Smith sharing her incredible adventure up the Alps Sound exciting to you?

女學生

我大概在下午三點左右會傳簡訊給你，對了，我聽説下週晚上 6 點會有演講，講者是 Ashely Smith，她會分享在阿爾卑斯山的故事，你覺得有趣嗎？

Male Student

Yeah I am interested in that too. The notice did inform us of the fact that the auditorium should reopen by Monday and their monthly lecture series will resume next Tuesday at 6:00 P.M. Wait a minute, do I still get the potential hot basketball game ticket tonight?

男學生

我對那個也很有興趣，公告上有説禮堂下星期一就會恢復開館，每個月的系列演講也會在下個禮拜二晚上 6 點重新開始，等等，我還有機會拿到今晚熱門的球票嗎？

Female Student

Haha... no worries, yes you do. Text you soon then.

女學生

哈哈，別擔心，你一定拿得到啦，等等傳簡訊給你啦。

中文翻譯

注意！

由於禮堂的空調出現問題，Frank Jackson 今晚的演説《音樂是我的人生也是藝術》將取消。很抱歉造成您的不便。

禮堂星期一就會恢復開放，每個月的系列演講也會在下個禮拜二晚上 6 點重新開始。敬請期待由 Ashely Smith 帶來的阿爾卑斯山歷險記。

歡迎參加！

單字小解

① **cancel** *v.* 取消

② **warrior** *n.* 勇士

③ **cavalier** *n.* 騎士

Unit 25
公告描述與討論 3
Notice Descriptions 3

A 準備方向提示

1. 此類型題目焦點為對時間、活動或事件描述的敏感度及反應能力。

2. 快速瀏覽提供的閱讀資料,結合聽力內容後快速重點整述。

3. 配合前述相關校園口說題組的技巧,了解校園中可能會有哪些狀況,訓練對聽力內容及時間表結合的口語表述能力。

 模擬題目 Track 91

Please read the notice carefully first and then listen to the following conversation about this notice.

請先仔細看公告內容，並聽以下和公告有關的對話。

Job Fair Notice

"Opportunity Knocks!"

All the final year students are hereby informed that a Mega Job fair will be organized by bestservice.com（Vocational Higher Education） at Memorial Hospital Lobby from 05 / 05 / 2015 to 08 / 05 / 2015.

In this event, more than 25 reputed companies, such as Banking, IT, ITES, Real Estate, Brokering, Education, Retail, Healthcare and Consulting, will be participating to recruit students from different streams like Sales, Customer Service, HR, Accounts, Software, Back Office, Operations, Trainer and other similar streams. This is a good opportunity with 1000+ JOB OPENINGS.

Please register on the below website to get your package in advance: http://tw.bestservice.edu.com

"Join us to POWER YOUR FUTURE!"

Question: What are this notice and the two students' conversation mainly about? Please briefly summarize it with evidence or examples.

請舉例並概述公告的主旨以及兩位學生的談話內容。

The summer is coming and students are going to graduate. So the two students are talking about some plans for graduation and their summer vacation. The female student mentions a good BBQ time at professor Emily's house. Students are chatting about their future plan at the BBQ party and most of them would like to go to the other states for job hunting. This reminds the male student of a job fair notice he reads about the coming of Mega Job Fair event from May 5 to May 8. Over 1000 job openings will be looking for their future employees at this event. As a result, both students are interested in going to attend this fair so they invite each other to go together. The female student encourages themselves to cherish and grab this one little stepping stone for their future career.

中文翻譯

夏天即將到來，學生也要畢業了。女性學生談及了她在 Emily 教授家 BBQ 時談及畢業後的未來計畫。大部分的學生表示他們想要到其他州去找工作。此事提醒了男性學生有關五月五號到五月八號舉行的 Mega 工作展。屆時將會有上千個工作機會尋找他們未來的工作伙伴。兩位學生對此也相當有興趣，並互相邀請對方一起參加活動。女性學生鼓勵他們倆好好珍惜及抓住這次對前途大有益處的墊腳石。

單字、片語說分明

① **graduation** *n.* 畢業
② **remind...of...** *ph.* 提醒……某件事、物
③ **cherish** *v.* 珍惜、珍視
④ **grab** *v.* 抓取

⑤ **stepping stone** *n.* 墊腳石

⑥ **career** *n.* 職場生涯

🔧 新托福口說參考範文解析與評點

托福口說答題拿分首要掌握以下要點

1. **What（內容資訊）**：本範文完全針對題目回答了所需的內容資訊。

2. **How（再解釋 1）**：文法上沒有錯誤，語意上可以理解。

3. **Why（再解釋 2）**：本範文沒有離題，絕對針對題目回答，沒有答非所問。文章針對所提供更新公告時間文章的內容及對話聽力內容加以整理論述。

🔧 此類考題考前及應考時準備筆記要點

1. 不同的校園活動主題

   job fair, club fair, international student fair, culture fair, renaissance festival, grandpa and grandmom day, parents day, music festival, international student festival, Chinese culture fair, video game festival, opp-campus housing fair...

2. 形容對活動感覺正面或負面的詞彙

   正面：

   excellent, incredible, irreplaceable, extraordinary, exceedingly amazing, successful, inspiring, peaceful, cool down, fresh my mind, reenergize, bring someone new idea, runner's high, relaxing, inspiring, peaceful time, spectacular...

負面：

terrible, troublesome, ridiculous, suck, bring / drag one down, ruin one's day, break one's heart, feeling down, ...

3. 描述相關休閒活動經驗的詞彙

fair, festival, club, experience, adventure, exploration, challenge, excitement, extreme sport, view, vision, journey, tour...

E 換句話說補一補 Track 93

The summer is coming and students are going to graduate.
夏天即將到來，學生也要畢業了。

1. When the graduation is coming, the school is also closed to a summer vacation.
   畢業典禮快來到，學校也要關閉放暑假了。

2. The graduation is around the corner as well as all the students is going to have a summer vacation.
   畢業典禮快來到，學校也要迎接暑假了。

Over 1000 job openings will be looking for their future employees at this event.

屆時將會有上千個工作機會尋找他們未來的工作伙伴。

1. More than 1000 job openings will look for their future employees at this event.

   屆時將會有上千個工作機會尋找他們未來的工作伙伴。

2. Over 1000 job openings will be offered at this event.

   活動上將會有上千個工作機會尋找他們未來的工作伙伴。

The female student encourages themselves to cherish and grab this one little stepping stone for their future career.

女性學生鼓勵他們倆好好珍惜及抓住這次對前途大有益處的墊腳石。

1. The female student motivates both of them to cherish and seize this great chance for their future career.

   女性學生鼓勵他們倆好好珍惜及抓住這次對前途大有益處的墊腳石。

2. The female student inspires themselves to treasure this one tiny stepping stone for their future career.

   女性學生鼓勵他們倆好好珍惜及抓住這次對前途大有益處的墊腳石。

錄音原文

告示或傳單對話 Conversation

Male Student

One more month, this semester will be ended. After graduation this summer, do you have plans?

男學生

在一個月這學期就要結束了，畢業後的這個暑假你有什麼計畫嗎？

Female Student

We just talked about that last night at Professor Emily's house. She is the nicest lady and professor we've ever met. There was a BBQ she invited us coming over in her family's backyard. That was an excellent time. Also, we shared some of our thoughts about summer vacation and graduation.

女學生

我們昨晚才在 Emily 教授的家談到這件事，她真是我們見過最好的女士和教授了。她邀我們到她家後院吃烤肉，我們過了很棒的夜晚，也和她分享了我們的暑假和畢業計畫。

Male Student

Yap. So how was that? And what about the conversation?

男學生

那你們討論的怎麼樣？都討論了什麼？

Female Student

A lot of us thinking about going out of the states, or perhaps visit and find job in another states.

女學生

有很多人考慮出國，或是到其他國家看看，在那找工作。

Male Student

So how are you going to do that? Wait a minute, I think I just had a great idea. There will be a Mega Job Fair from May 5 to May 8 at Memorial Hospital Lobby. Perhaps we can plan to go on together?

男學生

那你想怎麼做？等等，我突然有個想法，5 月 5 日到 5 月 8 日在 Memorial Hospital Lobby 有舉辦 Mega 就業博覽會，或許我們可以一起去？

Female Student

What is that about? Do we have to register first or something?

女學生

那是什麼？我們需要報名參加嗎？

Male Student

The job offers are A LOT there. I can't remember all of them. As far as I can recall, this event suggests that they have more than 25 well known companies. Also it varies from **Banking**, Real **Estate**, Brokering, Education, **Retail**, Healthcare and **Consulting**. All of them will be there to **recruit** students from different streams like Sales, Customer Service, HR, **Accounting**. Perhaps including Software, Operations and many other similar streams. They recommend that it's a great chance to see all those job openings to gather together.

男學生

那裡會有很多工作職缺，我沒辦法通通記下來。印象中活動會有 25 家以上的知名公司參與，產業多元，舉凡行業、資訊產業、房地產、教育、銷售

還有健康諮詢等都有，他們會招募業務、客服、人資、會計、軟體……等的新人，並推薦我們好好把握這個有 1000 多個職缺的好機會。

Female Student

Sounds like an amazing job feast. Sure, let's go! And find ourselves some perfect shoes before we become CEO later in our career.

女學生

這活動聽起來很棒，一起去找個好工作吧！

中文翻譯

就業博覽會公告

機會就在門口！

所有應屆畢業生注意，在職專班 bestservice.com 將在 2015 年 5 月 5 日到 5 月 8 日，於 Memorial Hospital Lobby 舉辦 Mega 就業博覽會。

25 多家來自銀行業、資訊產業、房地產、教育、銷售還有健康諮詢等的知名公司將會共襄盛舉招募新人，並提供業務、客服、人資、會計、軟體……等 1000 多個以上的職缺。

請點選以下網址報名參加：
http://tw.bestservice.edu.com

「加入我們，點亮未來！」

單字小解

① **banking** *n.* 銀行業
② **real estate** *n.* 房地產
③ **retail** *n.* 零售業
④ **consulting** *n.* 顧問
⑤ **recruit** *v.* 招募
⑥ **accounting** *n.* 會計

Memo

Unit 26
傳單內容描述與討論
Flyer Descriptions

A 準備方向提示

1. 此類型題目焦點為對節慶、活動、時間或緊急改變事件描述的敏感度及反應能力。

2. 快速瀏覽提供的閱讀資料，結合聽力內容後快速重點整述。

3. 配合前述相關校園口說題組的技巧，了解校園中可能會有哪些狀況，訓練對聽力內容及時間表結合的口語表述能力。

B 模擬題目 Track 94

Part
1

Part
2

Part
3

Please read the notice carefully first and then listen to the following conversation about this notice.

請先仔細看公告內容，並聽以下和公告有關的對話。

Off-Campus Housing Fair

Wednesday, January 27, 2015
10:30 A.M. ~ 16:00 P.M.
Loops 55678 Anderson Room

Housing.uow.edu

This event will give main campus students an opportunity to meet with property owners and local real estate agents. You can also arrange appointments to view available properties. A 30 percent (30%) discounted fee and a prior package will be given by the rental agents to anyone who signs a lease as a result of the fair.

Remember, agents are in competition with one another. That is their job. You are there to relax and learn the facts, find a trusted rental agent. Check with juniors presently living off and seniors who lived off-campus. No solicitation. Please notify your RA if you have flyers slipped under your door.

Question: What are this notice and the two students' conversation mainly about? Please briefly summarize it with evidences or examples.

請舉例並概述公告的主旨以及兩位學生的談話內容。

Students are given off-campus housing fair flyers. The male student is on his way to Professor Larson's office to let Professor Larson, his RA as well, know that he got the flyer about the housing fair. The female student enjoys her in-campus living very much. However, due to some family budget, the male student has to find off-campus housing for the coming semester and he's also thinking about getting some part-time job at cafeteria. Meanwhile, the off-campus housing fair provides a great opportunity for students to get a hold of some property owners and local real estate agents. Therefore, students can have a better understanding of their options and make better decisions. The school authority also suggests students to learn the facts first and be cool. A 30 percent discounted fee will be given by the rental agents and some prior packages can be some bonus provided by those agents and owners.

中文翻譯

學生們收到校外租屋展的傳單。男學生正要去學業指導教授 Larson 的辦公室，讓他知道他拿到了租屋展覽會的傳單。女學生對校宿舍的生活非常滿意；而男學生基於預算考量，他下學期必須到校外租屋，而且還要找學校餐廳的兼職工作。此外，校外租屋展將提供學生與租屋人士或房屋仲介商有直接的接洽，如此學生可以確實掌握租屋資訊，並有更好的決定。學校建議學生先別急著下決定，徹底了解情況後再說。當場簽約將享有租屋人士提供的七折優惠還有仲介或屋主提供的各種優惠方案。

補充：

文化大不同：美國校園通常宿舍品質都非常優質，相對起校外租屋，住宿舍相對花費還比較昂貴些。

單字、片語說分明

① **off-campus** *adj.* 校外的

② **semester** *n.* 學期

③ **property** *n.* 財產

④ **real estate agent** *n.* 房屋仲介

⑤ **discounted** *adj.* 折扣的、打折的

⑥ **rental agent** *n.* 出租人

⑦ **prior package** *n.* 優惠方案

⑧ **bonus** *n.* 特別優惠

C 新托福口說參考範文解析與評點

托福口說答題拿分首要掌握以下要點

1. **What**（內容資訊）：本範文完全針對題目回答了所需的**內容資訊**。

2. **How**（再解釋 1）：文法上沒有錯誤，語意上可以理解。

3. **Why**（再解釋 2）：本範文沒有離題，絕對針對題目回答，沒有答非所問。文章針對所提供傳單文章的內容及對話聽力內容加以整理論述。

D 此類考題考前及應考時準備筆記要點

1. 不同的校園活動主題

job fair, club fair, international student fair, culture fair, renaissance festival, grandpa and grandmom day, parents day, music festival, international student festival, Chinese culture fair, video game festival, off-campus housing fair...

2. 形容對活動感覺正面或負面的詞彙

正面：

excellent, incredible, irreplaceable, extraordinary, exceedingly amazing, successful, inspiring, peaceful, cool down, fresh my mind, reenergize, bring someone new idea, runner's high, relaxing, inspiring, peaceful time, spectacular...

負面：

terrible, troublesome, ridiculous, suck, bring / drag one down, ruin one's day, break one's heart, feeling down, ...

3. 描述相關休閒活動經驗的詞彙

fair, festival, club, experience, adventure, exploration, challenge, excitement, extreme sport, view, vision, journey, tour...

 換句話說補一補　Track 96

The male student is on his way to Professor Larson's office to let Professor Ldrson, his RA as well, know that he got the flyer about the housing fair.

男學生正要去學業指導教授 Larson 的辦公室。Larson 也是他的 RA，男學生想要讓教授知道他有拿到校外租屋會的傳單了。

1. The male student is goint to meet his RA professor Larson to notify him of the flyer he received.

   男學生正要去學業指導教授 Larson，同時讓他知道已收到傳單。

2. The male student is going to his RA professor Larson's office to meet him and inform him of the flyer he got.

   男學生正要去學業指導教授 Larson 家，同時讓他知道已收到傳單。

Part
1

Part
2

Part
3

However, due to some family budget, the male student has to find off-campus housing for the coming semester and he's also thinking about getting some part time job at cafeteria.
而男學生基於預算考量,他下學期必須到校外租屋,而且還要找學校餐廳的兼職工作。

1. Nevertheless, because of some family budget, the male student has to find off-campus housing for the next semester. At the same time, he's also thinking about taking some part time job at cafeteria.
   不過基於預算考量,男學生下學期必須到校外租屋,另外他還是會找學校餐廳的兼職工作。

2. Nonetheless, owing to some family budget, the male student has to find off-campus housing for the coming semester. Meanwhile, he's thinking about taking some part time job at cafeteria as well.
   不過基於預算考量,男學生下學期必須到校外租屋,而且還要找學校餐廳的兼職工作。

Therefore, students can have a better understanding of their options and make better decisions.
如此學生可以確實掌握租屋資訊,並有更好的決定。

1. Consequently, students can get clear understanding of their choices and make suitable decisions.
   如此學生可以確實掌握租屋資訊,並有更恰當的決定。

2. Hence, students will be able to get better knowledge of their options and make wise decisions.
   如此學生可以確實掌握租屋資訊,並有更明智的決定。

錄音原文

告示或傳單對話 Conversation

Female Student

One year of dormitory life was actually exciting. I met people all over the world. Bangladesh, Swiss, Netherlands, Taiwan...many other countries.

女學生

過去一年的住宿生活真的很棒，我遇到來自孟加拉、瑞士、荷蘭和台灣等等各國的人。

Male Student

That sounds so great. Well, dormitory fee is off my family's budget now. I'm thinking about getting an off-campus housing life for the coming semester.

男學生

聽起來不錯，不過住宿費已經超出我家的預算了，我考慮下學期要住校外了。

Female Student

Is there anything I can help? Maybe I can ask my roommates some information about campus part-time job at cafeteria? More or less, you can self help for the in-campus life.

女學生

有我可以幫忙的地方嗎？或許我可以問問我室友校園咖啡廳兼職打工的事。這樣多少能有助你自理你的校園生活。

Male Student

Yeah, that would be great. At the same time, I will still go to the off-campus housing fair. The flyer says that this off-campus housing fair will give main campus students an opportunity to meet with property owners and local real estate agents. Also, we can arrange appointments to view available properties. This can provide me better understanding of the deal and make an ideal decision. What is even better is that a 30 percent discounted fee will be given by the rental agents if I find some good deals and decide to sign the contract right at the fair. Perhaps some prior packages as well.

男學生

太棒了，不過我也會去校外租屋博覽會，這張傳單上説我們學生有機會和屋主、房仲碰面，還能安排時間看房子，這樣我也會比較清楚合約內容，然後才能做出理想的決定。更棒的是，如果在當場我真得找到不錯的合約想要簽下來，我還有租金 7 折的折扣和一些優惠呢。

Female Student

Right. It is a great opportunity. Perhaps you can also check with **juniors** presently living off and **seniors** who lived off-campus.

女學生

這真的是一個好機會，然後你也可能也可以問問現在住在校外的大三和以前住過校外的大四生。

Male Student

That's exactly what the flyer suggests too! Also, be calm and learn the facts.

男學生

傳單上也是這樣建議耶，要冷靜，並多收集資訊。

Female Student

That's absolutely a smart way to do it since none of any of us knows what kind of living setting they particularly offer. Checking with previous tenants from our school should really help a lot.

女學生

畢竟我們沒辦法知道對方會提供什麼樣的居住環境，所以這麼做才聰明。詢問和我們同校的前房客真的幫助很大。

Male Student

Thanks for the tips too! By the way, I'm going to Professor Larson's office. The flyer suggests us to notify our **RA** if we have flyers slipped under our doors.

男學生

謝謝你的建議，對了，我要去 Larson 教授的辦公室，傳單上建議我們拿到傳單後，能通知我們的指導教授。

Female Student

Alright, see you soon in class then.

女學生

好，晚點課堂見。

中文翻譯

校外租屋博覽會

日期：2015 年 1 月 27 日，星期三
時間：早上 10:30～下午 4:00
地點：Loops 55678 Anderson Room

Housing.uow.edu

　　主校區的學生將有機會透過這個活動和屋主與房仲面對面，並安排時間看看房子。若在博覽會中和房仲簽約，還能享有房租 7 折的折扣與其他優惠。

　　別忘了房仲彼此間會互相競爭，這是他們的工作。你只要放輕鬆、收集資訊，然後找一個值得信任的房仲就好。可以問問現在住在校外的大三和以前住過校外的大四生。恕不接受其他廣告宣傳。請於拿到傳單後，通知您的指導教授。

單字小解

① **junior** *n.* 大三生
② **senior** *n.* 大四生
③ **research assistant (RA)** *n.* 研究助理

Unit 27
時間表描述與討論 1
Timetable Descriptions 1

A 準備方向提示

1. 此類型題目焦點為對時間事件描述的敏感度及反應能力。

2. 快速瀏覽提供的表格，結合聽力內容後快速重點整述。

3. 配合前述相關校園口說題組的技巧，**了解校園中可能會有哪些狀況，訓練對聽力內容及時間表結合的口語表述能力。**

模擬題目　Track 97

Please read the timetable first and listen to the conversation.
請先看過時間表，並聽對話。

Week1	Morning 9:30~12:00 am	Afternoon 2:00~5:00 am	Evening 7:00~9:30 pm	Note
Day 1	Arrivals	Arrivals	Welcome Activities	Folder
Day 2	Placement Tests Tour & Course Photograph	Team Building Game and Piano	English Class	(Folder)
Day 3	Piano Tutor	English Oral Testing	House Theme Evening	Schedule Sheet
Day 4	Renaissance Day Trip		Oregon Multiculture Feast	Snack Water
Day 5	English Classes	Piano Tutor	Project	Proposal
Day 6	English Classes	Piano Tutor	Student Night	
Day 7	Piano Tutor	The Modern Academy of Music Center, Proms at the Peterson Meyer Hall		Dress up

Question: What are this timetable and those three senior counselors' introductions mainly about? Please briefly summarize it with evidences or examples.

試問此時間表及三位資深指導員的說明內容為何？請簡短以文章及聽力內容中的具體證據及範例陳述出來。

This is a schedule of a music summer camp. As the timetable shows, three senior counselors are giving tips and introductions to this piano camp. International students will have an English placement test and must be scheduled to have their English oral test too. Photo-taken will also take place on the second day. Folder is required on the first two days. The fourth day is a blast. It will be a fabulous Oregon treat, the Renaissance Festival and multiculture feast. All the freshmen have to do is to bring water or snack with them if they want. While day five could be very academic like, because students will have to bring their proposals and share with their supervisors. They are going to discuss their projects with their supervisors on that same day too. The closure will be at The Modern Academy of Music Center, and Proms at the grandeur Peterson Meyer Hall.

中文翻譯

這是一份夏日音樂訓練營的訓練時刻表。幾位資深指導員介紹及說明幾天下來的鋼琴訓練課程。國際學生會有英語能力分班測驗及口說測試。第二天需拍攝大頭照製作學生證件。前兩天需攜帶說明會資料夾。第四天將會有奧勒岡特別款待的歡樂宴會、文藝復興節以及多元文化饗宴。所有新生可自備水和零食。第五天將會和指導教授個別學術會談,並與指導教授討論企劃案。夏日訓練將於現代音樂中心落幕,並以豪華 Peterson Meyer Hall 的舞會為結尾。

單字、片語說分明

① **senior counselors** *n.* 資深指導員

② **introduction** *n.* 說明；介紹

③ **International** *adj.* 國際的

④ **English placement test** *n.* 英語能力分班測試

⑤ **Renaissance Festival** *n.* 文藝復興博覽會

⑥ **multiculture** *n.* 多元文化

⑦ **supervisors** *n.* 上司、指導教授、指導老師

⑧ **grandeur** *n.* 豪華的、壯麗的

新托福口說參考範文解析與評點

托福口說答題拿分首要掌握以下要點

1. **What**（內容資訊）：本範文完全針對題目回答了所需的內容資訊。

2. **How**（再解釋 1）：文法上沒有錯誤，語意上可以理解。

3. **Why**（再解釋 2）：本範文沒有離題，絕對針對題目回答，沒有答非所問。文章針對所提供時間表的內容及聽力內容加以整理論述。

 此類考題考前及應考時準備筆記要點

1. 不同的校園活動主題

   job fair, club fair, international student fair, culture fair, renaissance festival, grandpa and grandmom day, parents day, music festival, international student festival, Chinese culture fair, video game festival, off-campus housing fair...

2. 描述相關休閒活動經驗的詞彙

   festival, fair, club, show, experience, adventure, exploration, challenge, excitement, extreme sport, view, vision, journey, tour...

3. 形容對活動感覺正面或負面的詞彙

   正面：

   excellent, incredible, irreplaceable, extraordinary, exceedingly amazing, successful, inspiring, peaceful, cool down, fresh my mind, reenergize, bring someone new idea, runner's high, relaxing, inspiring, peaceful time, spectacular...

   負面：

   terrible, troublesome, ridiculous, suck, bring/drag one down, ruin one's day, break one's heart, feeling down, ...

換句話說補一補 Track 99

This is a schedule of a music summer camp.

這是一份夏日音樂訓練營的訓練時刻表。

1. This timetable shows the schedule of a music summer camp.
   這份時刻表顯示夏季音樂營的流程。

2. This timetable presents us the schedule of a music summer camp.
   這份時刻表顯示夏季音樂營的流程。

Folder is required on the first two days.

前兩天需攜帶說明會資料夾。

1. It is highly recommended that bringing the folder with you on the first two days.
   強烈建議前兩天需攜帶說明會資料夾。

2. The lecturer suggests that students bring the folder with them on the first two days.
   講員建議學生前兩天需攜帶說明會資料夾。

They are going to discuss their projects with their supervisors on that same day too.

他們將在同一天與指導教授討論個別的企劃案。

1. They will discuss their projects with their supervisors on that same day too.
   他們將在同一天與指導教授討論個別的企劃案。

2. They shall discuss their projects with their supervisors on that same day too.
   他們將在同一天與指導教授討論個別的企劃案。

Part 1

Part 2

Part 3

287

錄音原文

Senior counselor A

Good morning fellow students. First of all, congratulations for making your way to here. Our music program provides **the most complete and solid** training for future musicians and artists. Meanwhile, it's our great honor to have you here with us in the freshmen piano camp before the school starts. International students will have to have some English classes and English oral test. We want you to experience and get familiar with the campus environment and be comfortable about your English speaking. There will be a brand new country and culture to adjust, also some school work and club to participate. We want you to accomplish your study here with great honor and wonderful experience too. So that's why we are going to help and offer you this great freshmen piano camp. Ok, let's skip to the point. Today, you are doing pretty well so far. Please check your folder is in your hand, and schedule is also included in this folder. Be sure to have this folder with you for tomorrow's English placement test. Also, in order to smooth the registration process, we will take your photo and make your student ID tomorrow too. Make sure you dress up if you would like to look astonishing on your student ID. There will also be a tour to show you around the campus, surely, cafeteria is a very important place for lunch time, great meal and nice chat with classmates. This afternoon, for welcoming you, we will invite each of you to go to boardroom to have traditional Caribbean coffee and Dolly's House treat to have a great afternoon tea time. Most importantly, you can get to know each other well. For the day three, there will be a schedule sheet given to you after your English placement test, and it will have your English oral test scheduled too. So make sure you bring the schedule sheet. It's gonna be your first day meeting your personal piano tutor too. The third day night is gonna impress you with House Theme Evening, what is that? Hmmmmm...not tell.

資深領隊 A

早安同學們。首先，恭喜你們加入這個大家園。我們的音樂系提供未來音樂家及藝術家完整及扎實的訓練。同時，我們也很榮幸有你們在開學前一起加入新生鋼琴夏令營。國際學生將有英文課及英文口說測試。我們希望你們可以體驗及熟習校園環境進而輕鬆發揮你們英文口說的實力。這裡有全新的國家文化需適應，還有學校及社團需參與，我們希望你在這裡可以帶著榮譽心完成你的學業，並留下美好的回憶。這也是為何我們舉辦夏季鋼琴營的原因。好，廢話不多說。今天，大家都非常的棒。手上大家都有資料夾，所有需要的資訊都在資料夾中，記得英語分班測試時也得帶著資料夾。同時，為了讓開學註冊更順利，明天會為你的學生證拍照。如果你想把 ID 照拍好，那你最好穿著正式服裝。會有校園巡迴參觀行程，當然學校餐廳不可少。午餐會有美好餐點與同學們共度的快樂時刻。下午，我們將邀請你到會議廳享受新鮮的加勒比海域咖啡以及當地 Dolly's House 的美味甜甜圈。最重要的是，你們可以好好認識彼此。第三天將會安排你們的英語分班測試，以及英語口說測試，所以要記得攜帶你們的時間表。那天也將會是你們和個別指導教授第一次的晤面會談。第三天晚上將舉辦特別晚會，會是什麼呢？請期待。

Senior Counselor B

Good morning again pumpkins. I'm cultural exchange counselor and responsible for managing and planning for entire campus' international students the cultural festival or exchange programs. All of you are welcome to join this big family. Music will always lead you to a right place. The fourth day is going to take your breath away. Before surprising you with Oregon style of multiculture feast, we want to show you every

summer's heat, the Renaissance Festival. Renaissance Festival is a big event every summer. It's always held at StoneHill Resort. All you need to take with you is some water and some snacks if you may feel like to. I do remember Renaissance Festival offers yummy ice cream every year...

資深領隊 B

早安孩子們。我是文化交換指導員,負責整個校園國際學生文化及節慶交換等活動。歡迎加入大家庭。音樂總是引領你生命明亮面。第四天將讓你讚嘆不已。在以奧勒岡式的多重文化盛宴款待前,我們將帶你去經驗文藝復興盛會!文藝復興盛會是每個夏天的大活動。它是在 StoneHill 度假勝地舉行。你只要帶水或者是一些你覺得需要的隨身小點心,我記得文藝復興盛會都有提供很棒的冰淇淋⋯⋯

Senior Counselor C

Back to school project. The fifth day could be more academic like, because we will require you to bring your proposal of your project here. Each of you should already have some ideas before you sign up for this program, so that's the time and great opportunity to show it and discuss it with your supervisors. At the end of this summer camp, we would like to show you The Modern Academy of Music Center. This is a profound music museum. We are sure that this place will inspire you more than what you can imagine. Furthermore, Proms at the campus' prestigious Peterson Meyer Hall, we hope to invite you to campus' most gorgeous building. Welcome!

資深領隊 C

再來是學校時程。第五天會比較偏向學術研究些,因為你必須攜帶你的企劃大綱。在你們加入此系時,都有一些願景想法,所以當天會是你將你的想法與指導教授分享或討論的好機會。夏令營的最後一天我們想介紹你們現代音樂中心。這是一個有深度的音樂博物館。我們相信這地方會帶給你意想不到的靈感。此外，舞會會在著名的 Peterson Meyer 廳舉行，我們希望介紹你們校園裡最瑰麗的建築物。

> **中文翻譯**

第一週	早上 9:30~12:00	下午 2:00~5:00	晚上 7:00~9:30	備註
第一天	報到	報到	歡迎活動	資料夾
第二天	分班測驗 校園課程介紹 拍照	團隊活動 鋼琴課	英文課	（資料夾）
第三天	鋼琴課	英文口試	主題館之夜	課程表
第四天	文藝復興之行	奧勒岡多元文化饗宴		點心和水
第五天	英文課	鋼琴課	討論企劃	企劃書
第六天	英文課	鋼琴課		學生之夜
第七天	鋼琴課	現代音樂中心舞會，於 Peterson Meyer Hall 舉行		請盛裝出席

> **單字小解**

① **complete** *adj.* 完整的
② **solid** *adj.* 固體的；扎實的

Unit 28
時間表描述與討論 2
Timetable Descriptions 2

A 準備方向提示

1. 此類型題目焦點為對時間事件描述的敏感度及反應能力。

2. 快速瀏覽提供的表格，結合聽力內容後快速重點整述。

3. 配合前述相關校園口說題組的技巧，了解校園中可能會有哪些狀況，訓練對聽力內容及時間表結合的口語表述能力。

Please read the timetable first and listen to the conversation.
請先看過時間表，並聽對話。

ShapeUp Fitness Centre
　　Class prices vary according to membership. Please contact us by the following phone number or email address for further information. Thank you for your time.

Phone: 0392104
Email:fitnessgym@km.com

Timetable	7:00 to 8:30 am	9:20 to 10:50 am	11:00 to 12:00 am	Break	1:30 to 2:30 pm	3:00 to 4:30 pm	Break	7:00 to 8:30 pm
Monday	Yoga Vivi							Salsa Heat Liam
Tuesday	Step & Pump Josh	Junior Gym Alex			Kettlebells Tony	Crossfit Training Kevin		Hip hop Dance Emma
Wednesday	Yoga Vivi	Aerobic Burst Beyonce			Kettlebells Tony	Crossfit Training Faith & Amberson		Hip hop Dance Emma & Asim
Thursday		Aerobic Burst Beyonce			Kettlebells Tony	Crossfit Training		Salsa Heat Clair
Friday			Hot Yoga Patrick		Kettlebells Tony	Crossfit Training Kevin		Club Night Team B
Saturday			Dive & Splash Mya					Club Night Team A
Sunday								

Question: What are this timetable and those people's conversation mainly about? Please briefly summarize it with evidences or examples.

試問此時間表及三位談話者的說明內容為何？請簡短以文章及聽力內容中的具體證據及範例陳述出來。

 參考範文 Track 101

Sunday is the easiest day of them all. There's no class on Sunday, so if this male student would like to borrow the gym for their club event, then Sunday could be a great option. Also, Monday is the easiest day too. Only two classes are there for the day. The gym will be available from eleven a.m. to seven p.m. on Monday. If their club members are also interested, Kettlebells and Crossfit Training are two regular classes they have everyday other than Monday and weekend. Rita is interested in Salsa Heat and Hip Hop dance. She might join one of them next week. Meanwhile, aerobic and hot yoga are both tempting too, this female student would like to try Aerobic Burst out tomorrow. After the conversation and information from the desk, the male student decided to grab some flyer this time and have further discussion with his club members and go back to ShapeUp fitness center.

中文翻譯

星期天課程最輕鬆。星期天沒有任何課程，因此假如學生想借健身房以星期天尤佳。星期一的課程也很少，只有兩堂課。星期一從早上十一點過後至傍晚七點都是空堂。假如學生社團團員有興趣的話，壺鈴運動重量訓練這兩堂課每天都有，除了拜一及週末。Rita 對 Salsa 舞還有嘻哈舞蹈很喜歡，她下週想都參加。同時，有氧舞蹈及熱瑜伽都很誘人，她明天就會去試跳有氧舞蹈。和櫃台討論後，他們決定先拿傳單回社團與團員們商討。

單字、片語說分明

① **option** *n.* 選擇、選項
② **Meanwhile** *adv.* 同時
③ **aerobic** *adj.* 有氧舞蹈
④ **tempting** *adj.* 誘人的

C 新托福口說參考範文解析與評點

托福口說答題拿分首要掌握以下要點

1. **What**（內容資訊）：本範文完全針對題目回答了所需的**內容資訊**。

2. **How**（再解釋 1）：文法上沒有錯誤，語意上可以理解。

3. **Why**（再解釋 2）：本範文沒有離題，絕對針對題目回答，沒有答非所問。文章針對所提供時間表的內容及時間表的相關聽力內容加以整理論述。

D 此類考題考前及應考時準備筆記要點

1. 不同的校園活動主題（themes, activities）
   job fair, club fair, international student fair, culture fair, renaissance festival, grandpa and grandmom day, parents day, music festival, international student festival, Chinese culture fair, video game festival, opp-campus housing fair

2. 描述相關休閒活動經驗的詞彙
   festival, fair, club, show, experience, adventure, exploration, challenge, excitement, extreme sport, view, vision, journey, tour...

3. 形容對活動感覺正面或負面的詞彙

正面：

tempting, excellent, incredible, irreplaceable, extraordinary, exceedingly amazing, successful, inspiring, peaceful, cool down, fresh my mind, reenergize, bring someone new idea, runner's high, relaxing, inspiring, peaceful time, spectacular...

負面：

terrible, troublesome, ridiculous, suck, bring/drag one down, ruin one's day, break one's heart, feeling down, ...

E 換句話說補一補　Track 102

Sunday is the easiest day of them all.
星期天課程最輕鬆。

1. Sunday is the easiest day.
   星期天課程最輕鬆。
2. Sunday got the most relaxing schedule of them all.
   星期天課程最輕鬆。

Also, Monday is the easiest day too.
星期一的課程也很少。

1. Meanwhile, the fitness center has the most flexible schedule on Monday.
   同時，健身中心星期一的課程也很少。
2. At the same time, Monday is the easiest day too.
   同時，星期一的課程也很少。

After the conversation and information from the desk, the male student decided to grab some flyers this time and have further discussion with his club members and go back to ShapeUp fitness center.

和櫃台討論過後，他們決定先拿傳單回社團與團員們商討後，再回健身中心。

1. After they communicate with the front desk, the male student decided to get some flyers this time and discuss with his club members and go back to ShapeUp fitness center.

    他們和櫃台討論完後，男學生決定先拿傳單回社團與團員們商討，之後再回健身中心。

2. Informed of the details from the front desk, the male student made a decision to grab some flyers this time and discuss with his club members so to be able to get back to ShapeUp fitness center.

    他們和櫃台討論完後，男學生決定先拿傳單回社團與團員們商討，之後再回健身中心。

 錄音原文

Male clerk

Good morning, how may I help you?

男店員

早安，請問需要什麼？

Male Student

Hi, we are looking for an empty gym classroom for our club.

男學生

您好，我在為我們社團尋找空的體操教室。

Part 1
Part 2
Part 3

Memale clerk

Is there any specific time you may be looking for? I can give you one of our classroom schedules. Monday and Saturday are the easiest days. Well if you are looking for the whole day empty classroom, Sunday is the only option. For Monday, the gym classroom is available from eleven a.m. to seven p.m.

男店員

時段上有什麼需求呢？我可以給你一張教室時間表。星期一及星期六課都不多。星期天是唯一整天都空堂的時候。星期一體操教室從早上十一點到晚上七點是可使用的。

Female Student

So you also provide Kettlebells and Crossfit Training classes every afternoon except Mondays and weekends?

女學生

除了星期一和週末外，你們每天下午也有壺鈴和 Crossfit 訓練課程囉？

Male Clerk

That's absolutely right. Kettlebells and Crossfit Training classes are two regular classes we offer pretty much every afternoon other than Mondays and weekends. Salsa Heat and Hip Hop dance are also quite popular dance classes here too. We got a lot of campus students coming over for that.

男店員

是的。這兩個課程是每天下午都有的，除了星期一及週末。莎莎舞及嘻哈舞都很受歡迎，我們有許多學生過來參加喔。

Female Student

Rita is interested in Salsa Heat and Hip Hop dance, so I will come to these

classes next week with her. So is there any form that I have to fill or register before we attend those classes?

女學生

Rita 對莎莎舞及嘻哈舞很有興趣，我下週會跟她一起參加。那上課前我需要填什麼表格嗎？

Male Clerk

It's ok to just come with water and towel for the first time. I'll be here to serve you after your first class experience and discuss with you about some packages and membership if you may be interested too.

男店員

只要記得當天帶水跟毛巾即可。我當天會在這為您服務，妳們參加完第一次課程後，可能會對一些方案或會員制度有興趣，我也會跟妳們一起討論。

Female Student

It sounds great, if that's the case, I think I'm gonna go to Aerobic Burst to try it out first tomorrow, will that be good for me to do that? Aerobic and hot yoga are both **tempting** to me! While there will be an Aerobic Burst tomorrow, I guess I will give it a shot.

女學生

太好了！那我明天就想先參加有氧舞蹈試試，可以嗎？我喜歡有氧舞蹈及熱瑜伽，明天有課嗎？我想試試。

Male Clerk

Sure, no problem. Just come. So I guess I will see you tomorrow then. About the opening classroom section, just feel free to get back to us when your decision has been made from club discussion. We are looking forward to having your club to join us here.

男店員

沒問題，歡迎參加，明天見囉。有關教室空堂的問題，在您的社團討論過後，歡迎再跟我們聯繫。期待您社團的加入。

Male Student

Thank you very much for all the information and help. We'll definitely come around soon.

男學生

謝謝您的協助，我們很快就會再來這裡。

中文翻譯

塑身健身中心

課堂學費依會員級別而有不同。取得進一步的資訊請透過下面的電話號碼或 Email 聯絡我們。謝謝。

時間表	7:00 ~ 8:30 早上	9:20 ~ 10:50 早上	11:00 ~ 12:00 早上	休息 時間	1:30 ~ 2:30 晚上	3:00 ~ 4:30 晚上	休息 時間	7:00 ~ 8:30 晚上
星期一		瑜珈 Vivi 老師						Salsa Liam 老師

星期二	Step & Pump Josh 老師	初級 體操課 Alex 老師		壺鈴 Tony 老師	Crossfit 訓練 Kevin 老師	Hip hop 舞 Emma 老師
星期三	瑜珈 Vivi 老師	有氧舞蹈 Beyonce 老師		壺鈴 Tony 老師	Crossfit 訓練 Faith 和 Amberson 老師	Hip hop 舞 Emma 和 Asim 老師
星期四		有氧舞蹈 Beyonce 老師		壺鈴 Tony 老師	Crossfit 訓練	Salsa Clair 老師
星期五		熱瑜珈 Patrick 老師		壺鈴 Tony 老師	Crossfit 訓練 Kevin 老師	會員之夜 Team B
星期六		Dive & Splash Mya 老師				會員之夜 Team A
星期天						

>──── 單字小解

① **tempting** *adj.* 誘人的

Leader 029

iBT、新多益口說：

獨立＋整合題型，２８天拿下高分 （MP3）

作　　者　李育菱
封面構成　高鍾琪
內頁構成　菩薩蠻數位文化有限公司

發 行 人　周瑞德
執行總監　齊心瑪
企劃編輯　饒美君
校　　對　陳欣慧、陳韋佑、魏于婷
印　　製　大亞彩色印刷製版股份有限公司
初　　版　2015 年 10 月
定　　價　新台幣 369 元
出　　版　力得文化
電　　話　(02) 2351-2007
傳　　真　(02) 2351-0887
地　　址　100　台北市中正區福州街 1 號 10 樓之 2
E - m a i l　best.books.service@gmail.com

港澳地區總經銷　泛華發行代理有限公司
地　　　　址　香港新界將軍澳工業邨駿昌街 7 號 2 樓
電　　　　話　(852) 2798-2323
傳　　　　真　(852) 2796-5471

國家圖書館出版品預行編目(CIP)資料

iBT、新多益口說：獨立+整合題型,28 天拿下高分 /
李育菱著. -- 初版. -- 臺北市：力得文化, 2015.10
面；　公分. -- (Leader ; 29)
ISBN 978-986-91914-8-7 (平裝附光碟片)

　1.多益測驗

805.1895　　　　　　　　　　　　104018771